Mission Impastable

Mission Impastable

Sharon Arthur Moore

Oak Tree Press　　Hanford, CA

Oak Tree Press
Publishers Since 1998

Mission Impastable, Copyright 2014, by Sharon Arthur Moore. All rights reserved. Printed in the United States of America. No part of this book may be used or reproduced in any manner whatsoever without written permission except in the case of brief quotations used in critical articles and reviews.

For information, address Oak Tree Press, 1820 W. Lacey Boulevard, Suite 220, Hanford, CA 93230.

Oak Tree Press books may be purchased for educational, business, or sales promotional purposes. Contact Publisher for quantity discounts.

First Edition, January 2014

ISBN 978-1-61009-097-1
LCCN 2013956708

To my wonderful family, John, Kevin, and David, who ate everything (well, almost everything) I cooked and lived to tell about it.
Your delight in the food and your nourishment were of equal importance to me.

Acknowledgements

So many amazing critique group members over the years helped to shape the story line, characters, and final look of *Mission Impastable*. No writer I know makes it this far without much help.

Thanks so much to my Munds Park group: Annie, Al, Marcia, Lou, Jo, and Joann for all your suggestions. My Westbrook Village group: Sandra, Sylvia, Lee, Sharon, Sue, and Mary Kay encouraged me and provided valued help.

Carolyn Hughey, mystery author and personal chef, was a huge help in fixing some of my errors and figuring out how to cover myself for the ones I didn't fix!

My biggest critiquing thanks goes to Sandy Bremser who read drafts of this manuscript almost as many times as I did.

Thanks so much, too, to Sunny Frazier, Acquisitions Editor, and Billie Johnson, Oak Tree Press Publisher for giving me the opportunity to see my dream come true. Staff members Jeana and Suzi at Oak Tree Press offered ready help with a smile.

And David, your never-flagging support of me, during the good times and bad, and your willingness to eat these recipes helped the most of all.

CHAPTER 1

Lowering clouds above the arid Arizona landscape promised rain. But, Alli, on her way to Safeway, knew that often during the humid monsoon months, promises were broken. "Monsoon season, a metaphor for life," she said aloud. "That would be a good blog." She laughed at her unusual somber mood and ran a hand through orange-red curls, a hair color nature had never seen. Alli basked in this hue because it reminded her of the Valley's sandstone hills. Keeping her eyes on the street ahead, her fingers sought the CD buttons and hit "play." Ah! Duke Ellington!

In rhythm to the music, Alli bobbed her head and tapped her fingers on the steering wheel while Ellington's drummer, Sonny Greer, beat out a gut-rumbling solo. Her surrogate mother's twenty-year-old, mostly-still-silver, Toyota Camry didn't have the greatest sound system, but the Duke's orchestra rocked the car. *Or maybe it's just me rocking the car. Who says a trip to the grocery store has to be boring?*

Alli's eyes slid up to the rear view mirror again. That guy in the bright blue car still tailgated her. At least she assumed it was the same guy. The windows had the darkest tint she'd never been able to see through.

Right after she turned off their street onto 67th Ave., he'd pulled in behind her. *Hey, Fella! Pass or turn off or get where you're going.* The Phoenix metro area had some of the worst drivers in the country. On occasion, if she were truthful with herself, she had to be counted among them. Still, she never tailgated. A little speeding, an ambiguous light change, but, no, not tailgating. That could be dangerous.

She stuck her hand out the open window and signaled a right turn into the Safeway parking lot, her signal a sure sign in August in Arizona that neither the air conditioning nor turn signals worked. The tailgater zipped past and turned in at the next right. *Make up your mind where you're going! Did your wife call and tell you to pick up some milk? Probably your first trip here and you were watching your GPS instead of the road!*

Alli cruised up the parking lot to a spot near the entrance. It was too hot for exercise. Besides, the dark storm clouds presaged a downpour, the sort that could be legend during the desert monsoon season. Just in case it really *did* rain this time, she planned to be in and out fast so she wouldn't have to navigate flooded streets. She glanced north while turning the key to lock the car. Fluffy white thunderheads piled high and contrasted with the lower lying dark ones.

Alli's eyes dropped from the sky to the video store. She saw the tailgating car parked there. *Okay. Wifey called him to get a movie. Dinner and a show. Hmm! Maybe we should do that, too. Maybe Tangled. That would go with linguine and maybe the kids won't notice the clams in the sauce.*

Alli made her way to the produce section and began hefting heads of romaine lettuce for salad that night. She examined the leaves on the heaviest one for freshness.

"Excuse me. Miss?"

Alli turned to the man behind her. Tall, maybe 6'2", light brown hair that was longish in front. A recalcitrant hank of it fell forward despite a toss of his head to move it back. He had two items in hands held out toward her.

"I'm sorry to bother you, but you seem to know your way around produce. I'm making a dish that calls for mango. And, please don't think I'm rude, but I figured someone with that hair color has to know about mangoes. I don't think they look so good. Besides, I don't know how to open them. Something about a big pit inside? Anyway, could I use pomegranate instead?"

Alli looked at the guy. *What a pick-up line! Too bad I like dark-haired guys better.* "Uh, no. At least, not usually. What's the recipe?"

"That's the thing. I don't have an actual recipe, just kind of a listing of ingredients that I *think* are in it. It's a shrimp and mango quesadilla that I had at a local place a few days ago. Café Rumba? Over at the corner of 59th and Union Hills?"

Alli laughed. "Then definitely not. Pomegranate would totally change the texture and flavor. I'm not saying you wouldn't create something tasty, but it won't be anything like what you ate. You might try papaya. That would be closer."

The guy nodded understanding. "I'm Craig, by the way. I just moved here a few months ago. I'm easing into the lifestyle and food. I haven't been to the Southwest for, golly, years. Sorry to have bothered you, and thanks for the help. I guess I'll wait until the mangoes look better. You take care now."

'You take care now'. Mom used to say that. Alli shook the memories from her head and smiled through the pain. "No problem. When you make it, I hope it tastes like what you remembered. Oh, and welcome to the Valley of the Sun."

Alli moved out of the produce section and wandered toward the front of the store to watch the guy leave. There was something about him she found appealing. Still, she didn't make a habit of tracking after guys. By the time she made it to the door, he was out of sight. Maybe he had gone into another store in the strip mall. Alli shrugged off whatever this feeling was that had come over her. She shook her head and found her cart again. Time to get the rest of the dinner fixings.

She enumerated her remaining items. She believed in committing them to memory instead of being enslaved to little slips of paper that had a way of living up to their name. Slipping away, that is. "And I have to get over to the video store and pick up that movie for tonight," Alli said aloud, loading the groceries in the trunk. Putting in the last bag, she scanned the parking lot of the video store. Maybe she'd spot the jerk who had tailgated her. He must have already picked up his movie because the car was gone.

* * * * *

In a far southwest corner of the Safeway parking lot, the driver of a bright blue sedan sat low in his seat. He spoke aloud, watching Alli get into the old Camry and drive off. "It won't be long, Alli, now that I know where you live. Not long at all."

* * * * *

As Alli stirred the clam sauce on the kitchen stove, she heard the garage door to the house open. She yelled out, "Hi, Gina."

Gina dripped a trail of rainwater into her mother's aromatic kitchen and dropped her car keys onto the counter by the phone. She removed her sopping coat and took it through the sliding glass doors to the covered patio for draining, mumbling hello on her way out. Once back inside, Gina leaned over and shook her frosted hair, spraying water across the tile floor.

She walked over to the stove. "Brother! That rain is vicious. When we were kids, do you remember the teacher reading us that Langston Hughes poem that started, 'Let the rain kiss you. Let the rain beat upon your head with silver liquid drops'? I never understood that poem. Rain in Arizona, *when* it rains, beats you up with bullet drops or knife slices!"

Alli grinned and nodded. "Yup. Long day? Well, relax. I've got dinner under control." Alli held up a spoonful of sauce for her friend's professional evaluation. "Here. Sip this white clam sauce. What does it need?"

Gina shook her head. "Not yet. I need a drink first! I swear, if killing weren't illegal, and, you know, immoral, I'd murder her."

Alli laughed. "The Dragon Lady been spitting fire again?" She went over to the freezer and got out the Chardonnay, nice and icy, just like Gina liked it. She handed Gina a glass.

"I wish you wouldn't do that, Alli. An ice cube is good enough for me. Remember that time you forgot, and we had broken glass and sticky wine all over the roast?"

Alli waved a hand in dismissal. "A mere lapse in memory. Here. Try this. Will the kids eat it?" She held out the spoon for Gina.

Gina took the spoon and slid it into her mouth. She made a face. "Well, it doesn't need more garlic! Whew, Alli, I think you outdid yourself. Can you tone it down a bit for the kids? Ma will be fine with it and maybe add more garlic. As a professional dietician, I have to say I wouldn't let you serve this to our hospital patients."

Alli laughed aloud. "Yeah, but the salad would cut the olive oil, right? I'll make a light Caesar dressing with a small bit of garlic. Of course, there's the garlic bread."

Gina shook her head. "I'm taking this wine back to my room to change out of these clothes. I smell like I spent most of the day in the hospital kitchen, and that's true. Back to help out in a few minutes."

Alli held up a hand. "No need. This is a quick, simple supper for tonight. But, I do want to tell you about my adventures with a rude driver and then the cute guy who hit on me at Safeway. So, hurry. Oh, and I got *Tangled* to watch with the kids. They won't notice the garlic." She paused, then yelled down the hall after Gina. "Maybe not even the clams."

[See Alli's Tangled Linguini with Clam Sauce]

* * * * *

The next morning, Alli's eyes popped open. Her heart pounded so hard she felt it echoing through her body. She peeled her dry tongue off the roof of her mouth and wiped a slick of sweat from her forehead. The covers twisted in a colorful quilt labyrinth around her body. She struggled to sit up in her double bed.

The watch she had forgotten to remove last night twisted around her wrist. *Cal and Mom? I haven't dreamed about them in years. Not since...*She rubbed the pinched skin of her wrists. *Maybe that's why I dreamed my hands were tied up.*

She brushed back kinky wet bangs. Alli pulled loose from the covers and swung her feet over the side of the bed. *That was a rude awakening.*

Alli peered at the clock beside her bed. She groaned aloud, "Geez, 3:12?" Alli groaned again. "I'm up for the day, I guess. Might as well work on the paperwork for the small business administration."

Alli rummaged through a stack of clothes on the chair near her bed and found a pair of jeans that looked clean and a tank top. She sniffed the armpits. Good enough.

After a quick face wash and a finger comb through tangled red curls, she exited the French door into the sultry Arizona August predawn morning. She strode across the yard to Gina's house, slid the Arcadia door quietly, and she entered the kitchen without waking the household.

*   *   *   *   *

Alli, surrounded by papers on the floor and counter behind her, was sipping her fourth cup of coffee when Gina, yawning, entered the kitchen two hours later. Gina saw the neat stacks of completed paperwork on the table and the even greater spread of loose paper.

Gina looked at her. "Oh, my gosh! What are *you* doing up? I had the most horrible dream."

"Tell me about it," Alli said. When Gina opened her mouth, Alli interrupted. "Not really. I meant, me, too. I suppose it's all the stress of having to file our personal chef business plan when we don't even have a business name yet. Look at this rigmarole!"

Gina nodded and flipped through the shorter pile of papers. "That and Ma taking out a home equity loan to fund our business expenses. So I have to pay the monthly loan amount and find money for school supplies and clothes for the kids."

Alli nodded her sympathy. "Maybe you could just add some extra fabric to Nicky's jeans to make them longer. He could make a fashion statement about what the stylish third-grader wears. Maybe Carrie could go unisex this year and wear Nicky's old clothes to kindergarten."

Gina laughed and shook her head at the suggestions. "I don't know, Alli. Are we doing the right thing?"

Gina poured a half mug of strong black coffee and added a quarter cup of water to tame it down. Alli watched her, smiling over her cup.

Gina stiffened her spine as if to defend herself. She tore a paper towel off the rack to use as a coaster. "I know, I know. You like it strong. And it's easier for me to dilute it. I know there's no way for you to strengthen it if you make it to my taste. But, boy, if I wanted hair on my chest, this is the coffee I would drink full blast." Gina sipped from the brew, testing for drinkability Alli assumed.

Gina sat down next to Alli and cradled her mug. "Alli, we're both having bad dreams and not sleeping well. That is a recipe—ha ha—for disaster. Still, it is nice to get up and see the paperwork diminishing. Will it be ready drop in the mail on my way to the hospital this morning?"

Alli shook her head. "Not quite. See this bigger pile. It needs one thing on every page. The same thing, in fact. I saved that job for you. We need a name. For the last hour, I've been sitting here tossing around personal chef business names. Again! It's your turn to think of some! I've about exhausted my brain here, Gina!"

Given her "Luscious Mango" hair color, Alli laid what should have been a freckled cheek, but wasn't, on the top of the old oak table in Gina's kitchen. She closed her eyes.

Gina sat down across from Alli. She picked up her paper towel and swiped at a syrup puddle one of the kids had left behind for her to find with a silk blouse sleeve at some inopportune moment. She tossed the crumpled bit to the table. Gina's eyes looked stricken. She bowed her head. She ran her hands through the sides and to the back of her blond-streaked hair.

"How about 'Meals in Minutes'", she looked over at Alli whose head remained on the table.

"Or 'What's Cooking?'" Still no response from Alli.

"Maybe we could call it 'What's for Dinner?'" Gina asked with a question mark.

"Nah," Alli mumbled from her tabletop nest. "Somebody got that one with meals people drive in and pick up over by the Black Canyon Freeway." Alli's flat voice signaled a lack of her normal ebullience. Her head bobbed up.

"How about using our last names? 'Smithson and Wesson-food you'd kill for'? No, huh?"

Alli thought again, furrowing her brow and kinking more curls. "I know! I know! Unique! Ear-catching! Let's call it "Al-Gi Dinners'! Get it? Alli and Gina...Al-Gi!"

"Tell me that's your sick idea of a joke!" Gina frowned back at her best friend since second grade. Alli's cheek went back onto the table where she spied a stray cheesecake crumb—mmmm! blueberry, her favorite. Her finger darted out to capture it for release on her tongue.

Silence reigned, but a change in the air current signaled someone else had entered the kitchen. "'Dinner is Served'," Gina's mom announced, waddling over to the table, her pink, orange, and purple floral housecoat flapping limply in her considerable wake.

"Ma," Gina gave "the look" to Alli before further addressing her mother, "Ma, it's breakfast time. Since when have you lost track of your meals?"

"No, Genius! That's what you should call this personal chef thing, which I personally think is a wastrel of your time, since any good mother would not want a stranger cooking for her family if she had any self-pride at all and who will pay you enough to feed your own children which makes you wonder who will be cooking for *them* while you're out feeding the world, that would be me."

Maria Martini paused for breath. "Call your business, 'Dinner is Served'."

Alli's head popped up. "I like it," Alli smiled. "Classy. Specific. Easy to remember. 'Dinner is Served' Yeah, I like it!"

"Oh, Ma! That *is* perfect! How did you come up with it?" Gina asked, dark brown eyes snapping in her re-animated face.

Maria gave a smile that could have been smug or a snarl. "That's what I thought of the first time you two twits thought you wanted to start a cooking business even though you didn't ask me what I thought probably because you knew I'd try to talk some sensical into you because why would someone cook for other people in their kitchens when you don't even know if they have a can opener since people who don't like to cook probably don't even own a can opener, not that *you* open a lot of cans."

Gina and Alli stared at Maria. They knew she was going to start up again, and to interrupt her now would extend her explanation even further. Better to let her finish.

"But that's the name I thought of two weeks ago." Maria smiled, her lips twisted in what passed on her face for a sweet smile.

"Two weeks ago," Gina repeated flatly. "And you couldn't be bothered to tell us until now?"

"When I heard my sweet Alli say," Maria paused to pat Alli's cheek, "'Al-Gi Dinners', I couldn't keep it to myself any longer because why would you have listened sooner when people need to hit the dirt on the bottom first."

She sat happy-faced relishing the look of the two of them sitting gape-mouthed. It wasn't always easy following her logic or her language, but, more often than either of them would like to admit, Gina's mother made her convoluted points.

"You fill in the name on the forms in this pile," Alli tapped the larger stack. "I'll go register the name for a website." Alli darted off to the office they shared in Gina's house, enumerating her "to-do" list

Mission Impastable

aloud. "I'll be back in an hour or so," she yelled over her shoulder.

Alli," Maria's smile reflected her pride. "Isn't she just something? She plays that computer like a deck of cards. Why don't you learn to do the computer things she does?"

Gina felt the familiar rise of jealousy whenever her mother praised Alli's attributes over her own. "Why should I? Alli can do that part, or even the kids if it comes to that. I save myself for the other stuff," Gina replied a little defensively.

Maria settled herself at the table with a mug of Alli's strong and hot coffee. She and her mother had had similar conversations for years over Alli's talents compared to her. "I guess I get my computer genes from you, eh?"

Maria shifted her bulk. "Hmmph! I could do the computer if I wanted to waste my time instead of taking care of this family which is what I have to do since you run off to work and then slave here in this kitchen making food for other people to buy and now you want to go out to their houses, too, instead of just starting a restaurant like Uncle Frankie did when he thought he wanted to make food for other people who were always complaining that it was too cold or not spicy enough."

Gina believed that Maria paused for breath because it was necessary. She wondered over the years what doctors would find if they measured Maria's lung capacity developed through years of one-sided conversations.

"So why do you want to do this so bad, my Gina?" Maria sounded puzzled. "Why can't you just cook food here and then go deliver it so your children will see you at least sometimes instead of going into other peoples' houses to cook there?"

"Oh, Ma. Why do I want to be a personal chef? I don't know exactly. Control over my life? Independence? Need for creativity? Getting away from my boss at the hospital before I kill her? Maybe all of those," Gina sighed.

Maria reached a hand over the table and patted Gina's.

Gina placed a hand over her mother's. "And, truly, Ma? It's all Alli's fault. You know how she's always had nutty ideas ever since we were little. She began talking about our own cooking business, and one day it started sounding like a good idea, a natural extension of our 'Wild Cinnamon' food mix business. She said we could do more than sell cookie, seasoning, and muffin mixes."

Maria interrupted, "But they're so good. People like them."

Gina nodded agreement. "I know, but I can never quit my job at the hospital with that income. So this is our best shot. We can't cater. You know our kitchen would never pass health department standards. So, we have to be personal chefs, and cook at our clients' homes."

Maria squeezed Gina's hand. "I see. I do. That's what you need the house equity money for, to rocket launch this business."

Gina nodded. "We so appreciate this, Ma. And we'll pay back every dime and give you some interest, too. Speaking of 'Wild Cinnamon', that business is still going, and we got a new order in. Would you help me measure ingredients into these plastic bags for the oatmeal cookie mix."

Her mother jumped up and came to her daughter's aid. "I thought you'd never ask because you know I have some ideas for the oatmeal cookie mix that I thought you might want to try out by putting in some other things, not just raisins and walnuts, because I thought some peanut butter and chocolate chips might be tasty and, in fact, I tried some out. Here. Have one," she offered from a plate whisked out of nowhere.

Alli, just returned to the kitchen, reached around Maria's considerable middle to snatch the top cookie before Gina could get it. She bit down. "Ummm! That is so good, Maria! You know, that *is* a good idea. Branch out from our basic recipes to offer options."

"Alli." Gina's tone warned her that she did not agree. "I thought we were phasing out 'Wild Cinnamon.'"

Alli nodded vigorously. "Of course, but, you know, until the personal chef thing happens, this does bring in some money. My major income, I'll point out. And with new recipes, we could extend our 'Wild Cinnamon' customer base and keep the old ones coming back to see what else we have to offer. These cookies are fab, Maria. You're a marketing genius!"

Maria turned a coy smile to Gina.

[See Maria's Chunky PeanOat Cookies]

Alli swallowed the last bite and grabbed another cookie from the plate Maria still held. "Problem. 'www.dinnerisserved.com' is gone. Somebody already has the website name tied up even though they aren't using it right now. I don't want to get into a bidding war over it. But, 'www.dinnerisservedonline.com' is still available. What do you think? Shall I snatch that one? This one site said that a new domain name is registered every five seconds!"

"Go for it," Gina smiled. Alli grabbed a few more cookies and sprinted back to the office to make sure that someone had not pirated their name in the 30 seconds she had been in the kitchen.

"It's only money," Gina yelled after her.

Gina and Maria returned to filling the oatmeal cookie mix bags. Gina said, "Remind me to tell Alli to put our new website in the package with these cookie mixes. Maybe we'll get some business that way." They worked side-by-side as they had many times until the last bag was filled.

Gina sat down with another cup of coffee and filled in their business name on all the forms. Maria started pulling things from the cupboards and refrigerator for the family breakfast.

Before the hour was up, Alli returned with most of the website work done. She would finish it later that morning. Also, Alli had a handful of slips with their new web address to put into packages. Gina smiled to see that was done.

"Sit down, Maria," Alli ordered, the only one who could order Maria around. "SuperAlli is here! I'll take that," she grabbed the spatula from Maria's hand.

Maria handed it over without protest. "Alli, dear. I was wondering if you need me to do some laundry when I throw in the kids' stuff today along with Gina's to get them ready for the week so the people at the school don't show up here for neglection," Maria offered, sitting down with a grunt at the table.

"Nope. I'm caught up. Wish you'd made the offer yesterday!" Alli grinned back.

"Well, not to be critical of you, Alli, but if you did your laundry on a schedule like other people then I could help you because I'd even come and get it from your place and you'd have more time for your work since I know you have that log column to write for the computer that's due this week on top of trying to get your spider web finished for this foolishness about the personal chef business," Maria said, gazing out the kitchen's bay window to the casita in the backyard where Alli had lived since she was a teenager.

"Schedule, schmedule, Maria! I wash when something I want to wear is dirty. So, sometimes I wash three times in one week and sometimes I wash once in three weeks."

Maria raised her eyebrows.

"Hey, it works for me!" Alli defended. "By the way, you can go back to bed. I'll take the kids to school. I have to stop off at the computer store and pick up a new piece of software that will help us organize the recipes, menus, and shopping lists on our *website*," she emphasized the word. "Aunt Alli is on duty this morning. Get some beauty sleep, 'cause you must have had a bad run of insomnia, Maria," winking at her.

Maria shot a piercing gaze back as if not quite sure how much Alli was teasing.

Chapter 2

"Ms. Smithson? Ms. Smithson!" Her boss's voice lasered through Gina's concentration on another monsoon-y Arizona August afternoon. Clarice Franklin, the hospital's dreaded Dragon Lady, peeked through the open cubicle doorway.

"Gina," Clarice smiled in what Gina supposed she meant to pass for a warm smile. "Could you come into my office, please? Uh, whenever it's convenient," she added in what Gina assumed was an attempt to sound respectful of her time.

Is this what it was like for Carl in Accounting? Last week the Dragon Lady fired him and had Security supervise him while he cleaned out his desk. Gina weighed what the odds were that her job was on the line.

"I'll be right there. Let me just save this recipe file," Gina obliged, hating herself for not having the guts to keep the Dragon Lady waiting. She joined Clarice Franklin in the hall and followed her slim, professionally-coiffed, elegantly-clad, silk-suited body down the hallway and around to the corner office big wigs always got.

Hospital CEO's made more money than hospital dieticians, Gina noted for only about the nine-thousandth time, smoothing wrinkles from her beige polyester pantsuit with hands damp from nerves.

As they passed her supervisor's office, Craig glanced up and gave her a supportive, albeit, surreptitious thumbs up. They'd had many conversations about the Dragon Lady in the four months he had been there. Craig noted and recognized Clarice's tactics early on. He attempted to provide a mediating influence over what he called, "Clarice's Caprices". His staff cheered on his described efforts, despite there being no policy changes attributable to his interventions. The consensus was, he tried.

Once at her office, Clarice powered her way around her administrative assistant's desk, positioned to keep the un-summoned from making it into her office. "Rita--no calls," her icy voice tossed out to Rita's back. Following behind Clarice, Gina was able to see the dagger-adorned look Rita shot at her boss's back.

The Dragon Lady opened the door of her office and motioned Gina in. The hospital dietician looked around, unsure whether to head for the sofa area or the seat in front of the desk.

"This is a little bit awkward," Clarice began, after seating herself behind her desk and gesturing to the seat across from it. Gina wondered, just for a moment, what would happen if she ever called her Clarice to her face. Or what Clarice would do if she seated herself at the sofa like an equal.

"I know I should not take hospital time to deal with this, but with you being here, it's more efficient." Ms. Franklin glanced at her clock, as if by habit. Gina looked, too. Then she stole a look down at her watch. The perfect Dragon Lady's clock was off?

"Oh," Clarice issued a fake giggle. "You caught me! I just *hate* being late, so I always keep my clocks five minutes fast. But, back to our issue, I'm unsure how to begin."

Our issue? This isn't like Clarice. She seems almost supplicatory.

Clarice gave her another one of those "warm" smiles, meant to put Gina at her ease. She had also read the employee-relations training manuals.

Clarice began again. "Let me get right to it. I *heard*, but you know how the rumor mill operates around here, I *heard* that you were starting a personal chef business. Is that true?"

Gina stared at her clasped hands balled in her lap. *Does the Dragon Lady think she has jurisdiction over me during my off-work time? Or maybe she's worried I'm taking hospital time to attend to* business affairs. *Is she upset that she might lose me? Or is she concerned I'm using hospital recipes as my own creations, which of course they are. But she might not view it that way.* All of this flashed through her mind in the milliseconds before she nodded her head tentatively.

"Umm. Yes. I mean, not just me, but a friend and I. You may remember Allison Wesson who used to work in the P.R. department? She 'left' about six months ago?"

Clarice shook her head, a frown line between her eyes.

Gina began again. "No? Well, Alli and I have talked about starting a personal chef business, but we haven't begun yet. I'm sure it will be *years* before we can get a customer base going and begin..."

"Oh!" Clarice tapped her fingers on her desk, interrupting Gina's rambling. "I see. I thought you *had* begun your business. I was led to believe you were already cooking for others or that it was imminent."

"Well, we do have a website out of which we sell mixes to people, you know so they can make a cake or cookies in a flash with some water and oil. We've had that for about a year and a half. And we filed a business plan filed with the Small Business Administration for the personal chef business, but, no, I'm still doing my job here," Gina finished with a trumped-up lilt in her voice.

Clarice sat back into her leather chair and laced her fingers. "The reason I wondered was, well..."

What in the heck is going on? It is not like Clarice to be inarticulate.

"You see, my family needs such a service, and I wanted to sign on. I am well aware of the quality of your work, so I'm more comfortable with having you in my home than some stranger. Is there any way I could prevail upon you and your friend Alma to make us your first customers?" Clarice smiled, showing her teeth just like the training manuals suggested.

"Alli," she corrected without pausing. "For Allison." A stunned Gina nodded a reluctant agreement with the plan.

After making arrangements to come to Clarice's for an intake interview that evening, Gina high-tailed it back to her cubicle, giving Rita a quick grin on the way. She dialed the home phone to tell Alli. Their first customer! And the kind of well-heeled one they had talked about! This job could lead to recommendations to Clarice's friends.

And soon, this hospital could be history!

*　　*　　*　　*　　*

At 5:45, Gina walked in on one of the long-running, on-going discussions between Alli and her mother about Alli's hair color. Alli used to say, "So little time, so many shades of red!" just to drive her mother nuts. Indeed, it was one of the few areas where Maria expressed anything close to criticism of Alli. It was small of her, she knew, but Gina sort of liked that there was something her mother disliked about Alli.

Maria continued the tirade. "And why do you do that to your pretty hair whatever color it used to be that was so pretty, brown I think, but orange? purple? I don't think so. If God wanted hair to be that color he'd have made people with hair like that and do you see any of them walking around except like you who got it from a bottle?" One never knew for certain whether there was an actual question in her mother's meanderings.

But even she, used to Alli's intrepid use of whatever shade of red caught her eye when it was time for a touch-up, did a double-take when she saw Alli's purple hair. Well, reddish-purple.

Maria left the room, mumbling a hello and patting the side of Gina's blond helmet of hair, harumphing all the way back into her bedroom.

"Like it?" Alli preened, fluffing her curls. "This is hibiscus! Don'cha love saying 'hibiscus'? It's so delectable, it's almost like a food word!"

"It is distinctive," Gina moderated her initial response. "Uh, didn't you get my message? About the intake interview tonight?"

"Yeah. Cool! I guess I was doing my hair when you called. After I listened to it, I got right onto revising the intake form to reflect all the changes we talked about last month when we filed our plan with the SBA. Here it is! Say, who is this customer? I gotta get that answering machine tape replaced. Did you say 'Draggledy? Weird name!"

"Well, let's just say, I'd put money on you getting a reaction from her with hair like that. I just hope we don't lose the job over it. I said, for your information, 'Dragon Lady.' Ring a bell now?"

Alli blanched, her skin reaching a fairness Scarlett O'Hara would have envied. "Not *the* Dragon Lady? Not *our*, I mean, *your* Dragon Lady? From the hospital?"

"The same." Gina checked her watch. "What if we massaged some pureed black beans into your hair? We don't have to be at her house for, oh, a couple of hours yet."

Head tipped to one side, Alli considered that option, and then rejected it. "Nah. It wouldn't work. Don't worry. I can carry this off with panache! That's the secret to outrageous behavior, you know."

Even with her show of bravado, it was clear that Alli wished she had waited a just *one more day* before dyeing her hair this particular shade.

Alli grinned, her good humor restored. "I'll just present myself as a comestibles *artiste*! But for now, I gotta finish my blog. I'm late posting it, and we still need the money until the *dough*—get it?—starts rolling in!"

* * * * *

"Some say hunger makes the best sauce, but, in my vast and varied experience, any sauce with a dollop of sherry does the trick. And, if you add Portobello mushrooms, you just put it over the top."

Alli paused, fingers of one hand over the keyboard typing her blog. She ran the fingers of the other hand into the mass of corkscrew curls, all higgledy-piggledy over her head. She picked up the recipe notes she had jotted down last night during her turn to cook the family dinner. Living with Gina's family all these years had some culinary advantages.

"Your basic sauce has some fat, some seasoning, and some liquid, part of which I make alcoholic," she began again. "I play with this combo all the time, trying out possibilities. Some are delectable, some are...well, less delectable. But, this mushroom sauce over your sherry-marinated pork chops will have the family licking their plates. First—"

"Alllllliiiiii! Alli, come here. I need you."

Gina's voice carried across the large backyard into Alli's casita behind the main house. Alli saved her daily blog entry but didn't take the time to put the computer into sleep mode. She sprinted out her door to meet Gina on the patio.

"What? What? Who died?" Gina didn't often call for her, so Alli's voice showed her concern.

"It's the kids. I'm trying to get dinner done before we head over to the Dragon Lady's, and they are fighting just like we used to, and I was wondering if you had time to distract them, play a game maybe, before I chop both of them into this bowl for added protein." Gina gave her children a look meant to convince them they could be an intimate part of dinner that night.

"Send them out. I'll keep them busy sorting through recipes. That'll convince them it is easier to get along than be punished for not."

Alli peered into the kitchen through the sliding glass doors, her hands tenting to keep the afternoon sun out of her eyes. She snapped her fingers at the two glaring children. "Yes, you. Both of you. Exile Island is your fate. No snacks for you, just water until you get my recipe file in order."

Nicky, at eight, was three years older than Carrie. He sidled out the door and dashed for Alli's place. It was a rare treat to spend time there, and he knew there would be edible treats, too. "Aunt" Alli always had treats. But the three of them pretended otherwise or their mom wouldn't let them go there before dinner.

"You are so much better with them than I am." Gina sighed. "How do you do it? I lose patience and then just plain lose it!"

"Oh, it's a special talent of mine." Alli breathed on her fingernails and polished them on her faded jeans. "Fostered, of course, by not having discipline or any other responsibilities for their upbringing. They're good kids, Gina. But, they're kids. Of course, they fight! Remember our battles?" She cocked her head toward her place where the sounds of discord were growing louder.

"Gotta go before they destroy my files. What's for dinner, by the way?" Alli walked backward to her place.

"Lasagna Roll-ups. I tried them out at the hospital for some of the special diet people. A little time intensive, but all-in-all pretty easy. I hope you like them. I am eager for your *suggestions* for improvement."

Alli grinned. "Do I do that? Don't I ever just say, 'Gooolllyyy, that was delish!'?"

"Ummm. Actually, no,"

"Okay, let me keep the kids out of your way. I'm hungry."

Mission Impastable

Alli sprinted to her place and interrupted the fight in progress. With mock severity, she addressed the kids. "I don't care that you can't read, Carrie. Sort the recipes anyway. Figure it out. You kindergarteners ought to be able..." She pulled the French doors behind her shutting off the rest of her instructions.

Gina turned back to go into the house, smiling at Alli's voice raised loud over the sibling sounds, and then quiet reigned in the casita. She knew both of her children were engaged in some fun activity that didn't involve recipe sorting at all. Did they really think they had her fooled? Gina shook her head in amusement. She hoped they didn't pig out on too much sweet stuff right before dinner.

As she spread the ricotta mixture on the noodles, Gina worried about the upcoming meeting with her hospital boss. She slid the baking dish into the oven and sat down at the table, sipping her glass of wine. Was it a good idea to be doubly connected to Clarice Franklin? Were they even ready to begin this personal chef business?

Gina interrupted her reverie to take the lasagna roll-ups from the oven. She hoped the kids liked them. She knew she wouldn't be able to eat a bite. This meeting, she checked her watch, in forty-five minutes, was crucial to her future.

Chapter 3

The drive from Gina's house up 59th Avenue to the Arrowhead Lakes section of Glendale used to be prettier before all the grocery stores and gas stations bloomed around the Agua Fria freeway. Still, once one entered the housing area, it was clear from both the size and style of the homes planted on the rocks of the foothills, that while these might be working folks, too, they took home a lot more for their efforts than did Gina and Alli who lived in the sea of stucco and red tile roofs below them.

Gina and Alli entered the driveway and drove up the slope. The driveway was a circular one, allowing the driver to drop off passengers before parking, or did one just park there, Gina wondered? She decided to leave her fifteen-year-old teal and beige Ford Explorer by the front door unless directed to do otherwise. There was always the chance she would dent the Dragon Lady's Infiniti if she tried to squeeze in between it and the Beemer sitting outside the triple garage. She wondered what was *in* the garage that needed the additional protection.

From the car, Gina and Alli studied the acid-etched double front door glass panels that projected a sense of unconcern with crime or with others violating the privacy within. A perspective that was backed up with a discrete sticker indicating trespassers would be tracked to the ends of the earth by the protection services offered by Sentinel Security Systems. Ah, the wealthy! They had to pay a price for their nonchalance, Gina thought.

Alli stared goggle-eyed through her car window at a pit bull staring back at her, silently, from the front of the house. Another reason for the Franklins' seeming lack of anxiety, Gina supposed.

"Umm! Do you think that thing can get outside? Without them knowing, I mean?" Alli stuttered.

"Nothing passes by the Dragon Lady's eyes unnoticed. I'll bet that security camera by the front door has told her we are sitting here wondering what we are supposed to do now. So let's just go knock or ring or whatever we need to do and get this over with."

Gina took a deep breath, unfastened her seatbelt, and grabbed the interview clipboard from the back seat. Alli scrambled after her.

"But let's not forget to mention the dog. That dog has to be penned up or we can't come in here. *I* can't come in here!" Alli chattered. She had been anxious around dogs ever since the neighbor's Chihuahua had gone for her ankle bone in fourth grade, requiring three stitches. Gina's passive black lab mix was the only exception to Alli's terror of dogs.

At that moment, having walked up the three extra wide flagstone steps, finger poised to ring the doorbell, one of the front doors opened. Dragon Lady stood before them in a muumuu, a silky-swirl of jewel-tone colors. She cuddled the pit bull to her scrawny, and from Alli's perspective, malnourished, breast.

After the briefest of double-takes at the shade of Alli's hair, Clarice Franklin invited, "Please, do come in."

Noticing Alli's discomfort she added, "And don't be nervous about Baby, Alice. She is just too, too sweet, aren't you my darling?" giving Baby a kiss on her nose.

Gina stifled her gag reflex. *The Dragon Lady has emotions? She kisses dogs? Why doesn't this compute?*

"Ahh, thank you," Gina walked in. "This is Allison Wesson. Alli. I mentioned she had been in the P.R. department," Gina introduced her friend to her boss.

"Oh. Of course. What did you do in P.R., Alva?", and then turned away from them and led them into the formal living room off the foyer.

Alli got the signal that this wasn't a real question and didn't bother to try to answer. She and Gina seated themselves, gingerly, on the cream silk sofa Clarice indicated across from the wing chair the Dragon Lady claimed. *Throne?*, Alli wondered.

Alli sneaked looks around, taking in all the evidence of the world travels of the Franklin family. Fine *objets d'art* dotted a room that was cream and beige to display both paintings and statuary to best advantage. A room like this also gave the impression that there were no children, or if there were children, that the family owned the local Stanley Steemer company who showed up for a daily cleaning.

"Lovely, isn't it?" Dragon Lady purred. "Even if I do say so myself. And I do." Hearing Clarice chuckle was disconcerting.

Gina was right, Alli thought. The Dragon Lady missed nothing. She decided she had better be on her best behavior. Alli fought to keep her hands from tousling her purple curls, a trait that came out when she was nervous. Instead she affected interest in the decor.

"Your space is distinctive, so non-Southwest. It's a beautiful room. I am especially impressed with the jade dragon. Is it from the jade mines in the Szechwan region?" Alli asked in a nonchalant tone. She imagined the effect her question would have since the Dragon's Lady's disdain for her was evident.

Discomfited, Clarice nodded. "You do seem to know your jades, Alice. Yes, it was mined in the 1700s and created by an artisan in the region. Well, but on to other things. There is no need to visit the five bedrooms and six baths," she gave a self-conscious laugh. "You'll be using the half-bath by the garage door if you have need. The alarm system is by there, and here's the code you need to ensure the police don't show up and have the security company charge us for an unnecessary call.

"Let me tell you about my family and our culinary preferences, and then I'll show you the kitchen where you'll be working. If you have other questions on your little questionnaire, we can get to them then. I assume that will be satisfactory."

"Uhh, yes, that could work, but it might be more efficient to let us..." Gina began before being waved to silence by the raised hand of her boss.

"Nonsense. I can do this in a moment. We eat foods prepared with fresh ingredients. Fresh herbs too, no dried ones. No cans. No frozen foods. However, you can freeze meals you have prepared along with complete thawing and warming instructions.

"We like a variety of cuisines--Italian, French, Thai, you get the idea. Even good old American classics like steak and potatoes. Not too spicy--we like to taste the food flavors. However, the food, even when a classic dish, must have a unique aspect to it. If you serve meatloaf, make it an unusual meatloaf. If steak, stuff it with something like a peppercorn brie. Is that clear?"

The Dragon Lady looked at the two women, who nodded their agreement. Gina jotted information in the appropriate slots on their intake interview form, moving from section to section with haste.

"Also, while my husband and children would eat meat every day, I want to introduce a wider range of vegetarian items to them, so a couple of meals each week ought to be meatless or very close to it, perhaps a stir fry with a tiny bit of chicken. We eat fish once or twice a week.

"Each dinner must be able to be on the table 30 minutes after I walk in the front door. To ensure freshness, I do not mind adding in some prepared last minute ingredients or cooking the noodles per the detailed instructions you will leave.

"You do the grocery shopping for the meals, of course, and you'll charge us a fixed amount per meal, say $20-30 per person, depending upon the entrée, rather than submitting a series of tiresome receipts for reimbursement. Agreed?"

Alli and Gina nodded, the amount being more than they thought they could get away with.

"I am assuming you have your own utensils you bring with you and take away. Additionally, I have a full array of kitchen appliances in pristine condition. Any that you use, I expect to be maintained that way. You may load the dishwasher to run after you have finished preparing the meals. You don't need to stay to unload it," she offered generously. "In fact, the less evidence there is of your presence, the better.

"We'll require five dinners for four people. We'll start with a one-week trial. If your work is satisfactory at the end of that period, you will come every two weeks to fix ten nights of dinners." The Dragon Lady appeared to be finished. In her head, Alli computed their take for a half-day's work.

Gina had no further questions on their interview form and had even picked up a couple of ideas from the Dragon Lady that they should have included. She had to admit, the woman was thorough. She and Alli trailed behind the Dragon Lady on the way to the kitchen.

"Ms. Franklin," Alli ventured on the walk, "How do we, uhh, handle Baby? I mean, is he? she? locked in a cage during the day? Does it stay in the backyard?"

"Backyard? This is Arizona, Alfie. Baby stays in the house. She will stay out of your way, I'm sure. She is very shy around strangers and just a pussy cat, aren't we, Snookums?" This last to the dog who was trotting in front of their parade. Baby deigned to give her mistress a glance and a nose-in-the-air sniff.

"Here we are. I'll just leave you two to find your way around here. I must return a couple of phone calls, and then I'll be back to show you out. Baby will come get me if you finish earlier than I. Have fun," she added incongruously.

Gina and Alli made an inventory of the cooking appliances, serving dishes, and pans in the kitchen and then gathered their things to go. Baby, seeing this activity, arose from her crouch. She had stared at them the whole time. Now she dashed out of the kitchen and down the hallway where her mistress had gone.

"That dog gives me the creeps," Alli told Gina. She gave a mock shiver, watching the dog hindquarters disappear around a corner.

Moments later, Clarice rejoined them in the kitchen, and led them to the door, parade-style, behind her. They promised to come in on Monday morning to prepare the first week's dinners.

"I'll have to clear it with Craig, of course," Gina began, "But I do have several comp days due, and I'll plan to take a half day on Monday so we can get this started."

"I'm certain Craig will assent," Clarice stated flatly. "Tell him I am in agreement with that suggestion."

After awkward good-byes, the two escaped to the Explorer, its dented and scraped sides evidence of their many backcountry camping forays, looking less disreputable in the waning light.

Seatbelt buckled, Alli broke the silence by remarking, "She didn't seem to mind my hair."

* * * * *

Gina and Alli spent Saturday morning planning the five dinners they would prepare Monday morning. They would shop early on Monday, to get the freshest ingredients, and then head on over to begin cooking at 8:30, after the family had all cleared out.

"We could accelerate this if we just made a *couple* of things in advance," Alli begged Gina. "I'd wear a hairnet and everything," she wheedled.

"No, no, and no, Alli! Do you want to get our business disbarred, or whatever they do, before we even get a good start? You know that we can't. This kitchen, with two kids and a dog, could never pass the super-rigid standards of the health department. Approved home kitchens almost never happen. That's why we have to do the personal chef thing. Our clients' kitchens don't have to be approved." Gina knew that Alli knew the rules, but if Alli thought a rule was dumb, she was inclined to circumvent it. Gina had too often been all that stood between Alli and the long arm of the law.

As if to make her case, Tasha, Gina's black lab mix, rose from her corner behind the floor plants, scratched an ear, and then shook herself, spraying hairs on the linoleum's faux tile floor. She wandered over and laid her head on Alli's lap, expecting, and getting, a head rub.

And to cement the Health Department's good judgment, Gina's two kids burst through the Arcadia door from the backyard pool and dripped their way over to the freezer where they found the juice bars Alli had concocted and frozen for them last night. To free his hands, Nick laid his wet towel on the counter where either Gina or Alli prepared dinner every night. Carrie just dropped hers in the doorway.

"Okay, you win. Jeez, you didn't have to choreograph your answer!" Alli conceded. "Okay, kids, how much did your mama pay you to come in right at this very moment?"

"Mama didn't pay us, Aunt Alli. We just got thirsty. Right, Nicky? Hi, Tasha-Washa, hi, baby girl," Carrie crouched by the dog, her voice dropping into baby talk and shared licks off her juice bar.

"Carrie. Stop that! Get Tasha an ice cube if she wants something cold. You know where she had that tongue just five minutes ago!" Gina admonished.

Nicky snorted. That kind of remark tickled his scatological funny bone. Juice began to run out his nostrils.

"You kids are just so gross sometimes, I can't stand it." Gina, face crumpled, left the room.

"Uh, oh." Alli turned back to the kids and reassured them. "Don't worry. We have a big job coming up. Your mama's just a little tense. She'll be okay."

"Mama is 'little tents'? Is she going camping, Aunt Alli?" Carrie asked puzzled.

When Nicky snickered again, Carrie turned around and punched him. She knew he was making fun of her, though she couldn't understand why.

Alli interrupted before full-blown warfare erupted again. "Why don't we play a game in the pool. Wanna play 'Snacky'?" she asked.

Snacky was their favorite game with Aunt Alli. She chased them around the pool until she caught one of them. "Me hungry. Me want Snacky," Alli said, preparing to nibble on one or the other child's juicy arm or neck.

"Oh, no," the current Snacky would protest. "I'd taste much better with catsup."

"You right. But me no have catsup. You stay right here. Don't move. Me go get catsup," Alli threatened, "attaching" the Snacky to the side of the pool by placing the child's hands on the edge.

When Alli turned her back, of course the Snacky swam away. Meanwhile, Alli, enticed by the other Snacky who was darting in and out trying to get her attention. She "forgot" that she needed to fetch catsup. She captured another Snacky who insisted that Alli needed salt to enjoy the snack more. The kids could play this game for hours. Alli, however, wore out faster than that.

"Whew! I'm starved!" Alli said, climbing out of the pool. "You'd think with all those snacks, I wouldn't be hungry!" She winked at Nicky and Carrie who were begging her to come back in.

Gina greeted her on the cool deck with a towel, a glass of Kendall-Jackson Chardonnay, and a bowl of soybeans in the pod. "Eat up and then get changed. Ma is going off to her Bunco game. We're not to wait up," Gina made a moue.

"Oh," she added nonchalantly. "Craig Phillips is coming over for dinner. Did I tell you that? We need to get another appetizer ready.

The entree is marinating. We'll start the grill when he arrives. Maybe he can give us some tips for working with Dragon Lady since he has to do it all the time!"

Cooking always settled Gina down. Alli, too, for that matter, so it was good thinking on Alli's part, she congratulated herself, for getting the munchkins out of the way.

Craig was the latest obligatory one-time, welcome-to-our-happy-work-family dinner that everyone new to the hospital got from Gina. The fact that Gina seemed to be unsettled about this second dinner might mean something could be brewing.

"Sorry Maria and I missed the first dinner you had for him. I'm looking forward to meeting him. So, umm, Craig and you working on something? Some big project in nouveau hospital cuisine?" Alli probed.

"Yeah. Right. Ohhhh! You think…" Gina was an easy blusher. "No, no. It's nothing like that. I mean, he is my supervisor, after all. No, I just enjoy his company. He's lonely here, too, I think, being new and all. I always have the new folks over, you know that. But he is fun, and he does have that sardonic sense of humor that I've always been a sucker for."

Both women were quiet then, remembering Gina's husband, and the first sardonic sense of humor she had fallen for. After Alli's, of course. Nick Smithson hadn't come into their lives until fourth grade.

"How about whipping up another appetizer that will go with teriyaki chicken," she directed Alli, "while I go put what's left of these soybeans on the coffee table."

Alli loved making appetizers. There were so many possibilities, and she was an intrepid cook. Alli appeared unable to follow a recipe. She always told people that she considered a recipe a suggestion for what to mix together and how to prepare it. Her cook-from-the-gut attitude caused some literal and metaphorical heartburn when she and Gina talked about forming a cooking business. Since Alli never made anything the same way twice, writing down a recipe so it could be re-created was a foreign concept to her. Anathema, even.

Alli cooked a lot like the cook at whose knee she had learned, Gina's mom. Maria had always enjoyed working with Alli in the kitchen more than Gina. Gina liked to measure. Gina asked why she was adding an ingredient that the recipe didn't list. Alli just *felt* the ingredients and tasted the combination with what both she and Maria called their "taste bud in the brain".

Alli pulled out the ingredients for her super-easy-but-elegant, never-fails-to-impress cream cheese cracker spread. The hardest part of this appetizer was finding an elegant plate in Gina's kitchen to display it on. Elegance tended to get buried in the detritus of everyday family life.

[See Alli's Super-Easy-But-Elegant Cream Cheese Spread]

The doorbell chimed, and Gina brushed back her hair and went toward the door. Alli and Maria stood in the kitchen doorway that led to the foyer to get a glimpse.

When Craig came in, Alli gasped. Maria looked at her.

She whispered to Maria, "I know him. I mean, not really know, but we kind of talked in the grocery store last week. He's Gina's boss? Cute!"

Maria nudged her. "Why don't you just keep down and not be so visible? This is the first man Gina has had over since Nicky...well, you know just in case she has some interest that you could mess up. You can always get guys. You just can't keep them."

Alli continued to whisper while watching Gina and Craig interact. "I have to acknowledge we met. Don't I?"

"No, just pretend you forgot. It's not like you haven't ever told something that wasn't the whole truth in your life."

Gina turned and saw the two in the doorway. "Come here. Meet my boss, Mr. Phillips."

Craig waved a hand in denial. "No, Craig, please. And you must be Gina's mother. Now I see where Gina's looks come from." He took Maria's hand in his. "She speaks so often of you."

Maria harrumphed. An odd reaction, Alli thought to herself. Maria's typical response was to preen when given a compliment.

Craig turned toward Alli and did a double-take. "Say. Don't I know you? Didn't we meet, yes, at the grocery store last week. I was the guy pestering you in the produce aisle."

Alli shifted her eyes and shrugged. "Oh, maybe. I meet so many people in the grocery store. Because I'm there so much. And people just seem to come up to me. I'm always saying that, right, Maria?" She stopped babbling and blushed.

Gina regarded Alli with a quizzical look. She was acting odd even for Alli.

Alli tried to regroup. "But yes, I may remember. I hope what I told you was helpful."

Craig looked surprised. Alli guessed he wasn't used to not being remembered.

Carrie and Nicky burst into the room from the back of the house. They stopped short when they saw the visitor standing there talking with the adults.

"Well, yes, it was helpful." Craig smiled at the kids and then turned to Gina. "Uh, I brought something for your kids, Gina. I hope it's okay."

He held up an opened and partially-used bag of 75th anniversary balloons left over from the gala last month celebrating the hospital's longevity. The kids screamed when he tossed the bag to them.

"Water bombs!" Nicky yelled. "C'mon, Carrie. Let's get the other kids!" They ran out to call some friends together for an hour of warfare before dinner.

"Pick up all the rubber pieces when you're done," Gina yelled after them, knowing it was futile. "Great idea, Craig," she smiled to show her pleasure at his thoughtfulness. "How did you know that would be the perfect thing to bring?"

"Hey, give me some credit here. I know a little something about kids. I'm a fantastic uncle to my sister's five kids back in Des Moines. But tell me some more about your new business. A job already! I'm impressed!"

"Well, last time you were here, I think I outlined the general idea for you, but I was sure we wouldn't be able to prepare meals for a couple of years yet. And then Thursday, when Clarice asked me if we could cook for her family, well, I was blown away. How did she even know? I tell you, that hospital is like a small town where everyone knows everything."

Alli chimed in. "We planned some menus this morning, and we'll let those ideas 'percolate' and see if they still sound right tomorrow. Then on Monday morning, we'll hit AJ's and Safeway on our way to the Dragon Lady's house. Cook for a few hours. Send her a hefty bill. And, presto bingo! We're in business!"

Craig smiled at Alli's exuberance. "Umm hmm! Monday morning? Don't you have a real job, young lady?" Craig asked Gina mock-sternly.

"Oh, yeah. I forgot to say something yesterday, so there's an e-mail waiting for you at work. I have *weeks* of comp time coming to me. I don't have any meetings scheduled, so I wanted to take a half-day Monday, if that's all right with you?" Gina asked tentatively. She didn't want to throw Clarice's near-threats into this discussion unless she had to.

Craig's smile reassured her. "I've already accessed my e-mail. Of course, it's all right! Your overtime is so piled up, we'll never get you caught up. You need to take those days, you know. In an ironic twist, the hospital is not a very humane place to work. It'll kill you if you don't watch out for yourself!"

Alli wanted to get off the subject of the Dragon Lady. She knew from experience that they could spend all their time complaining about what seemed to be an untenable situation. Hospital morale, since Clarice arrived a year ago, had plummeted.

Alli interjected before they went down that path. "You know, Craig, I never asked what you do with your time when you're not chained to the hospital. You mentioned family in Iowa. Do you see them often? Have hobbies like painting nekkid ladies? Play X-Box games into the morning?" Alli leaned back to listen.

Craig didn't look the least bit startled, interrupting Gina's, "Now, Alli" with a very unselfconscious laugh. "No, no, and sometimes."

Alli and Gina both leaned in, wanting more.

"I don't get to see my sis's family much. Iowa is pretty far away. I think they are coming here for Christmas. Maybe we could get our families together then. I'm sure my nieces and nephews would love to play with your kids. And even the hint that they could swim on Christmas Day has them all excited. I'm putting them up at a hotel over by the mall. My place would never hold all of them, and I have to keep the kids away from my hobby."

Craig sipped his wine and picked up some more soybeans. "I almost hate to talk about it. It's not very masculine." Craig shrugged. "I grow exotic plants. My condo is pretty humid and hot, so I don't entertain there much. Being here is a real relief." He wiped imaginary sweat from his brow, sweeping a golden blond forelock back onto his head.

Gina and Alli looked at him, wondering where this was going. His hobby wasn't close to what they guessed this intelligent, kind, and very hunky guy would do with his spare time.

Alli, always one to know how to carry an awkward conversation forward, feigned interest. "Exotic plants? Like orchids? Plumeria?"

"Yes, of course orchids. That's *de rigueur* for exotic plant growers, but I also have an interest in lesser known plants like castor beans, the rosary pea, and of course plumeria. Their history is just fascinating. And to keep pests down, I have some Spanish Flies, a kind of beetle."

"Umm, isn't Spanish Fly a...?" Alli began.

Craig laughed. "Yes, that's the rumor, but contradictory to folk lore, Spanish Fly is not an aphrodisiac. However, do we want to talk about ground up beetle wings right before dinner? Alli, this cream cheese with chutney is delicious. No offense meant to your culinary skills, but even I could pull this off when my family visits."

Throughout dinner and the rest of the evening, Alli watched Gina and Craig. They jostled one another clearing the table, seeming to enjoy the contact. They had compatible senses of humor, and shared job interests. Alli began to think about how to accelerate this burgeoning relationship. Maybe she should buy Gina a book on tropical plants for her upcoming birthday. Just in case.

Craig gathered his things. Maria walked in from the garage, glowing from her Bunco game.

"You two ought to go out and have some fun like I know how to and see if you can distract yourselves from all this worrying about what you are fixing for other people to eat who probably won't appreciate all the work you put into it anyway. That kind of thing just makes me flusterated but, Bunco, those girls know how to lose your mind in the game! Whooee! Did we have some fun tonight! Pearl and me cleaned their clocks and reset the hands. I see you're leaving, Mr. Hospital Bigshot who makes my Gina work too many hours," Maria finished.

Gina shushed her mother. Craig laughed aloud, his booming peal sounding too large for the room.

"Yep! I gotta get home so these two can fret over those Dragon Lady menus some more! I'll bet her family would love that chicken you made tonight, Gina. Teriyaki with a hint of coconut and pineapple, I know, but was that ginger in there, too? Mmm mmm, good!" he rubbed his hand in circles over his tummy just like the old TV soup commercials.

[See Gina's Teriyaki Sauce and Fettucine ala Alli]

At the door, he gave both Gina and Alli a brotherly hug and peck on the cheek. He gave his bear hug and a loud smackeroo kiss on the cheek to Maria, who, Alli noted, held herself aloof.

Playing coy, Maria, are we? Alli thought. *I wouldn't mind being hugged and kissed like that by Craig.* And then she shook herself free of that fantasy. Craig was for Gina. And she knew just how to make sure that happened.

* * * * *

Monday morning saw the two cooks lugging their Safeway and A.J.'s grocery bags into the Dragon Lady's house. They pulled out their menus and recipes and measured out the recipes each had taken responsibility for.

A rap on the Arcadia door leading to the backyard startled them. Alli looked up and saw it was Pedro Lopez, Pete, a friend of Gina's husband from long ago. He owned a landscaping business and now they found he, too, worked for the Franklins'.

Alli let him in. "Pete! How are you? How's Carmen? The grandkids okay?"

"I thought that was you and Gina. Hi, Gina! How's Maria? Tell her I said 'Hi'."

Gina's voice showed she was pleased to see him, too. "Hi, Pete. You guys need to come over and swim one afternoon. The weather is a beasty right now. Excuse me, I have to keep working on this recipe. I'm at a critical point."

Pete nodded acknowledgement and turned to Alli. "Oh, not so good at home. But, I really gotta go. Ms. Franklin keeps the door locked, but my pee can won't work for my problem." Pete laughed. "Could I go to the bathroom?"

"Yeah, sure. Through there and around the corner. The left side door is to the garage, and opposite that is 'the powder room'. That's all we're allowed to use. Go ahead."

Gina was standing at the counter mixing her dish, and she turned to Alli after Pete left. "Alli. We were told not to let anyone in. Clarice would not like this."

"Oh, Gina, lighten up. We've known Pete forever. She'll never know. I'll go in and scrub the toilet bowl if necessary. It will be fine. Relax."

*   *   *   *   *

Three hours later, they congratulated themselves on a job well done. The freezer was full, the salad tossed in a bag in the refrigerator, the noodles and water for cooking them were measured out for later cooking, and the beef stroganoff was in the slow cooker.

Alli arranged flowers in a vase on the table with a note listing the week's meals.

"Dinner is Served," Gina said. They locked up the house and left the Franklins'.

Chapter 4

After an unexpected and sharp-toned, early evening phone call from the Dragon Lady, Gina and Alli jumped into the aging Explorer and headed back to the Franklin house. Alli noticed that Gina, always so observant of traffic rules, was speeding through yellow lights and was a tad more over the speed limit than even Alli normally drove. Alli's sideways look at Gina confirmed the stress on her face.

After a few minutes of silence, Gina asked Alli the same questions for the fourth time. "And you're *sure* you plugged it in? How about turning the slow cooker on? Did you do that?"

"This is getting tiresome, Gina! How many times and ways will you ask those questions? *Of course*, I plugged it in; *of course*, I turned it on. Am I a dolt?" Alli asked of her long-time friend. "You think I'm not taking this seriously, but I am. But I will not take responsibility for something I didn't do, or, rather the fault for something that I did do, or, well, whatever! You know what I mean!"

After a very quick grocery store run to pick up the replacement dinner items, Gina and Alli rushed over to the Franklin's, both wondering aloud and at the same time, which made for a rather confused conversation, how in the world their very first dinner could have gone so wrong.

Mission Impastable

Ten minutes later they pulled into the Franklin's driveway and climbed the three semi-circular flagstone steps to the frosted-glass doors.

No need to knock, Alli noted, as the Dragon Lady flung open the door, clearly waiting for them. Her folded arms and tapping foot did not portend well.

Gina rushed to speak first. "We are terribly sorry for this inconvenience and to try to make up a little for it, we brought a replacement dinner which we will prepare, serve, and clean up after. Obviously there is no additional charge! Then, Alli and I will figure out how this could have happened, but for right now, please have a seat in the living room and let me serve you some of this lovely little Chardonnay we like. Sparkling cider for the children!" she added gaily.

"This is not an auspicious beginning, Gina and Ellie," Clarice Franklin interrupted. "I am not a 'three strikes and you're out' kind of person. I typically allow one strike only! I am only willing to grant you another opportunity because of your stellar work at the hospital, Gina. Otherwise, I would not pay you the rather substantial check you've requested!" The whole family gathered behind Clarice at the door.

"I am certain, just certain, that we can make this up to you and figure out what needs to be done to prevent experiences like this in the future. Believe me, this is not the level of work you can expect," Gina assured the family.

As Gina talked, she ushered Clarice, Paul, and the two young Franklins into the living room. Alli, meanwhile, rushed into the kitchen and put a large pot of water with a little salt on to boil. She mixed a half cup of olive oil with a sliced clove of garlic, one whole peeled clove for artistic effect, and minced fresh basil. She put it all in a small bowl for dipping bread into. Then she began slicing bread which she popped into the oven, turned onto broil. As it browned, she chopped tomatoes and basil and tossed them with the olive oil and minced garlic. She took the bread out, spread some of the tomato mixture onto each slice, sprinkled on more cheese and shoved the pan at Gina, newly arrived from serving the drinks, so she could put some bruschetta on one plate and dipping oil with bread on another to take in to the family. That should stave off the most crucial hunger pangs, Alli thought.

Meanwhile, in the living room, Gina served the appetizers. As the wine and the olive oil worked their magic on the hungry and angry family, she tried again to assuage them. "I cannot tell you how sorry we are. We'll figure out what went wrong. This will never happen again."

"By the way, Gina," the Dragon Lady began just as she bit into a piece of the bruschetta. "Oh! Mmmm! Delicious! This is *very* good! But, back to my thought. I must ask you and Elva not to feed Baby table scraps when you're preparing food. I know she is a shameless begger, but she was very sluggish when we got home. We are careful with her diet, too."

"Oh! Okay. I'll tell Alli," Gina replied uncertainly. Had Alli fed Baby? Not likely, but she'd remind her later not to try to buy Baby's favor with food. That *would* be like Alli. The Dragon Lady seemed bent upon finding every little thing she could to discredit their work.

Alli was chopping peppers and mushrooms when Gina got back to the kitchen. Between them they finished up the preparations for the main meal, including more bruschetta, in the time it took the pasta to cook. Dinner was ready to serve 27 minutes from the time they arrived! A new record, Alli thought.

As Alli served the family, Gina prepared the pastry and fruit dessert and put it into the oven. Then she stared at the offending slow cooker, their *raison d'etre* for this rushed meal. It was indeed plugged in, and it was turned on, but the thing was stone cold. "Slow cooker failure. Not our fault, Alli," she told her friend when she walked back into the kitchen. "Here, fix the coffee and plug it in so it'll be ready for dessert. I'll whip the cream and then start cleaning up these dishes."

Alli could tell Gina felt better knowing there was nothing they could have done to have averted this disastrous first meal. She decided to keep the evidence there to show the Dragon Lady, and then they could clean out the spoiled food inside the appliance.

Alli plugged in the coffee pot in the same outlet as the slow cooker and leaned back against the counter waiting for it to drip through. "Bummer! Do you think she'll believe it? I mean, she is a suspicious, ummm...witch. Won't she think we just fixed it up to look good for ourselves?"

"I suppose she could, but the point is, we *know* it was not our fault. We can show her, after we clean it up, that it just doesn't work. That will clear us with her. I think." Gina sounded more cheerful than she had since the emergency phone call an hour and a half ago.

"Don't any of this woman's appliances work?" Alli asked, bending down to look at the coffee pot. "Brother! We are not making a good impression here!"

"That coffee pot, too? That's too much of a coincidence. It's not the electricity 'cause the lights are on, and we've used the stove," Gina noted worriedly.

At the same time, they recognized the problem. "The plug!" Alli cried out as Gina said, "The outlet doesn't work!"

The Dragon Lady took that moment to enter the kitchen carrying two plates, followed by her husband with the other two. "What doesn't work, Alex? That is practically a brand new slow cooker. Don't go blaming the appliance for your ineptitude, though I must say *this* dinner was delicious! I am amazed at how quickly you put it together! And a dessert, too?" she eyed the fruit in pastry cooling on the stove top.

"No, Ms. Franklin, the slow cooker is probably fine. We just discovered, when we were trying to make coffee, that this outlet doesn't work."

"That's not possible," broke in Mr. Franklin, a tall, slender, athletic man with kinky black curls setting off dark eyes against mocha skin.

Alli admired his jibe, as they used to say. She drew her attention back to his words.

Paul shook his head. "I make coffee there every morning, this one included. It worked fine then. There's no way it could go bad an hour later when you arrived." He was adamant, but being a man, he bent down to look at the outlet anyway.

"Well, well. It *isn't* working. How can that be?" He studied it some more, and then he pushed in a small red button on the outlet. Almost immediately they heard the sounds of the coffee maker.

"Reset button. The electricity must have gone off and this outlet, because it had an appliance in it, overloaded and so stayed off. That's strange, though." Paul Franklin looked around the kitchen. "When the electricity goes off, the digital clocks all have to be reset. You know, they flash '12:00' until you change them." Alli and Gina nodded. They knew.

Gina, Alli, and the Dragon Lady all looked at the three digital clocks in the room. Every one was showing the correct time, Alli knew, as she checked her watch. So much for that theory! No doubt the outlet had just had one of those inexplicable failures and was fine once reset. Well, at least they knew to watch for that now. If they were coming back, that is.

"Ms. Franklin, Mr. Franklin, again, please accept our apologies for tonight's dinner mess-up. We hope you will give us another chance. In the refrigerator are meals for the rest of the week. Try them out and let us know if you'd like us to return. We'd very much like to show you that we can provide interesting, nutritious, easy-to-heat meals for your family." Gina paused, hoping for a positive response.

Paul Franklin spoke first, "Well, these things can happen to anyone, I suppose. Just bad luck that it was on the first day. I sure would like you to make some of that beef stroganoff another time!"

He looked over at his wife. At her slight nod, he continued. "We'll be in touch about future contracts, but this incident will not be a factor in our consideration, I can assure you."

"We'll leave you to the kitchen clean-up. Do I need to show you out when you finish, or can you find your own way?" Clarice Franklin inquired, her tone chilly.

Like this is a mansion or something. Alli restrained a snort.

"Oh, we'll manage just fine," Gina assured her, and they watched the departing backs of their new clients, well, *maybe* clients.

*   *   *   *   *

The phone rang shrilly as Alli and Gina entered the laundry room from the garage off the kitchen. They dragged in, tired from their evening's work at the Franklin household.

"I wish you two would get cell phones. I'm tired of being your secretarial pool of workers." Maria picked up the phone.

"What you are saying? Impossible! Yes, they just walked in, but…" Maria sputtered as she listened to the voice on the other end.

"No, they can't come back. They are tired from taking care of your family and haven't even seen their own tonight and now you want them to come back to your house and they haven't had any dinner that is getting cold. I don't think so," Maria informed her listener.

This did not sound like a good conversation. It was apparent Maria was talking to the Dragon Lady, and the Dragon Lady was upset! Again.

"How could she have already found out that I mixed recyclables in with the garbage?" Alli whispered to Gina. "I didn't want to go poking around hunting for it, and I didn't want to interrupt their dinner to ask. Busted. Sorry!"

Gina reached for the phone after giving Alli a look that went back through years of Alli's screw-ups.

* * * * *

They headed—for the third time today—to the Franklin house.

"Well, we're getting to know this route pretty well," Alli quipped, trying to lighten the mood in the wheezing Explorer. She just couldn't take this as seriously as Gina seemed to be.

So one of her jade dragons was gone. What did that have to do with them? There was no evidence, no *corpus delicti* to tie them to the crime, if there even *was* a crime. A part of Alli's mind wondered if that were the right phrase. It didn't *seem* quite right.

One of the Franklinettes could have broken the statue or taken it for show-and-tell at school or maybe Mr. Franklin was doing an insurance scam. There were dozens of possibilities, none of which even remotely involved Gina and Alli. *So why is Gina so worried*?

But when Alli saw the three squad cars, lights flashing, parked in the circular drive, she began to get a little bit of the feeling that Gina must have. Maybe being innocent wasn't good enough.

* * * * *

When asked, politely, if they would go to the station to answer a few questions about their time at the Franklin residence, both agreed, of course. What choice was there? Though, Alli thought it a bit much to question them separately. After all, they had the same story.

When they entered the front of the station, Alli saw a familiar uniformed back. Her old boyfriend Evan was on duty tonight? Swell!

"Ms. Wesson, isn't it? Do you mind if I record this conversation as well as take notes? I'd rather do that than make a possible error because of mishearing something. We can get a copy printed out for you to review as soon as we finish. Is that okay with you?"

Alli nodded and said it would be fine.

"Would you please state your full name, age, phone number, and address?"

"Allison Wesson, 34, 623.555.1212, 7620 W. Hidden Manor, Glendale, AZ, 85308."

"Do you live alone, Ms. Wesson?"

"Yes, well, sort of, I mean, I live in a casita behind the main house, Gina's house."

"So, you and Ms. Smithson live together?"

"Not exactly. Just the same address. Not really together."

"What is your relationship to Ms. Smithson?"

"She's my best friend, and my business partner. We've been together forever. Well, a long time, since high school."

"You began your relationship with Ms. Smithson in high school?"

"No, second grade, but what does this have to do with the Dragon, err, Ms. Franklin's theft?"

"How close is your relationship to Ms. Smithson? Would you call yourself personal as well as professional partners?"

"You know what? That's none of your business, but, no. For gosh sakes, she's a mom."

"Sorry. I am just trying to get your relationship accurate. So you are her tenant."

"No. I don't pay rent. My casita used to be the pool house, but Gina's parents let me live there. I moved in when I was fourteen."

"Ms. Smithson's parents were your guardians?"

"No. I just moved in. No one from the school checked. My parents, well, my parents were no longer around, so Gina's folks let me have a place to stay. They watched out for me."

"What is your profession? How do you earn money for expenses?"

"Well, I sort of take whatever jobs I can find. Umm. Gina and I have a mail order food business, you know, soup and cookie mixes, stuff like that. And, uh, I have a blog that brings in some money from advertisers and a section of my website that people pay to access that has a newsletter. I, uhh, used to work at the hospital, in P.R., but, I, uhh, left that job to pursue other interests. And Gina and I have this new personal chef business we started. That's why we were at the Franklins' today."

Mission Impastable

"So that is your means of support. Is that sufficient for your expenses?" The detective looked at his pad of paper while Alli fidgeted.

She broke the silence. "What does any of this have to do with a jade dragon?"

The officer, Detective Clinton, his name badge read, looked up at her.

"Oh, right!" *Whatever happened to innocent until proven guilty? And I don't need a lot of money, Detective.*

"Take me through your day beginning with your arrival at the Franklin home this morning."

"Okay. We arrived about 8:30. The dog, Baby, growled at us. I'm really terrified of dogs ever since one took out a chunk of my leg when I was little, so I..."

"I'm sorry I wasn't clearer. I don't really need every detail. Just the outline of what went on, who you saw in the house or grounds, if anyone else came in the house while you were there, if you saw anyone hanging around the sidewalk, things like that. I'll ask for more info if I need it. Got it?"

"Oh, sure. Okay, the only person we saw while we were there was Pete, Pedro Lopez, the yard guy. He wanted to use the bathroom, so we let him use the one we were told to use. Then he went right back out. We weren't really supposed to let him in, but it's hot out there. We didn't think Ms. Franklin would mind, even though she had told us not to let him in. Oh! You don't think Pete took the dragon do you?"

Detective Clinton looked down at his notes.

"Is that Pete and Pedro?"

"No, just Pete. Pedro's his real name."

"Here is a floor plan of the Franklin house. Can you show me on here where you let him in and where the bathroom was that he used?"

Alli showed the route used.

"This bathroom here? By the garage door? Isn't that where the house alarm system is?"

Alli nodded. "But, we set the code again before we left. And, I think, I'm pretty sure we locked the back door. I'm sure we did. We would be responsible about locking the doors."

Alli answered the remainder of Detective Clinton's questions, elaborating when asked, and finally was released to go home with the promise of contacting him if she remembered anything else. She agreed to be available for further questions. Did she have a choice?

*   *   *   *   *

Alli drove the two of them home from the police station on Union Hills, thankfully only a couple of miles from their place. It was after midnight, and they were both exhausted.

"Wasn't that something to see Evan there? I thought he only worked homicide. You remember Evan from hospital security, don't you? He went to the police academy before I was fi . . , er, left the hospital." Alli looked over to Gina, her profile stark white marble in the waves of light from overhead street lamps they passed.

"So we had opportunity, and I suppose greed is always a motive, but how could anyone seriously think *we* would steal something? I mean, for crying out loud, you're a mom, and I'm...I'm...Well, I don't need to steal even if I'm not the most upstanding of citizens. Boy, makes you wonder what else they have on you if they can pull up all your parking tickets for the last three years, huh?"

Alli was babbling, she knew. But it was only to counter the stony silence of Gina. She always babbled when she was nervous or to fill dead air space. Both conditions were operative.

Of course, Maria was up when they dragged into the kitchen. She had cups of hot cocoa waiting. "Made with real milk and cocoa not that mix stuff the kids like because they don't know what real chocolate milk is like since kids today don't have taste buds worth spitting at," she offered. She wanted every detail.

"Sounds like these cops kinda grilled you good. Funny, huh, two wannabe cooks getting grilled? Or is that 'crooks getting grilled'?"

Maria's attempt at humor fell flat. Very, very flat. They made their good nights, with Maria stating that she was calling in sick for Gina the next morning, that morning. No way around it. That was her final word.

*   *   *   *   *

Unable to sleep, Alli was swimming laps at six in the morning when she saw Maria slip out the kitchen door and over to the recycling can. There was something about her furtive movements that caught Alli's attention. It was more than she was just trying not to wake the household. So, after Maria went back inside, Alli went to see what was so important to recycle this early. Tucked under yesterday's cereal box was a section of the day's newspaper.

"Hospital Head's Home Hit" the Valley and State section of the *Arizona Republic* proclaimed on page three. "Those guys are good," thought Alli. However did they get this story and write it up so fast? She'd have to contact one of her buddies in the newsroom, left over from her hospital P.R days, and find out their source. It was odd to have this detached and professional curiosity about a story that involved her.

"Smiths and Wessen, who run a catering business called 'Serving Your Dinner', have not been charged yet. Police are calling them an investigatory lead. Both women, who live together only a few miles from the victim, have been extremely cooperative, an unidentified official source stated."

"Well," Alli thought, looking for the bright side, as was her wont, "They messed up enough details that most people probably won't even know it's us." And then she heard the phone ring impatiently, no doubt from a friend of Maria's, a ring that demanded details!

Chapter 5

Alli was back to her blog. She rolled her shoulders and stretched up her arms before starting again. She was behind, so this was a marathon session.

"Garlic, the food of lovers, vampire repellent, tuberculosis and broken bone cure, giver of strength and courage, and recently-touted health food! Through the centuries, garlic has been lauded for magical properties. Garlic, the bane of dating teens and the friend of flea-infested dogs! Garlic, the lowly bulb that elevates food to a sensual experience!

"Amazingly, for as common as garlic is, many cooks are not sure what to do with it beyond dicing it into the spaghetti sauce. This week I will de-mystify garlic and share some unusual recipes of my own and from the readers of this blog. But first, take a little garlic test:

    1) Garlic is...
        a) an herb.
        b) a member of the onion family.
        c) a member of the lily family.
    2) Garlic powder is...
        a) more healthful than fresh.

　　　　b) easy to make on your own.
　　　　c) anathema.
　3) Garlic releases its strongest flavors when...
　　　　a) kept whole.
　　　　b) sliced.
　　　　c) minced.
　4) Garlic was first used in cooking in...
　　　　a) Italy.
　　　　b) France.
　　　　c) antiquity.
　5) Other than in cooking, garlic has been used as...
　　　　a) perfume.
　　　　b) an aphrodisiac.
　　　　c) medicine.
　6) Garlic is sold in...
　　　　a) cloves.
　　　　b) heads.
　　　　c) cubes."

　　Alli arched her back, held her arms out wide to her side, and wiggled her fingers to loosen up after her marathon session at the computer. This was the fourth food blog she had worked on today, and she was a little tired of thinking about food. After she was done with garlic, maybe she'd kidnap Gina's kids and go get design-your-own pizza at Cucina Tagliani's tonight. Gina could use the break. She had been really stressed out over this whole dragon mix-up.

　　Alli always worked several days ahead on her blogs. It gave her the illusion of being caught up to know that she had some breathing space before they were due again. She found it much easier to write in marathon sessions than just article by article, day by day. Sometimes, when she was on a roll, so to speak, she could crank out six of them in an afternoon, but she never let herself quit until she had at least three done in first draft. Then she let them sit and "steep" overnight before revising and posting online.

　　She hated revisions. Hated them, hated them, hated them! She'd rather do a hundred first drafts than even one revision! Sometimes she bribed Gina and got her to revise. The articles were always much better with Gina's revisions than her own.

Gina and she made quite a team, Alli ruminated. Best friends practically forever, after that first fight they had in second grade that had bloodied both of them. But, then they had become blood sisters, Gina and her family providing her stability. They had been closer than any actual sisters Alli had observed from her outsider stance.

"Okay, me bucko," Alli told herself. "Back to work, then a nice dinner for you for being such a good little girl." And she poised her fingers to begin the serious part of the blog, including recipes for baked garlic, the bruschetta they served the Franklins, and a modification of various linguine aglio e olio she had dredged from her own files and past reader submissions.

[See Linguine Aglio e Olio]

* * * * *

"Whew! You smell like garlic, Aunt Alli. I thought you said you were writing," Carrie noted. "I don't like garlic. It's yucky!"

"You don't even know what garlic is, Twit," Nicky replied in his big brother voice, using one of his grandmother's favorite epithets.

"Mama said not to say that, Nicky. It's a bad word. Do, too, know what garlic is! It's white and round and stinky," Carrie responded. "And I don't like it!"

"Then you better not get any pizza 'cause you won't like it, will she, Aunt Alli?"

"Just eating garlic by itself is something we don't often do, Carrie, but Nicky is right, we use garlic in all kinds of things at our house that you probably didn't even notice. Spaghetti and pizza sauce among them," Alli confirmed. "I know you like those, so you can't even tell they have garlic.

"But don't think about the garlic, Carrie. Instead, imagine the grilled fungi and the tiny, salty fishies they lay across the top, thick and deep. Hmm, Nick?" Alli teased Nick whose hatred of mushrooms and anchovies was well-documented from the time he had thrown them both up all over Cucina Tagliani's floor. Alli had never seen a restaurant clear of customers so fast. Receipts must have been down a lot that night! It had taken a couple of months before Alli and Gina could get up the courage to come back to one of their favorite Italian restaurants. And then they only did it sans kids.

"So what will it be, Nick? Your usual?" Patty, their preferred server, asked as she collected their menus. Nicky liked her not just for the service but because she was one of the few adults in his circle who called him by a more grown-up name.

"Yep. Bacon and pepperoni on thin crust, Patty."

"And I want pepperoni and sausage with green peppers and no onions and no garlic," Carrie stated emphatically.

Patty smiled at both kids and then turned to Alli. "Hi, Alli. What can I get you? Oh, and how's the personal chef thing going?"

"You must be the only person in Glendale, Arizona who hasn't heard about how Gina and I stole Clarice Franklin's antique jade dragon while we cooked dinner for her family this week," Alli responded.

"Umm. Okay. You want the vongole with white clam sauce or the eggplant parmigiana?" Patty asked without noticing the comment.

"Eggplant."

Patty did a double-take. "Say, was that *you* guys in the paper? That article today about the robbery of the hospital boss? You didn't really do it...did you?" She seemed to be considering the possibility. "Nah! 'Course not! Eggplant and two pizzas coming up!"

"Do people really think you and Mama stole something?" Carrie asked gravely.

"Nobody important does, Sweetie," Alli replied, muttering under her breath "except for the police and Clarice Franklin and her friends, our former and future customers!" She decided to change the subject.

"Look. I brought cards so we can play a few rounds of Golf while we're waiting for dinner."

Alli dealt four cards to each of them, all four face down. They arranged their cards in an array, two on top and two on the bottom. They each were allowed to look at the bottom cards before the game began. They had to get the lowest score by trading out cards they turned over or were discarded for ones on the table in front of them. The game was over when the Queen of Spades turned up. It was pretty easy to trade right for the bottom two cards, but sometimes they got rid of low cards on the top row because they couldn't look at them in advance. It took both skill and luck to win this game.

"Well, how sweet!" Alli heard an unfamiliar voice purr.

Alli looked up to see what's-her-name, oh, yeah, Rita, the Dragon

Lady's administrative assistant, by their table.

"Hi. Rita, right?" Alli responded.

"I didn't even know you had children, Alli," Rita said. "I'll bet Evan was surprised when you trotted them out for inspection. Is that why he's not with you now? He wasn't much of one for commitment."

"Evan? Oh, yeah, Evan. From Security," Alli replied, nonplussed at what this was about.

"Oh, my, yes! Well, he and I were quite the hospital item. I dropped him right after you started working there. Fear of commitment, as I said."

Alli and Evan had talked briefly about him dating someone else at the hospital. But everyone's names were so new then, that the name hadn't stuck. But, she *thought* she remembered that Evan had been the one to end the relationship. And that the other woman wasn't pleased about it, not at all.

"Oh, well, yes, the kids and I were a bit much for him, I guess," Alli backpedaled, winking at the kids to keep them from correcting Rita. "We single moms have a tough time dating." *What does this woman want? What is this all about?*

"Uncle Evan?" Carrie asked. "He was nice. Even when my ice cream cone fell right in the middle of his pants, he hardly even said any bad words."

Rita ignored Carrie. She leaned in close to Alli and "How is Gina doing, you know, what with her problem with Ms. Franklin?"

"Problem? They couldn't run that place without her."

"Oh, Alli, Dear, sorry to have blown the secret, but I am sure Ms. Franklin is this close to firing her," Rita nearly touched her forefinger and thumb together.

"For what?"

Rita shrugged. "Beats me. I just heard their voices raised in there one afternoon. Then Craig, Mr. Phillips came in and there was more yelling."

"Well, it can't be serious. Gina never said a word."

Rita shrugged again. "I did tell the cops about it when they asked if I knew anything. I understand you and Gina are having a little trouble with the law. I hope I didn't have anything to do with that."

Now Alli shrugged.

Rita continued, "I know the police told Ms. Franklin they are watching all the pawnshops for when you, I mean, the crooks might sell it off. Something like that is *so* distinctive, I guess, that it should be easy to find. You know, those ruby eyes alone would go for a bundle from a collector. Well, enjoy your dinner." Rita left, dodging Patty who was maneuvering the tray of food toward their table.

Suddenly, Alli wasn't much hungry anymore. *Ruby eyes?* She hadn't known about that. Apparently Rita had been in Clarice's house herself or someone told her about the jade dragon. And she could well have been told *or* have been in the house numerous times. As the Dragon Lady's administrative assistant—now there was a job that deserved every penny it paid—she would have had ample opportunity to be there.

Alli realized that she and Gina had to try to figure this out. She was not at all sure that the police were looking beyond the two of them. Maybe she should give Evan a call for coffee, just to chat, of course.

"Hey, Nicky, let me have the score pad. I need to make some notes on the back side of it." Her delicious eggplant parmigiana cooled in the dish as Alli pushed it aside. *I need a crime book to keep track of stuff.*

* * * * *

"And so, I figured we should check out where she was the day of the robbery," Alli concluded.

Gina shook her head at her friend. "Alli. Her jealousy of you is hardly reason to suspect her of robbery."

"But don't you see? She had opportunity, I'm sure. And the motive *could* be to get back at me. As the Dragon Lady's assistant, she had to know we'd be there that day. Besides, no other suspects are leaping into my mind. How about yours?"

"No. No other suspects come to mind. And let me tell you how uncomfortable I feel at work. You know, I hardly ever saw Clarice before this. Now it seems as if we run into one another a dozen times a day. She is always polite, but very, very cool. This has to change.

"And other people keep giving me looks, as if they half believe I could have taken her dragon. There are the ones who come up to me, squeeze my arm in support, and then go off with a heartfelt glance. But the worst are the ones who want the details—What's her house like? Is there a lot of security? How could this have happened? Who do we suspect? I just hate it. I've been barricading myself in my office and only coming out for bathroom breaks. Maybe I could get a colostomy bag so I don't even have to do that." Gina's attempt at humor brought only the faintest of smiles to Alli's face.

They both turned at the sound of the door to the garage opening.

"You'll never guess who I saw today at the Stadium Casino," Maria announced as she walked into the kitchen carrying a bag of groceries from Safeway. "Pearl and me went out there on the senior's bus trip and I was just putting my nickels into the machine that I just sit at the whole time which is the secret of my success winning so much money when who should go marching past us back to where the big shots play their poker for so much money that I could have a lot of nickels and maybe even play the quarter machine for the day, but Paul Franklin," she finished finally.

Both Alli and Gina had long ago learned they only had to hear the first and the last part of any message to get the gist. The trick was in knowing what *was* the first and the last part of the message. Over the years they had fine-tuned their reception of Maria's intonation patterns so they could mostly pick up what she was telling them.

"Paul Franklin? The Dragon Lady's husband?" Gina was incredulous. "I don't think so, Ma. This is a Wednesday. I know the man has a business to run. Or, I guess, maybe," she looked tentatively over to Alli, "maybe he was entertaining some out-of-state business people. You know, showing them what the area has to offer. Besides, how would you even know who he is?" Gina asked.

"Oh, I know who he is all right. Pearl told me. She knows who came into that hospital and forced her to retire when she really wanted to just finish out her years instead of wandering around like a lost person because she doesn't have a job. I see him a lot at the casino, not just this time. He goes by in his Streams or Rivers or Brooks Brothers suits, smelling like some spicy muskrat walking around in heat hunting for something to get rich on. And he always goes to the back. Where the big spenders go," Maria smiled knowingly. "That's who took the dragon. It's obvious he needed the money!" she finished triumphantly.

"You know. That *could* be what happened," Alli chimed in. "One of the first things I thought was that a Franklinette had broken it or that

Paul could be running an insurance scam. It would make sense, Gina. And, after all, who else is there to suspect? You didn't like the Rita idea."

"Oh, gee! Who else is there to suspect? Well, golly, Alli, Ma, like the *whole world*! Most robberies are by felons! We don't know any felons! Felons are out of our realm of experience! Felons break into peoples' homes, and we were just unlucky enough to be at the right place at the wrong time!" Gina said, exasperation evident in her voice. "If you two would get a grip, maybe we could figure out how to help the police solve this thing or at least clear us of suspicion."

"You're absolutely right," Alli agreed. "Let's do a little investigation on our own. Call Craig and ask him for the rest of the week off— use some more of that comp time. Let 'em recycle old menus and recipes. That place can and will run without you mothering it, Gina," Alli argued.

Gina needed little excuse to get out from under the microscope she felt under at work. But just as she picked up the phone to place the call, the phone rang beneath her fingers.

"Hello?"

"Ahh, yes, is this the "Serving Your Dinner' company that was in the newspaper yesterday? The one in the robbery story?" a woman's voice asked.

Gina raised her eyebrows and punched the speaker phone button for Maria and Alli to hear.

"Yes, well, I mean the real name is 'Dinner is Served'; the paper got that mixed up," Gina responded. "And, really. We have no comment. Good-bye."

"No! Wait! I want to hire your company to cook for my family. Clarice Franklin is a friend of mine, and she had told me that she was going to use your service and gave me this number. I haven't talked to her since this, ummm, all came out in the paper, but she spoke so highly of your qualifications that I thought I'd see if you had any other openings in your schedule. My home doesn't have valuable things like her house, so that's not a problem. And, I'd be around the whole time, just to help show you where things are and all."

Maria snickered.

"Well, I don't know, Ms....?" Gina hesitated.

"Pierce. Sheila Pierce."

"Ms. Pierce, my partner and I..." Gina began.

"...would be delighted to meet with you and talk over your culinary preferences and when an appropriate cooking day might be. We *could* fit you into our schedule, with a little finagling," Alli finished.

Gina glared at Alli, but handed the phone over for her to complete the arrangements. Maria had to leave the room so she wouldn't tip off the new customer that Gina and Alli lived with a maniac who couldn't control her laughter!

And so they got their second customer.

CHAPTER 6

The Pierces' lived in the same Arrowhead Lakes area as the Franklins' but their house was not as ostentatious. It was as if they had followed the age-old realty advice, "Buy the cheapest home in the most expensive neighborhood." Still, it was larger and newer than Gina's place and sat on a small piece of ground that backed into the Hedgepeth Hills, so it was more private than some of the homes lower down the hill. To maximize his investment, it looked as if the builder had placed a smaller home on a tiny bit of land in a prime location rather than making larger lots on either side.

Whatever the story, the Pierce's view out the kitchen window of the Sonoran desert was spectacular. It would be restful to cook there, Alli decided. Some newcomers to Arizona didn't find the tans, browns, and reds of the rocks and sand, dotted with the sparse greens of cacti, palo verde, and brittlebush, attractive at all, but Alli loved the desert. She and Gina, both desert rats, couldn't imagine living someplace where the greenery choked off the view and suffocated you with its overpowering closeness. Alli liked to let her eyes roam for miles across the desert.

"What a wonderful view, Ms. Pierce," Alli complimented. "You must really enjoy cooking here."

"Me? Cook? Oh, no, dear me, no!" her voice trilled with the fake laughter that a certain strata of social climber had inculcated into her language patterns. Sheila Pierce was anorexic thin. Feeding her ought to up their profit margin considerably, that is unless she had an incredible metabolism or was bulimic and so ate anything that passed before her eyes.

"No, I've never been much of one to cook," Ms. Pierce explained. "I do so admire you people who can do it day in and day out. We used one of the Mexicans to cook for us. But the woman was *so* undependable. Her car, when it was working, was always leaking oil on the drive, and she would have to add more before she drove home. My husband even had to take her home on occasion. You wonder why some people live like that! And sometimes she showed up with two or three of her children in tow. Not that they were bad or anything, but one can't always be watching out for children as they wander off to the bathroom. And, of course, she *wouldn't* learn English. Such a disaster, really. She was likely an illegal we decided, and so, even though she was much cheaper than this service is going to be, we told her not to come back.

"Of course, it took a while to get that through to her!" Sheila Pierce went on. "Fortunately, one of her children knows enough English to have gotten her to understand, or I don't know what we would have done. I went through her purse and got our key back. You'd think those people would have more pride than to cry in front of their bosses, wouldn't you?"

Alli and Gina could read one another's minds. Did they really want to take this job? No! But did they need to? Yes. Sadly, yes.

"It seems," Sheila continued, "that just anybody who is anybody is using a personal chef! We were up at the Club last weekend when Clarice mentioned she had hired you. I knew I just had to try you out as well."

"Well," Alli began briskly, "Let's get started with the interview. How many people are we preparing dinner for? How many are children and how many are adults?"

"There are five of us. My husband and I, and our three children ages, 10, 12, and 14. I hope you can fix healthful foods. I'm afraid we all need to watch our weight around here." She chuckled again. "I'd also like you to serve half portions compared to what you are preparing for other people. That should keep the cost down some, too, I would think," Sheila suggested.

"Umm. Okay. Half portions," Gina wrote on the intake form. "Are you sure?" Gina began again, "Ms. Pierce, I am a certified nutritionist and dietician. Alli and I are perfectly capable of preparing nutritious full portion meals that meet the daily requirements for dinner. I would strongly advise against half-portions."

"Yes, well. But it is my family, correct? And you will be working for us, right? Let's just try it my way for a week or two. Then we can decide what to do," Sheila answered.

"What kinds of ethnic foods does your family like to eat or not eat?" Gina continued. "For example, if they hate Italian we would make sure not to serve foods with that kind of tomato or cream sauces. Or if they love curry, we would include those foods."

As the interview went on, Gina and Alli were getting a picture of how controlling the mother of the family was. This was going to be a fun, fun, fun job, Alli decided satirically.

"Now, finally, as to the price for this service," Alli began. "Since we do all the grocery shopping for the dinners as well as prepare the food, we normally charge $10-15 per person per meal. The price is dependent upon what we prepared. Obviously, a London Broil dinner would cost more than a spaghetti with a marinara sauce dinner."

An audible gasp from Sheila drew Alli and Gina's attention.

"Why, I had no idea! That's...that's a lot more than I thought it would be. Why, Lupe prepared dinners for the whole week for the cost of one of yours!" she got out.

"Yes, well, personal chefs *are* a luxury item," Alli replied with some satisfaction yet trepidation. This could all fall through, and they would have wasted 45 minutes with an absolutely dreadful woman.

"But, you said *normally* cost. My cost will be half that for half portions, right? After all, we will be eating a lot less food." Sheila recovered. "And, please, use the food in the cupboards here instead of shopping for more. That should keep the cost down as well."

"Well, but you see, it still takes us a set amount of time to prepare the food, which is where most of your cost is. So, I guess, for half portions, we've never done this before," Alli was ruminating as she talked, "but let's say three-fourths cost of our normal charge. Is that okay, Gina?"

"Possibly. But we will have to keep an accounting and see how it figures out at the end of the first week. But that is what we will charge you initially. And, Ms. Pierce, we will do our own shopping for all our own food needs. We have certain brands we prefer to ensure quality. We pick the best for our customers," Gina put in.

"Well, but 'best-quality' is not necessary for us. Just pick 'good enough'. For example, olive oil. It is shocking what some companies want you to pay for the exact same product." Sheila shook her head ruefully.

"We don't work that way," Gina told her. "We use the freshest and the best. That's part of why you pay for a personal chef. You can depend upon the quality of our dinners."

They finished up the details of when they would begin, how the billing worked, and other loose ends, and Gina and Alli skedaddled as quickly as they could.

Sitting in the car, they were silent at first, each staring pointedly out the front windshield as Gina negotiated the driveway and onto the street. Knowing Sheila was likely watching, they didn't want to explode with hysteria in front of her upon catching the other's eye.

"Well, hmmm. Interesting, eh?" Gina began.

"We gotta put the cost thing up front, Gina. She had no idea what she was getting into," Alli responded, always looking at their presentations from a marketing standpoint.

"I'm gonna make up a brochure. It will outline the services and the price. Then we can give it to people and follow up with the intake interview if they still want it," Alli thought aloud. "In fact, maybe we could make it totally convenient and have most of the intake done as a written form. We'd still need to get in the house to see what the set-up is and find out if there are things they remembered after sending the form to us. What d'ya think?"

"Yep. That might work. *I* would have preferred a lot less time with her," Gina concurred.

"One good thing," Alli smiled. "She doesn't have a dog!"

"It would probably cost too much and poop where she wouldn't want it to!" Gina laughed.

*   *   *   *   *

It was late afternoon. Alli's fingers hesitated over the numerals on her phone. He might not even have the same number. And, with an on-going investigation, would he even see her? Better to run into him. Casual. No pressure. "Oh, coffee? Sure!" But how could she run into Evan casually?

Alli dug into the back of her closet and pulled out a cute exercise outfit. She knew he always went to the gym after work at the hospital. She assumed the same pattern held now. In fact, the unworn spandex was a leftover from those days when she was dating him. She thought it would be fun for them to work out together, all hot and sweaty, until she actually did it. One time at the gym convinced her she'd rather be waiting with a brew and a brat for him at home dressed in some cute little sundress.

Alli squeezed herself into the shorts and top. "No more pizza until our names are cleared," she vowed. This had better work out. She looked like a stuffed tomato.

All the way to the gym, she second-guessed this move. Maybe Evan was involved, or even married. Maybe he didn't want to start up with her again. And, in truth, she didn't really want to date him again. This was strictly for survival purposes. Gina was in a bad place, and it was affecting the whole family.

Alli approached the desk to beg a free time on the machines as a trial when she heard her name.

"Alli. I've never seen you here before. Is this your usual time?" Craig came toward her with a huge smile on his face. He gave her a quick hug and peck on the cheek.

Over his shoulder, Alli saw Evan emerge from the men's locker room. As he swung his bag into his left hand, he caught her eye. Evan began to smile, but then realized another man had her under his arm. He gave a small salute and exited the front door.

"I gotta go. Sorry, Craig. Nice to see you. Have a good workout." Alli dashed out the front door, sprinting across the parking lot toward the navy shirt she knew was Evan's.

"Hey! Wait up! You know I'm not in shape to go running all over this parking lot."

Evan stopped, hesitating before he turned toward Alli.

"Hi. Working out with a new boyfriend?"

"Hi, Evan. Imagine seeing you twice in one week! How long has it been?"

"Almost a year. I'm glad to see you back to taking care of yourself.

I've seen your new guy here a lot these last few months."

"Oh, he's not my 'new guy'. He's Gina's, or at least that's what I'm working on, but he's also her boss so it makes it tricky. What?"

"Alli, you sounded just like Maria there for a minute. How is Maria, anyway? I miss her cooking and commentary."

"She'd like to see you again, too, I know. Whenever she gets mad at me for something she brings you up, and how I screwed up with you." Alli shrugged. "Can I be honest?"

"I've always preferred that."

Alli winced. "I didn't come here to exercise. Like you're surprised! I came to see if I could 'accidentally' run into you. Go get coffee or something."

"And this is because you're having regrets about dumping me? Or could it have something to do with a certain case involving you?" He stared at her for a moment. "Whatever."

Evan turned away from Alli and unlocked his car door. He threw his bag into the back seat and climbed behind the wheel. "Well, get in. If you went to this much trouble, I'd be happy to get a coffee and explain why I can't tell you anything about an on-going investigation before I tell you that I can't even see you while the case is open. First, though, I've got to go to the shooting range and get my monthly practice in. We did that a lot while dating, remember? I'll pick back up with your shooting lessons, too, then we'll get coffee. Coming?"

*   *   *   *   *

"So when is Evan having dinner with us?" Maria probed. The kids played a game of "Chutes and Ladders" while the adults had after-dinner coffee with a new treat Alli had created, Chocolate Chocolate Kick Cookies.

"I told you, Maria, he can't come to dinner because he can't even talk to me."

"Well, he could talk to me. You don't have to talk to him."

Gina smiled at Alli.

"Ma, are you finagling to get Evan for yourself?"

"Hrumph! Where is your mind? In the garbage disposal? You know your father was the only one for me."

She looked at Gina's face. "Oh, you're teasing. Well, I still say I could get him to tell me things about what they are checking on for this crime that he won't tell you because we have a different relationship like a son to me he was or he could have been if Alli hadn't run like a bunny from him."

"But, he says they are checking on things and to leave it to the professionals. The good news is we're not the only 'investigatory leads'. I thought that was encouraging. Still, it's our lives at stake here, not the police department."

"Alli, did he tell you how he got involved in this to begin with? I mean, last I heard when you two were together, was he was in Homicide."

"Yeah. I wondered, too. Apparently, and this is the good news, there aren't a lot of homicides in Glendale, but burglaries are up. So, they sent him over to Burglary to give a hand since he had some time. He doesn't like it. Says that burglaries are messier to figure out and tie up than murders. He didn't sound too encouraging that this case would get resolved. The usual leads aren't coming through and there's no action at the pawn shops."

"For someone who wouldn't talk to you about the case, you got a lot out of him."

"Well, Gina, I do have my ways." Alli batted her eyes. "And, we did, sort of, tentatively, maybe said we'd see one another after this is wrapped up. Just to catch up. See where we are."

"I knew that man would be back. I always said what Alli really needs is a man like Evan who has his head about him who can give her the shoulder support she needs so she can have the kind of life she deserves for her to have and him, too."

"Thanks, Maria, but don't go printing the wedding invitations yet. Evan may think he can't tell me more about this jade dragon thing, but he doesn't stand a chance. When I want information, I know how to get it. Mmm. Don'cha love these cookies? I think I'll take a batch over to the police station tomorrow."

[See Chocolate Chocolate Kick Cookies]

Chapter 7

Alli made two batches and boxed up seven dozen Chocolate Chocolate Kick Cookies for the officers and staff at the police station. She put another dozen in a separate bag. Detective Clinton was at the desk signing some paperwork when she walked in. He glanced over his shoulder, saw Alli, turned back to the papers, and turned to face her.

"Ms. Wesson? Is that right? Did you remember something more?"

"Oh, no. No. Nothing. Well, nothing important. Just uh, a question. Is Detective Katz available? I think he talked to the family, and I wanted to ask him something."

"Uh uh. No. That's not the way it works. This is my case. Detective Katz was just lending a hand from another department. I have his notes, but I can't tell you anything about the family interview."

"Oh. Well, could we talk then? I brought cookies. I hope there are enough for everyone here. Do you have a break room? I can put them there."

"Well, how nice. You're a chef, right? That's very nice of you. We don't usually get gifts from suspects, err, people we have interrogated, uh, interviewed. I'll show you where you can put them."

Alli followed his broad beam down a hallway to the left of the desk clerk. *Don't eat too many, Detective Clinton. Wouldn't want to add to your load.*

The detective held the door for Alli to enter, and she immediately recognized the beam, not at all broad, standing before the sink. Evan turned at that moment and saw Alli in the doorway. His face flushed red, and he ducked his head as if to ignore her presence.

"Hey, Guys. Ms. Wesson here, a local chef, brought us some cookies. Hey, Katz. Didn't know you were here. Want to join us for a minute in my office. Grab a coffee and a couple of cookies for me, will ya?"

Alli turned to Clinton. "No need, sir. I brought you your own little bag." She leaned toward him and whispered, "One dozen for you". She turned to Evan and said more loudly. "There's enough for you, too, Detective Katz."

Stiffly, Evan followed the two of them into Clinton's office. Alli sat on one chair in front of the desk, and Evan took the other.

"Now what's this question you have about the family interview? I guess we might as well go to the horse's mouth, eh, Katz?" Clinton stuffed a whole cookie in his mouth.

"You might want to limit your coffee intake. These cookies have a pretty heavy dose of caffeine going for them already. But, right. The question is, Detective Clinton and Detective Katz, did any of the Franklins' mention their dog? How Baby was when they came home?"

Clinton scanned the pages of Evan's notes. "I'm not seeing anything. Katz?"

Evan cleared his throat and looked directly at Alli for the first time since her arrival. "No. Why should they?"

"I just wondered because when we showed up to cook the replacement dinner, I was given an explicit warning not to feed the dog again. The dog appeared 'sluggish', I think that was the word they used. They thought we had fed Baby. Like I'd go anywhere near those teeth!" Alli rolled her eyes. "So, I wondered if they had mentioned that to you."

"Apparently, not, but why would that matter?" Detective Clinton asked.

"Don't you see? Someone could have drugged the dog so they could steal the dragon. Can you do a blood test on the dog? Check it out?"

"I'm not at all sure we have a budget for testing overweight dogs for drug use," Clinton told her. "Besides, we have a much better lead on who might be behind this theft, and this person wouldn't need to drug the dog."

"Oh, who is that?" Alli asked. "You don't mean Gina and me, do you? Because I can assure you we would never steal from a customer. Rather, we would never steal from anybody. So who is the suspect?"

Before speaking, Clinton cut his eyes to Evan as if to say, "What a card this one is!" He held up one hand and wagged his finger back and forth.

"No, you don't. I'm sure you watch enough TV to know I can't tell you that. Is that it? Anything else?"

Alli shook her head no, and got up from her chair. She crossed to door, then turned back. "Well, thanks for your time. And, if you can find a way to check the dog, it might help your case. Enjoy your cookies."

Alli was at her car door when she sensed someone behind her. She automatically positioned her body to deliver a karate blow if circumstances required it.

"Stand down. I don't know how I'd explain that the nice little cookie lady gave me a larynx blow." Evan touched her arm.

"Evan! Did you want something?"

"Yes. I want to know why you came here with cookies? Were you trying to start something up with us again? I told you I couldn't see you until I'm off this case."

"Well, a girl can try, can't she?"

"I appreciate that." Evan smiled at her for the first time. "And, for your information, I was just relieved of the case. The sick guy's back, so they turned everything over to him. Clinton just told me. He's okay, Alli, don't underestimate him. He's a good cop. Word is he's moving to homicide soon."

"Yeah, he's put the hounds onto someone else. That's good for Gina and me. I just wonder who it could be?"

"Well, all I can tell you is that it's a good lead. The guy's home life shows he could use an infusion of cash right now. And he had opportunity."

"Not Pete?"

"Alli, I didn't say that."

"No, not Pete. He's such a nice guy! I mean, Gina and I have known him for a long time. His family has had a landscaping business for years. He's was a friend of Gina's husband. That's the only reason we let him in the house when the Dragon Lady didn't want us to. Pete's good people!"

"Yeah, I know, I know. Everybody is good people to you! But, Pete's financial situation is bad. His granddaughter needs an operation, and you know he's not flush. Times are tough. People are cutting back on services. He admitted that he is struggling. So, we don't have concrete evidence yet, but, yeah, he's a front-runner right now. And you, you got that out of me somehow! Alli, I swear on your Julia Child cookbook that if you tell anyone, and I mean *anyone*, what I just said, I will make sure you are sorry for that. I will arrest you for impeding an on-going investigation. Let's not go there, okay?"

Alli studied Evan's very serious face. "So, you came out here because...?"

Evan's face softened. "Because, I love your cookies. I wondered if I could get a special batch of my own like you gave Clinton, now that we can be friends again. You won't have to stalk me anymore."

"I'm sure that can be arranged. That bag of cookies I gave Detective Clinton? That was meant to be your bag. But I can always make more. Could you pick them up tonight?"

* * * * *

Gina dialed her home phone number and waited for the pick up. "Ma, are you available tonight to sit with the kids? I, uh, Craig and I are going to pick up dinner to eat while we go over some accounts."

"Oh, ho. Accounts. Right. Yeah, Pearl and me can stay in with the kids. I see a lot of activity over at Alli's, so I think she has something cooking on her stove and not just dinner which she told me she wouldn't be coming to."

Gina smiled and put down the phone, wondering what Alli was up to. A rap on her door pulled her eyes up to Craig's, his head poked around her door.

"'Dinner is Served', so to speak." Craig walked over to her small conference table and plopped down the two bags he had brought. "The choices were not legion," Craig said, "but I tried to get somewhat nutritious stuff for my head dietician. And to make dinner a tad less banal, I brought a small bottle of wine we can drink after we finish, just to celebrate getting those darned accounts done. I don't know how you have had the patience to tackle them on your own all these years."

Gina blushed at both the compliment and inference she couldn't help but draw from the wine he brought. *Wine at work?*

Craig unloaded the salads from the bags, and removed two bottles of water and two cookies.

"Craig, you shouldn't have. This really won't take long, but I'm happy to show you how the accounts work. It's not hard; it's more just, well, tedious. But I'm glad for your interest. Let's eat our salads. I'll go over some basic principles while we eat. After that, I can show you examples in the books. Okay?"

Craig was a quick study and asked the right questions. He grasped the overall concept of how the accounts worked, and he would point out what he thought to be examples in her books.

"Mr. Phillips, you are one bright guy. Are you sure you don't have an accounting background?"

"I have had lots of different experiences over the years, that is true, but not really, no formal accounting training. You're a good teacher, Gina. But, then, I'll bet you know that. I've seen you working with the kitchen staff when you have a new recipe for them."

Gina blushed again. She changed the subject. "How are things going? I mean with your job, with Clarice?"

"Great. Just great. I think I'm her new pet after that dog she talks about so much. Why? Have you heard otherwise?"

"Oh, you know. Office gossip. Somebody told somebody who told somebody that Clarice was yelling at you one day." Gina shrugged. "She's yelled at all of us, so I didn't give it any credence."

"No, maybe we got excited once or twice when I was trying to get her to back down on some policy change or other, but I'm good with her."

Gina smiled. "That's good to hear. Sounds as if you'll be staying then. I mean, we've had so much turnover in your job, it will good to have some stability."

Craig smiled. "Shall I open the wine? Are we done?"

"Pop the cork, Pop. That's what my mom used to say to my dad."

Gina paused and reflected. "We still miss him. But, what about you. I know a teaspoon's worth about your background. I know you have family in Iowa. What did you major in at college that would land you in hospital administration."

"I started out in pharmacology. I really thought I wanted to do that, but then...well, life happens, you know? I couldn't afford the tuition, so I dropped out of the program. I switched to business admin courses, and here I am. Here. Close your eyes and sip this. Tell me what you think. Can you taste the cherries and a note of licorice?"

* * * * *

One week later, Clarice was in her office trying to concentrate on her work. Her stomach grippe had her bowels in a twist. The whole week she had felt uncomfortable but today she had piercing cramps and the diarrhea was worse.

"Rita, fix me another cup of tea. And this time remember to add in a bit of sweetener. My stomach can't take it so bitter. I told you that yesterday."

Clarice, leaning back into her chair, groaned when she sat up to take the teacup from Rita.

Rita stayed in front of desk waiting while Clarice sipped the tea. "Will that be all? And, excuse me for saying so, Ms. Franklin, but you look like hell. Should you be here today? I mean, we're a hospital. What if you're contagious?"

"You'd like that, wouldn't you, Rita? Let the mice play today? No, no. I know I'm not contagious. It's just some sort of stomach thing. Probably aggravated by that spicy dinner last night that Gina and her friend fixed. You can relax. I won't infect you before some big date weekend. Still, I'm glad it's Friday. What time is my meeting with Craig this afternoon?" Clarice leaned back into her chair and closed her eyes.

"He'll be here at 1:30. Uh, do you need any files for that meeting or...anything? I wondered, if it's okay with you, if I take a late lunch."

"Nothing needed, I have everything right here." Clarice patted a file in front of her. "You can go, but I'll be timing you. One hour exactly. You have to set an example for the others who take timed lunches."

"Yes, ma'am. One hour." Rita turned on her heel and left, closing the door a bit harder than usual.

"Whew! Someone is testy today." Forester Bailey Young leaned against the doorjamb from the hallway.

"Yes, she is! What are you doing here, Fores...Mr. Young? You know she'll have conniptions if she sees you around. I have to work, even if you don't."

"Oh, relax. I just thought I'd check in to see how it's going around here. See if we're still on for lunch. Can you get away?"

"At least close the door and lower your voice if you're going to come in here. What can I say if she comes out and finds you?"

"Oh, just tell her I came by for some personal files I had left when she threw me out on my keester. In fact, here are some dummy files for that very purpose." Forester opened a file cabinet and jammed some folders into the front of the drawer. "There, you're covered, Miss Nervous Nelly."

"C'mon, Forester. You know how she pitched a fit when she found you in her office last week. And you never did tell me how you got in or why."

"Rita, Rita, Rita. These things are beyond the ken of a sweet little thing like you. But, that woman is up to something or has been or will be. No one is squeaky clean, Darlin'. Especially not the way she took this job from me. I will be back in that office. Oh, when you come to lunch, would you just bring along her appointment book, her personal one, not the one you keep? I just want to check something."

"I don't know if I can do that. I mean, she keeps it in her desk drawer. I'd have to get her out of there in order to take it."

Clarice's door swung open. "Rita, will you get..." She stopped when she spotted Forester. "I thought I made it clear you are not welcome in this hospital. Shall I call security to escort you out?"

"Good morning to you, too, Ms. Franklin. I was just asking Rita for some files I left here, personal files, of course." Forester's smirk showed no fear of her threats.

"Uh, yes, Mr. Young." Rita crossed to the file cabinet, opened a drawer, and took out some of the folders he had placed there. "Here you are."

"Not so fast. Give them to me, Rita." Clarice flipped through the folders, then with a huff, handed them to Forester.

"I can see why they tossed you out, Forester, if you kept personal files like these at the office. If you had run the hospital instead of tracking your investments," she waved a hand at the folders, "you would likely still be here. Get out. Don't come back." Clarice pushed past him into the hallway then held the door for him to leave.

"Rita, I'm going down to Accounting. I'll be right back. Get that cup of tea on my desk. With sweetener. Goodbye, Forester."

"Goodbye, Clarice." Forester grinned at her, and then sauntered toward the elevators.

Rita noticed Clarice following Forester with her eyes, then shook her head before turning the other direction toward Accounting. As soon as the Dragon Lady left, Rita scurried into Clarice's office and got her appointment book. She slipped it into her big purse, then fixed another cup of tea with extra sweetener. Clearly, the Dragon Lady needed it.

* * * * *

Alli hummed as she drove the old Explorer she'd borrowed from Gina for the day. Life felt pretty good right now. *Evan coming over for cookies. Umm umm sweet!*

First, though she had to run a million errands and be back in early afternoon to take Maria and Pearl to the casino. She was glad that Clinton was looking at someone other than Gina and her, but she knew he was looking in the wrong direction. Just a little bit of detective work might help the police out.

She pulled into an auto parts store parking lot on Thunderbird to get new wipers for the car. The summer heat was deadly on the rubber. She tried to argue with Gina that they shouldn't bother. How often did it rain anyway in a city where the average yearly precipitation was eight inches? But, no, Gina insisted she pick some new ones up.

She undid her seatbelt and was about to climb out of the car, when she saw a sight that caused her to duck down and reach for her camera.

Across the street, at the local No-Tell Motel, Rita and a man were standing next to a snazzy looking Porsche. *Pretty fancy car for that setting.* Snap. Snap. *Who is that guy? He looks familiar? Too big time for Rita.*

She saw Rita reach into her huge handbag, glance around surreptitiously, and slip a book to the man. Snap. Snap. *What is that about?*

The man seemed to be berating her. *For giving him something in public?* The man gestured to a door, and Rita followed him to it. They went inside for what Alli assumed to be the usual reasons for a noontime tryst. Snap. A picture of the motel sign in front of the room number.

Alli thought about waiting for them to emerge, but decided they would likely do the usual thing and slouch back to their holes after they had done the deed. No. She needed to see Gina to find out who was in the picture with Rita. He looked so familiar. And what was the book?

Back at the house, Alli plugged in her camera to the computer and downloaded the photos. She enlarged them as much as she could and then e-mailed them to Gina. Her subject line said: URGENT!!!!

Do u know who this is? Book looks familiar, any ideas? L8R G8R

Three minutes later, the phone rang.

"Alli, how did you get a picture of Forester Bailey Young and Rita? At a motel? Ewww!"

"I wasn't tracking them, honest, Gina. I was getting the wiper blades at the car place, auto parts, you know, the one we..."

"Alli. Focus. Okay, you took the picture from the parking lot of the auto parts place. Yeah, right, there *is* a motel across the street. But, Forester and Rita? C'mon. Get real. He's married to some society celeb."

"Yeah, like that matters. Okay, we'll give them the benefit of the doubt. They're just going into the room to have a cool place to read the book together. What's the book? Any idea?"

"Well, I think I am looking at its twin on my desk. The hospital issues appointment books to all administrators. I'd put money on that's what it is."

"Gina, whose *appointment book* would be worth stealing? And whose appointment book could Rita get...Ohmygosh! It's the Dragon Lady's appointment book. Gotta be! But why? And why would a fired hospital CEO want to look at it?"

"Alli, I know how your mind works. You think its connected to the burglary. Uh uh. Couldn't be. No way."

Alli paused. "Why not 'way'? None of this makes any sense. See you tonight. I gotta date with Maria and Pearl."

* * * * *

Alli looked more like a bag lady than she had intended, but Maria's dresses were just too big on her, even with stuffing and a belt to hold it together. And to top it off, the smoke at the casino was setting off her allergies. Improved ventilation, right!

"Why are you hiding that pretty face under a hat and who wears sunglasses inside except for big shots like Jack Nickles and gangsters not that I'm saying he's one? Whoee. Him in that scary movie with the ax now that was one great movie, right Pearl? Anyway, why did you want to get dressed up like this to come gamble with us?"

Pearl cut her eyes to Maria, before looking Alli up and down again. "Oh, Maria. Don't pretend you don't understand. Even I know that Alli is in disguise. She is doing detective work like that young man she likes, right, Alli?"

Pearl looked around the room. "Who are we looking for? What are we trying to see? Will this crack the case so you and Gina are cleared of grand larceny?"

"Shh. My name, today, is Sasha. Please remember to call me that. You never know who might be listening. And, yes, I am here to investigate. I am looking for Paul Franklin."

"How exciting! We can be dicks, too!" Maria's loud voice drew disapproving glances from some senior citizens even older than her and Pearl.

"No, you can't. Gina would kill me if she knew I involved you in this. She doesn't even want *me* to do it. And Evan…" Alli rolled her eyes thinking about what Evan would say to her. "But, tell me, point me in the direction of, where Paul Franklin goes to gamble with the high stakes guys. Then, you go off for your afternoon of fun, and I'll be back to whisk you away from the ball and back to the scullery."

Pearl resisted the dismissal. "Not so fast, Alli. Just how are you going to prove Paul Franklin is gambling?"

"I have my camera. I'll just snap a few shots."

"Alli, Alli, Alli. They don't just let you take pictures here. This is not a scenic site for photo ops. Use your cell phone camera. But carefully," Pearl said.

"You don't want to call attention to what you are doing so you get in the paper again so that people will think you are a crook for real and not just somebody who screws up a lot. She doesn't have a cell phone, Pearl," Maria put in.

"Cell phones cost money, Pearl. I can't afford one now, nor can Gina. But, if this business takes off, that is going to be my first purchase."

"Oh, for heaven's sake. What kind of a detective are you?" Pearl rolled her eyes again. "Here, take my cell. Look through here, and push that. It takes great pictures. Don't get caught! I expect to get this phone back."

"I'll be careful. Thanks, Pearl." Alli winked at the two women and meandered off in the direction had identified earlier.

She knew she was near her prey when she noticed the change of clothes. It made her think of the church sign a minister had posted one fall, "Arizona changes colors in the fall, too. Check the out-of-state license plates." In the same way, she knew by the upgrade in clothing that she was nearing the high rollers. Suit jackets, expensive watches, loosened ties. The average casino denizen was of the denim variety. And their shirts had messages.

Alli plunked down at a slot machine facing the entrance to a door with a gatekeeper. She got out a nickel, and it wouldn't go in. *A dollar machine? I didn't even know they were allowed to have dollar slots!*

Alli stopped fumbling in her purse when she noticed Paul Franklin approach the gatekeeper. After high school, Alli had been busted by the "eye in the sky" guys who scour the casino floor looking for suspicious behaviors.

She slipped Pearl's cell phone out of her purse and faked a phone call so she could take a picture of Paul Franklin greeting the gatekeeper. *They seem to know one another.* Additional shots documented him greeting others who were entering the room. As the door closed behind the men, Alli checked her watch. 3:30.

What would Paul's secretary would say if I called the office and asked for him. Pearl's phone is pretty handy.

Paul's secretary responded to her query. "I'm sorry. Mr. Franklin is unavailable. Who did you say is calling?"

Alli hung up. *Wonder if I could get a peek in that room?* She wended her way past the slots and back to the gatekeeper at the high stakes room.

She waited until the gatekeeper was looking another direction, then Alli sidled up on his blind side. She was almost to the door handle when the gatekeeper grabbed her hand.

"No way, Lady. Try the nickel slots. That way."

Alli affected an old lady tremor. "Oh, I was told I could play poker in there. I just love poker. Don't you?"

"Well, the poker in there isn't for you, Lady. Move on. You're blocking the door."

Alli read his name badge. "Mr. Butch, I have money. Lots of money. I could bet $25!"

Butch laughed. "Yeah, well, add three zeros to that, you could talk to management about me letting you in. Go find the slots, Lady. Good luck with all that cash." He laughed again as Alli waddled off.

25k? Now how where could Paul Franklin get that kind of money?

Chapter 8

Early Monday morning, Gina and Alli pulled into the Pierce's driveway and gathered the bags they had brought to prepare the week's meals for the family. Once inside, they found that yet, again, there was no envelope of money on the kitchen island.

"This is ridiculous, Alli. This is the third time we've arrived with no money left for us. I get that you might not have that kind of cash on hand, but why she doesn't just write us a check, I don't know. I am so tired of fighting with this woman over money. I'm going to call her and tell her we're leaving unless she arrives here with our money within 15 minutes."

"Let me. You are a tad hot, Gina, and I don't mean just the weather. I'll use those famous skills that got me the P.R. job at the hospital."

"Are those the same skills that lost you the P.R. job at the hospital? I can handle this. I deal with companies all the time that don't pay their bills. I promise I'll be civil and professional."

Gina dialed the work number for Sheila Pierce. Someone picked up, said hello, and then disconnected the call when Gina identified herself.

Alli watched Gina's face during the attempted call. "Do you think she is hiding out from us? This is nuts. Let me see if I can find her husband's number in the phone's contacts list. Maybe he'll clear this up finally."

"Oh, I'm not sure you should go rummaging…"

"Here it is. 'Rod—work'. Brother, can you imagine growing up with the name 'Rod Pierce'," Alli snickered as she dialed his number. "Hello. May I speak with Rod Pierce, please? Oh, good. Mr. Pierce, I'm Alli Wesson, with 'Dinner is Served'. We're at your house, but there is no money on the island. Since this is the third time, we're calling to tell you we…What? 'Dinner is Served'. You know, the people who make your meals…I don't understand that you don't understand. You eat the food. We expect to be paid. In fact, we're leaving if you don't show up with the money you owe us…What do you mean get out of your house? Yes, we are getting out of your house, and we're taking your dinner makings with us. What? No, don't call the police…"

Gina took the phone from Alli. "Mr. Pierce? This is Gina Smithson with 'Dinner is Served'. What seems to be the problem?"

Gina listened, her face turning paler as the man on the other end of the line continued speaking. "I see. Well, we have a signed contract with your wife and…"

She listened again and finally said goodbye and hung up.

"Apparently Sheila didn't let her husband in on our arrangement. He just thought her cooking had improved. He was quite complimentary, but adamant that our services were no longer required. He's a personal injury lawyer and said there has to be an escape clause, and he's exercising it. We're to pack up and leave. That does explain the cash payments, by the way. No trail for her husband to follow."

"Oh, Gina. What are we going to do? Can we sue?"

"Sure, but do we have that kind of money to sue over her piddling contract amount? Let's call it a lesson hard learned. C'mon. At least we have food for a couple of days for home, and I think we can use some of it, if we change our menus, for two of the families we cook for tomorrow. The good news is we can go to the Dragon Lady's house early. I'd just as soon get her stuff done and then head on over to the hospital for a couple of hours to catch up."

*   *   *   *   *

"Oh, sorry. We didn't know you were here." Gina and Alli started to see Clarice sitting on a bench in the foyer. Gina closed the front door and reset the alarm.

"Are you all right, Ms. Franklin? You don't look well." Gina went over to her and touched her clammy brow.

"I didn't go in today because I just can't shake whatever this is. Could you, would you please help me up to my room? I prepared a cup of tea, but now I am simply exhausted. I would like to lie down."

"Of course. Alli, would you take the groceries into the kitchen. And then, would you bring up this cup of tea for Ms. Franklin?"

Gina took Clarice's forearm and supported her as she arose. Together they made their way to the master suite where Clarice went immediately into the bathroom. At the sound of both gagging and explosive diarrhea, Gina, with hesitation, knocked on the bathroom door.

"Can I help? Do you need anything? Should we call Mr. Franklin?"

"Not a thing is required of you. Please close the door on your way out and try not to bang pots around."

"Sure. We'll be quiet as we can. Just call if there's anything..."

"Must I repeat myself. Nothing else is required, Gina. Please leave me to this indignity. I am counting on your discretion."

Gina closed the door to the master suite and made her way back to the kitchen where Alli had already begun the first of the meals they were preparing. The chicken thighs were soaking in the buttermilk, sugar, salt, and pepper marinade. They would cook the chicken last since it had to soak for a couple of hours before being rinsed, dried, and baked.

Gina quickly joined Alli in the preparation of the other meals. "What do you think she has? Sounds like the flu."

"I just hope she isn't contagious. Evan and I are having ice cream tonight after he gets off work. Don't want to miss that. I have to tell him who I think took the jade dragon. C'mon. Let's get these meals done. We can check on her before we leave, take her some water or something after we finish."

After three hours of prep and cooking, Gina and Alli washed down the counters. All the food was in the freezer except for tonight's refrigerated buttermilk chicken over brown rice. A zippered plastic bag contained chopped salad awaiting dressing. All Clarice, or given her health, more likely Paul, had to do was pop the chicken dish into the oven for warming. Four small bowls of lemon curd with whipped cream sat beside the chicken.

[See Buttermilk Chicken and Rice]

"I'll go up, Gina. I just brewed her some more tea and I have a glass of warmed ginger ale. That's good for tummy aches. She can pick her poison."

Moments later, a huge *crash* resonated through the house.

Alli's scared voice carried to the kitchen where Gina was washing the last of the dishes. She had already packed their materials preparatory to leaving. "Gina! Gina! Call 9-1-1!"

Gina picked up the Franklin's portable phone and punched in 9-1-1 as sprinted up the stairs to Clarice's room. She stepped over the mess the dropped tray made on the hardwood floor beside the bed. Clarice was dead. Gina wasn't sure how she knew that. She'd only seen a couple of dead bodies in her life, her dad and Nick. But she knew. Clarice's eyes were open and fixed. Her hand was clutching her cell phone and a tiny voice was calling out from it.

"Ma'am. Ma'am? Are you there? We're sending someone right away. Stay on the line. I'll be right here. Ma'am?"

Alli was backed against the bathroom door, hands clasped together over her mouth. Her body shook. "She was like that. She was just like that. She didn't say anything. She didn't talk to me. She was just like that."

Pounding on the front door insisted upon immediate entrance. Gina knew she had to snap Alli out of her shock and get her out of the room. Her friend knew the memories were paralyzing Alli.

"Alli! Alli, go get the door. Answer the door!" Gina led Alli to the hall door and pushed her through. "Go. Answer the door."

Alli came to, looked at Gina, and sprinted through the door. Gina could hear her take the steps two at a time. Then the sound of male voices from the foyer. She moved to the landing and looked down at the police officers standing there. Evan was among them. *Why are police here? Why not paramedics? Wasn't that why Clarice called 9-1-1?*

Alli moved toward Evan as if seeking to be held, but Evan turned away from her and moved up the stairway. Alli stood watching, her arms slowly dropping to her sides. She sank onto to the floor and leaned back against the wall.

Gina wanted very much to go to her, knew she should go to her, but her first responsibility was to the officers who wanted information about what had happened. So, Gina turned back into the bedroom. Clarice was dead.

Evan walked into the room last. "Oh, no! No." He turned to Gina. "Gina! What did you two do?"

CHAPTER 9

Gina and Alli were having their third disagreement in as many days over how much they should be involved in clearing their names. Gina wiped the kitchen counter over and over, even though no food particles were visible. Putting down the sponge finally, she picked up her car keys and straightened them out so they were as if one piece. She glanced occasionally at Alli seated at the table making her points yet one more time. There was no new insight, just days-old hash served up again.

"The theft and her death have to be connected, Gina. And, we have to clear Pete's name. He is a double suspect now since he works, well, worked, at the Dragon Lady's house. Since it was homicide, I'm sure we're still on the 'possibles list' these cops keep."

"Is it at all possible for you to have some respect for the dead? Please do not refer to Clarice Franklin as the Dragon Lady. That is over. Let it go."

"But, Gina, just because she's dead doesn't mean we should pretend she was a nice lady. She wasn't, and somebody wanted her dead because of it. Good people aren't poisoned. I'm going to prove that."

"Alli, stay out of it. STAY. OUT. OF. IT. Is that clear enough for you?" Gina pounded her balled fists onto the kitchen table, glaring at

Alli over the remains of dinner.

"But I can't. This is really important. It's our names, and Pete's."

Gina stared at Alli. "I am so sick of your arrogance, of your ignoring my feelings and reservations. You think you're above the rules that govern us mere mortals. 'Super Alli', right? Isn't that what you told Ma? You are still as mercurial and unfocused as you have been your whole life. You don't have the gumption to solve any crime because that takes doing the boring stuff. You can't stand being bored."

"Sure, Ms. Perfect! Except for the little glitch with losing your husband, everything has always worked out for you. Perfect parents, perfect college education, perfect marriage, perfect children. What would you know about gumption, anyway? You never had to have any," Alli retorted.

Gina came back at her. "What makes you think you can solve a crime, you with a barely earned high school diploma and a year late at that? Let the professionals handle this, Alli. You did enough damage to me in high school. Do not screw up my life any more than you already have."

Maria arrived at the doorway and surveyed the two red-faced women, probably brought there by the sounds of argument. Gina turned on her heel and marched toward the door, brushing past Maria as she headed to her room.

"Good you're here, Ma. You're just in time to comfort her. You can go see her in jail, too. I won't be visiting."

Alli met Maria's gaze and interpreted the look to be disappointment, maybe even disapproval.

"Oh, what have you done, Alli? You know Gina hasn't been herself since this all started. She's not sleeping. She snaps at the kids. Why did you upset Gina even more?" Maria re-traced her steps down the hallway, continuing past her room to enter Gina's.

Alli arose from the table and stared after the two of them. Blood always tells. She shared no blood with this family, and they just reminded her of that.

Grabbing the Explorer's keys, Alli left the kitchen for her casita. She exited a few minutes later, purse in hand, jingling the keys to the car. She didn't care what Gina thought now. She'd thank Alli later. For now, Alli had to do something to salvage their names. *We'll just see who has gumption!*

As Alli drove, she tried to remember the past week. It was little more than a blur for both Gina and her. Gina ended up taking more comp time to accommodate all the police interviews.

And the newspaper. The second incident involving them moved them up to the front page, and this time they got their names, personal and business, correct. Maria shooed reporters from their lawn every morning and drove the kids to school so they wouldn't be accosted.

Carrie and Nicky, of course, had heard some of the details, and Nicky was having trouble sleeping. He told them he was afraid that the murderer would come after his mom and Alli next. Carrie responded to the tension in the house by having meltdowns at school and home. The stress on all of them was horrific, and the shouting match with Gina, though the worst, wasn't the first.

Fifteen minutes later, Alli pulled into Gina's parking space at the hospital. Fortunately, the car keys also had Gina's office keys on it, so she could get in and plan her break-in to the Dragon Lady's office.

* * * * *

It was after eight o'clock. She was tired, but Rita continued to sort Clarice's personal belongings from those of the hospital. She was happy enough for the overtime pay, especially since the reason for it meant she'd never have to see that blasted woman ever again. Rita was so happy to be free of Clarice that she *almost* would have volunteered her time to clear out any remnants of the Dragon Lady. *The old bat deserved what she got. And no one is going to get punished for it. It is the perfect crime.*

A glint of green caught her eye, and she moved aside a book. She stared at a dragon statue crouched behind the budget books in Clarice's office. Rita reached out and removed it from behind the books. *Why did she hide a dragon here? A present for her husband? Something she got illegally? That would really do a number on her reputation if I could only prove it.*

"Rita?"

Rita dropped the statue. Alli Wesson walked into the office and looked at the green statue on the carpet. "What are you doing?"

"Alli, uhh, you startled me. I was just cleaning out the Dragon, uhh, Ms. Franklin's office things. What are you doing here? Where's Gina?" Rita peeked around Alli.

"Oh, she was tied up with the kids. I told her I would come over to pick up some files she needs. Then, I saw your light and wondered who else could be here. You know, did I need to call the cops or security or whatever?"

Rita shrugged. "This place feels like Grand Central Station tonight. Craig, uh, Mr. Phillips came in about an hour ago. He just had to get something from her office for some big meeting tomorrow. Mr. Franklin was in right after that, and Mr. Young just left. Gosh, how am I supposed to finish this job with all these interruptions?"

"Looks like you found something. May I see it?"

"Oh, I don't think so. It's a present for Mr. Franklin, I think. She must have put it here until she could wrap it."

Alli bent down and picked up the dragon. "Nice red eyes. Amazing what they can do with crystal these days. If it's for Mr. Franklin, I can get it to him. I'm headed over there to cook dinners for them." Alli wrapped it in tissues from a box on the desk and popped it into her purse.

"Tonight? Isn't it pretty late for you and Gina to be at a customer's house?"

"Well, Rita, see this is a special dinner. Things have been so hectic for the family. We are going to prepare a hot meal for them rather than one they thaw. It's been pretty tough. So, I'll just take it along to him. No worries."

Rita began to protest, but then shrugged and went back to clearing off shelves. Alli edged over to Clarice's desk. Rita turned and watched her suspiciously. Alli's eyes dropped to scan the desk.

"Since I'm going over to the Franklin's anyway, maybe I could take her appointment book with me. You know, save you the trouble. There may be numbers in there Mr. Franklin needs to contact."

Rita felt her cheeks burn. "Uhh, maybe he already has it. Or maybe the police picked it up when they came. It's not here."

Alli met Rita's gaze. "Uh huh. Well, just trying to help. Bye, Rita."

Rita sat down in the chintz chair and dialed a number on her cell phone.

On the third ring, it was picked up.

"You better get that appointment book back here. People are asking about it." She slammed her phone cover closed.

* * * * *

Mission Impastable

Craig rang the bell at Gina's house. She opened the door, a smile on her face.

"Ready? Sorry to be so late. I had to get some stuff at my office first. Is it *too* late?"

"Hi, Craig. No, but I am pretty tired. Can we just go to the Chocolate and Wine bar instead of a movie? I think you'd have to carry me out of the theater over your shoulder."

"Hmmm. Now that's an enticing idea! Sure. Let's just get wine and talk. My life is so drab, and you always have such interesting things going on in your life between family doings and Alli's investigations. Can't wait to hear the latest!"

Craig hugged Gina, lightly kissed her lips, then ushered her outside. Maria watched from a doorway, mouth pursed, and shook her head.

* * * * *

The next morning, Alli waited until Gina and the kids were gone. She knew Maria had her volunteer work at the church office, so it was safe to leave without meeting anyone from the house. Since both cars were gone, Alli got her bike out of the shed, slung her backpack on, and peddled toward downtown Glendale.

So it's still hotter than a griddle on the campfire. I can do this. It's only 10 miles. Each way. Alli grimaced and peddled faster. *Hope that deodorant is as good as the commercials claim.*

An hour later, sweating, Alli parked her bike in front of Prentice Carlisle's antique shop in Catlin Court in downtown Glendale. These old homes had been converted into boutique shops and Glendale was *the* destination place for antiquers. The doorbell clanged her entrance, and Carlisle came from a back room into the entry way.

"Welcome. It is surely a hot one already, eh? You must be looking for something special to brave the heat on your bicycle." He looked through the front window at the bike propped against the porch railing.

"I heard that this was the place to come for antique dragons, jade ones in particular," Alli replied.

"Indeed, that is my *spécialité*," Carlisle smiled. He looked her up and down. "They are pricey, you know."

"So I gather. I have one I'd like you to look at. See what it's worth."

Do you do that?" Alli asked.

"Appraisals? *Certainemente.* Do you have the dragon with you?"

Alli fished around in her backpack and brought out the tissue wrapped dragon and placed it on the counter.

Carlisle gasped when she uncovered it. Alli glanced at him quickly. "Is there something wrong?"

"No. No, nothing wrong. I was just, uhh, startled to see it wrapped so casually. Of course, it may not be authentic, just a good copy, but I'll let you know in a few days. Would you please fill out this form, Miss, uh, Miss...?"

Alli glanced at her monogrammed backpack. "My name is Wes... West. Anita West."

"Fine, Miss West. Just fill in this form with contact information. I'll call in a few days, a week at the most." Carlisle said.

"Well, I have no 'contact information'. You see, I just moved to town, I'm staying with a friend, and I can't for the life of me remember her address or phone. And I must be the only person you know who doesn't own a cell phone. I just stopped here on a whim."

"You carry antique dragons around with you on a whim?" Carlisle asked.

"Well, I mean, not a total whim. Anyway, I'll be back in touch with you to check on your appraisal. A few days, you said. Talk to you soon."

Alli forced herself not to dive for the bike and pedal off in a rush. She unlocked the bike, took it down the steps, and then leisurely began to ride north toward home. She felt Carlisle's eyes boring into her back. At the next street, she turned left and then rode quickly down the alley behind the shops on Carlisle's street. She sneaked up to a rear window where she saw movement. Her hunch was right. Prentice Carlisle was on the phone and he wasn't keeping his voice low.

"...name she gave was West. Anita West. Know of her? Well, you better get over here fast. I don't know how she got hold of that dragon...Of course, I know it's the same dragon. There is pattern on the jade near the left front eye that I recognized. When can you...? Not sooner? Fine. See you Thursday." Carlisle slammed down the phone, and Alli ducked as he turned toward the window. She backed away to the alley and rode home.

Who did Carlisle call and why? She wiped the sweat off her nose.

I need to call Evan. Please, God, let me earn enough money to get a cell phone.

Forty-five minutes later, Alli neared the mall. She knew right where the bank of phones was. She dialed Evan's number, almost hanging up on the fifth ring, when she heard his voice.

"Detective Katz, Homicide."

"Oh, Evan, I thought you weren't there. I have evidence, well, almost evidence, that Pete is innocent. He didn't take the dragon, and if he didn't take the dragon then that means he couldn't, well, wouldn't have killed the Dragon Lady, so you can let him go now."

"Alli? Alli, I thought for a minute Maria had called. Slow down. What do you mean you have evidence? Where did you get evidence? And how do you even know it is evidence?"

"Can we meet, Evan? You know the Starbucks near the mall on Bell and 75th Avenue? Can you come there? Now? I'll tell you everything."

"No, this is not a coffee shop conversation, Alli. This is a murder investigation. You have to come to the station, or I can come to your house."

"Oh, Evan. I'm on a bike. I don't think I can pedal anymore in 110 degrees. Don't get your shorts in a bunch and go all regulations on me. This is Alli. Meet me."

"No, Miss Wesson. This is a burglary investigation tied to a murder investigation. For the burglary, you should have called Detective Clinton if you have information. Come in, Alli, and we'll figure out what you have. Alli? Alli?"

Alli held the phone out from her ear and then gently laid it back into its cradle. So much for working together. She decided she had to gather more information, more evidence before bringing in the cops.

When she thought about it, she realized she had no proof that Carlisle knew anything about the dragon. She didn't know who he had called or why. And she didn't know when or where the Thursday meeting with the mystery person would occur. Realizing that Evan could have alerted the mall cops to her presence, she dashed for the escalator leading to the outside doors. Once at the bike rack, she unlocked her bike for the ride home. *Another 20 minutes. I can do this.*

Chapter 10

Early that evening, Alli ignored the banging on her door. Her draperies were pulled, and she stood on the wall beside the window so she would cast no shadow to anyone outside.

"I don't think she's here, Katz. Let's go."

"Alli. If you're in there, you have to talk to us. If you are withholding evidence in an on-going investigation...Don't make me finish the sentence. Alli, answer the door." Evan pounded extra hard one more time.

Alli held her breath and stood motionless, willing them to leave.

"C'mon, Katz. She's not there. Let's ask the folks in the big house to tell her we need to talk to her. Families are usually willing to help."

"They're not her family. She doesn't have any family." Evan's voice faded as the two officers made their way across the yard.

Alli peeked out an edge of the draperies. Evan and some other cop stopped on the patio near the pool. Gina had her arms akimbo listening, Craig at her side. Maria was gesticulating wildly, snatches of her berating reaching Alli's closed door. *Is she yelling at them or me? Everybody's so mad at me, she'll probably tell the cops I'm in here hiding.*

After several more minutes, Evan and his partner left. Gina took them to the front door through the house. Maria looked over at the casita then headed to Alli's door.

"Allison Marie Wesson. Open this door right now, or I'll be back with the key."

The French door opened a slit, then wider, enough for Maria to come in sideways. Alli shut and locked the door behind her.

"Turn on the lights so we can see one another because your eyes always tell me when you are telling the truth and besides I could trip over something since I am an old lady."

"I don't want to turn on the lights, Maria."

Alli shut her eyes against the glare of the overhead fixture.

"Okay, okay. If we gotta have lights, let's do the table lamps," she told Maria, who was standing next to the light switch. Maria reached over and turned on the sofa end table lamp to the lowest of the three-way illumination levels.

"What is going on that the police are pounding on your door and all the neighbors wonder why a police car is in our driveway again when your name isn't in the paper today?" Maria looked at Alli and held out her arms. Alli stumbled into them.

Alli, enveloped by Maria, sobbed and gulped, her tears flowing freely for the first time since the whole crime nightmare had started. Alli was not a crier. She had learned at an early age to not be a sniveling brat; crying only made things worse.

Maria was crying, too, and the release Alli felt was palpable. At some point, she didn't know how, they were on the sofa and Alli was cradled in Maria'a arms, being rocked and shushed like a baby.

"My Gina's heart hurts, too. You two should never fight. The pain goes so deep it cuts into your veins and you bleed out like a stuck pig. Gina is so afraid for the kids, for me, from what would happen if you go to jail like happens on those cop shows all the time when they put the innocent person in jail who can't prove they didn't do it but then by the end, they exaggerate them."

Alli looked up at Maria with a teary grin. "Exonerate. They exonerate the innocent ones. Do you just talk like that to get me to smile?"

Maria tilted her head and kissed Alli's forehead. "You two have always been stronger together. Whoee! I didn't stand a chance when the two of you took me on. So be strong together now."

"Gina hates me, Maria. She resents me. She doesn't respect me.

She sees me as a leach, a parasite on this family. And, let's face it. I am a screw up. Going back to high school when I literally screwed up."

Maria interrupted. "That was then. This is now. Gina doesn't know any of it, and she doesn't need to. We did what we had to do. But in the now, you two have to get past the anger and the hurt and bad words you said. Can you do that? For me, if not for you? I could die any minute, you know. I am an old lady and I'm sure my heart or my blood pressure could blow up anytime. This *could* be the last time we talk."

"Yeah, right. You'll outlive all of us, maybe even Nicky and Carrie." Alli disentangled herself from Maria and sat straighter. "I have to confess something to you. The reason the police, led by Detective Fink, my former boyfriend, want to talk to me is I may, well, okay, probably, took a piece of evidence from Clarice's office, and I gave it to somebody else."

Maria's mouth opened showing her surprise. "Alli, there is a killer out there. Somebody could hurt you. Call Evan. I'm sure he will understand when you explain how you accidentally were in the Dragon Lady's office and accidentally took something that you had no idea of so you accidentally gave it to another person who might be the real murderer because why would you give evidence away unless you were collecting more evidence?"

"No one cares more than us about clearing our names. I don't even care, well, not much, if they find out who dunnit. Truly. I just want this to be over for us. I don't trust the police to have that same level of commitment to clearing our names."

Alli slumped back into a corner of the sofa and hugged a pillow to her chest. "And that is part of the problem. Gina doesn't want to get involved at all. Nor does she want me involved. Let's just leave it to the authorities. If Gina found out what I've done, oh, Maria, I don't know what she'd do.

Maria nodded agreement.

"Maria, this may be my second worst screw up in my life. Honestly, right now, if I could do it over, I'd never have taken that dragon to Prentice Carlisle. In fact, I'm going to go get it tomorrow and take it to the police. You're right. Gina's right. I don't know what I'm doing. Can I use your car tomorrow morning?"

"That's my girl. I knew you could figure this out by yourself otherwise I would have told that nice young man, Evan, who you aren't seeing now because you can't but I know he's important to you, that you were here. See. You are doing the right thing."

Maria fished the keys from her pocket and pushed herself to her feet. She waddled to the door and turned to wave good-bye.

"I hope so, Maria. I surely hope so." Alli rested her head on the sofa back, tucked her feet under her, and watched Maria close the door behind her.

* * * * *

The next morning, Wednesday, Alli jumped out of bed resolved to fulfill her promise to Maria. Pulling on jeans and a tank top that were mostly clean, she scrubbed her face, brushed her teeth, and grabbed a banana for her breakfast before heading out the door.

She had every intention of going to Prentice Carlisle's shop immediately after she got some coffee at the gas station, but then she reminded herself it was only a bit after 7. He wouldn't open until 10, so she sipped her coffee in the parking lot and thought about what she could do in the time she had.

From her satchel purse, she grabbed the crime notebook she had begun last week, a bright pink with orange flowers spiral leftover she had found in the bottom of a drawer. After ripping out the first few pages of how to apply henna tattoos, freeze drying flowers for bouquets, and ten surefire ways to lose weight, she had a lot of space to figure out the crimes she was involved in.

Alli flipped to her first page of suspects and re-read her notes hoping for some new insight, something, anything to pop out:

> Pete Lopez—Nah! No case against him except he came in the house while we were there cooking. Cops think he needs money for family so he'd steal. They think he killed to conceal that he was a thief. Doesn't square with what we know of him.

Alli clicked the top of her pen and wrote more on the page:

And, he couldn't get into Clarice's office to put the dragon there, so he's innocent. And if he needed the money why would he put The dragon in her office anyway? TELL EVAN THIS IS PROOF!!!

There. Pete is cleared. Now who else is here?
She turned to the next page.

Paul Franklin—Possible. She was a witch, but maybe not to him or the kids. Check on their relationship. He was spending lots of money gambling. Where did the money come from? How much insurance was there on the dragon? On Clarice's life? Why he wouldn't do it—doesn't seem like the type; would leave the kids motherless; maybe he doesn't need money—could be richer than we think

That was it. Two suspects, well, and the cops had her and Gina on their list. And she'd already cleared—in her own mind—both of them. *How could I find out about the insurance? Did the cops examine the Franklin's financial records? Probably. Maybe I could find out something from Evan? No, dead end. I pulled the plug myself on that fountain.*

Well, who else could it be? Ah, that Young guy, Forester Bailey Young. She wrote his name on the next page.

Forester Bailey Young—cheating on wife with Rita? needs money to pay off wife? or he might want to cause aggravation for Clarice by stealing the dragon. But how could he get in there? Maybe Rita grabbed it for him when she went to Clarice's house. He might kill Clarice to keep her from turning him in OR maybe he killed her because she took his job after he was fired. Or maybe he killed her because she was mean to Rita. Lots of questions, but he could be the one.

Or maybe he is covering up for Rita?

Alli turned to another page. She wrote Prentice Carlisle's name and began to jot her thoughts.

> Prentice Carlisle—what is his connection with the stolen dragon. He recognized it as Clarice's. How? Did he sell it to her? Who did he call? Insurance report might tell who bought from. Might Rita know? Check newspaper to see if he's listed.

Alli didn't think she was being biased about Rita as she considered her as a possible suspect. *Just because she dated Evan, well, that has nothing to do with this.* She wrote her name on the next page.

> Rita Kinney—she didn't like Clarice. She could go to Clarice's house with no problem. She could get the dragon and hide it in the office. But why would she kill unless Clarice found out? Why would she give Clarice's appointment book to FBY? What was in there he wanted? Take Rita to lunch to milk her?

Alli looked at her few notes, over and over. Nothing helped. The more she found out, the more tangled it all was in her head. Alli snapped the loose leaf notebook closed, her crime book. Maybe going to see Prentice Carlisle wasn't the right move this morning. Maybe she could get a little more information first.

The mall was close by, and those early morning health nuts were there doing their mall-walk exercise, so she knew it was open and she could use a phone. Maybe she and Rita could have a little girl-to-girl talk over lunch. But first, Evan.

* * * * *

"Yeah? Come in."

"Hi, Evan. Long time no see!" Alli's lips smiled, but her narrowed eyes gauged his reaction.

"Alli. You. Where have you been? What have you been up to?"

"Remember how when you were in the Academy, and they would give you homework on cases to solve? Remember how you and I did them together? Remember how good I was at figuring out connections and finding clues."

"That was homework, Alli. This is real life. You cannot go around investigating because you do not have the authority. And if you tamper with evidence, that can destroy a case. Besides, it's dangerous. There is a killer out there. What makes you think he or she wouldn't come after you?"

"I know, I know, I know. Everything you say is true, but I got caught up in things. It's like there are all these balloons up there with their strings hanging down. And when you pull one down, you find there are three other balloons attached to it. I thought I could help. But, I know I didn't."

"Alli, that's what I said from the beginning. Trust us. We are trained to do this work. I know you're smart, but you just can't get into the same stuff we can."

"You're right, Evan. I just came from Detective Clinton. I told him everything I know about the jade dragon Rita found. He's going to follow up with Prentice Carlisle and Rita Kinney. I know there is some link between this dragon and the death. One of those two knows something, I'm sure of it. I just hope you can get it out of them."

"You told Clinton all this? Good. What is the link you think you see?"

"Something is going on with Rita and Young. I caught them at a motel and she gave him Clarice's appointment book. Maybe Young took the dragon. Maybe Rita did; I don't know, but something smells."

Evan was taking notes. "Okay, but if they were continuing their affair, it is probably unrelated."

"Continuing their...what?"

"Alli, remember when I told you that I was no longer seeing someone at the hospital, that I'd like us to get together?"

"Yeah. And I figured out it was Rita because she kept 'running into' you, accidentally. Plus she froze me out whenever she saw me. So?"

"Well, I broke it off with her when I realized she was having an affair with her boss, F.B. Young. She was just using me as a shill, a romance cover story so no one would suspect them. I doubt there is anything there. The appointment book may have been hers so they could plan their next rendezvous."

"Evan, I'm done. This case has broken up my family, because Maria and Gina *are* my family, even if you don't think so. It's also bashed our new start. I just want out of it now."

"That's the first smart thing you've said during this mess."

"But, Evan, I wanted so much to help clear Pete. They've got a lot on their plate, that family."

"I guess I can tell you this, Alli. It will be in the paper tomorrow. Pete is out of jail. We couldn't really hold him any longer with so little evidence, and now, if what you are saying about Carlisle pans out, there should be no doubt in anyone's mind that Pete is innocent."

Alli got up to leave. "Just one last thing, if you can tell me. What happened to Clarice. Why did she die?"

"That will be in the paper tomorrow, too. She was poisoned. Apparently it was in her tea, at home and the office."

"So now you are wondering who could get into both those places. Gina is still a suspect, isn't she?"

"I didn't say that, Alli. I'm glad you're not involved anymore. This could get nasty. Killers are usually unpleasant people to get mixed up with."

"So that clears Gina. In your mind, right? She's not an unpleasant person."

"Alli. You're out of this. You promised."

"Yeah. Yeah, I did. Bye, Evan. See you someday?"

He smiled as she left.

*   *   *   *   *

Alli didn't think keeping her lunch date with Rita was a violation of her promise to Evan. Well, maybe a technical violation. But she couldn't call her up now and cancel. Rita did have access to Clarice's office and home, but if she were one of the suspects, she probably didn't even know it. What could be wrong with having a lunch with an old acquaintance? Besides, it was better to get some info before the cops started muddying the waters with their questions after they got to Carlisle. She promised herself to turn it all over to Evan and

Clinton if there were anything of import.

Alli pulled into the parking lot of the "The Dragon Inn", a Chinese place really close to the hospital, waiting for Rita. Alli thought the name might inspire Rita to talk more.

She picked up her crime notebook and recorded the facts as she had related them to Detective Clinton along with info she had gleaned while at the station. Clarice was poisoned? What kind of poison? How was she poisoned? Alli hoped they had checked all the food she and Gina had prepared. That would clear Gina. She was finishing a sentence when she started at a rap on her window. Rita had arrived and spotted her.

Alli opened her door and climbed out, slipping her crime notebook in the side of her voluminous bag. "Hi, Rita. A bit early. That's good." She led the way into the restaurant.

Alli and Rita settled themselves into seats and Alli reached into her purse and moved the small tape recorder onto her lap and turned it on. If Rita caught her, she'd have to make up something, but what were the odds?

Alli began. "I'm so glad you could get away. You know, I've been thinking about you a lot since the kids and I saw you at Cucina Tagliani and then that lucky meeting earlier this week. How come we never hung out at the hospital while I worked there? It seems we have a lot in common."

Rita snorted. "Yeah? Like I am an Administrative Assistant and you wrote newsletters so we both type? Sorry, Alli. That was mean. This is very nice of you to do."

The waitress interrupted to take their order. She brought them tea and they settled back into conversation.

"How are you holding up, Rita?"

"That hospital is a horrible place to be right now. The cops come in on a whim. Other people come in and out to get stuff, take stuff, read stuff. I don't know what's off limits and what's not. The cops even went through the boxes of her personal stuff I'd packed and took her tea and a dish of candies! I mean, really! Are the cops that hard up for snacks?"

"Wow. All that must be hard on you. Losing your boss must be tough, emotionally, I mean."

Rita looked at Alli as if gauging her seriousness. "No. Actually it's a relief. I'm not sorry someone did the old bat in, frankly. I mean it's probably tough on her family and all, but, really, they may be glad, too."

Alli affected shock. "No. You don't mean it? Tell me, tell me. What was going on with her family?"

Rita scooched her chair in closer, looking around to see if others were paying attention to them. "I wondered if Paul Franklin was in some kind of trouble, money trouble. You know he could have done it. Lots of men off their difficult wives. And money can be the trigger."

"Rita, they were rich. Between his business and her job, they had to be pulling down high six figures, right?"

"Money only lasts as long as you let it. I heard her screaming at him on the phone one day. About his gambling, I think. I wondered if maybe the Mafia or somebody might be on him. I mean, she sounded really upset. She said something like, 'We don't have that kind of money, Paul. See if he'll take less. If you cave now, you'll end up paying more than we can afford.'"

"When did this happen, Rita?"

"Oh, right after she took the job. I was surprised, because she was always so controlled."

Alli nodded in sympathy. "You see these high-ups, Rita, from the lower echelons where we are, and you think 'They have it made. Good money, no worries.' I guess you never really know."

"Yeah, they have no money problems, but we do, Alli, and they don't even care. Did you know the Dragon Lady cut my salary the first month after she started?"

"No! How could she do that? Why?"

"She said my pay was out of whack with the other Admin Assistants. She thought Forester, uh, Mr. Young, overpaid me. I earned every penny of that money working for that guy. The things I covered up for him, the times I saved his...well, you know what I mean. Admin Assistants have a tough job."

Alli nodded again, showing she understood.

Rita dug into her purse, peering into its contents. "There was something I wanted to show you, a note I found. I put it in here somewhere." She continued digging before dumping the whole mess onto the table. Alli noted used tissues, change, lipstick tubes with and without caps, breath mints, crumpled grocery store receipts, and... was that a gun? It didn't quite look like one, yet it did. Maybe it was a toy.

Rita stirred around in the mess until she found what she was looking for. "Ta da! Now read this and see if I should give it to the police. It was on the floor under Clarice's desk the afternoon she went home sick."

Alli pointed to the weapon on the table. "What's that? Do you have a permit for a concealed weapon?"

"No, but you don't need one in Arizona. It's from a friend, someone who worried about me walking all by myself to my car in the parking lot at night. When Evan still worked there, he would come by to take me to my car, but after he left, well, a friend thought I should have it."

"I see. So what's this note?" Alli reached across the table for it.

Rita began shoving stuff back into her purse, but there was a lot of it. She put up her hand. "Not so fast. Do you promise not to tell anyone about it?"

"Yeah, sure. Who would I tell?"

Rita handed it over to Alli. "Read that and tell me what you think."

Alli opened the folded half-sheet of paper. It was a list:

> Appraisal vs insurance value vs price paid?
> Verify theft how?
> How soon does policy take effect?

Alli handed it back to Rita. "So what do you think it means?"

"Oh, Alli, you are such an innocent. Don't you see? Clarice was planning an insurance scam all along. That's what this means. Do you think I should take it to the police?"

"Maybe. I mean, I guess it is better to have everything that might be related. Still, you don't know that this refers to the jade dragon or if this indicates planning for insurance fraud." Alli shrugged, "But I guess it's better to give it to the police than not."

Rita seemed miffed that Alli wasn't more impressed. She stuffed more junk back into her purse, but several things were still scattered on the table.

Rita leaned across the table to get closer to Alli. "You want to know the really juicy stuff? Now, I didn't start it, but, I admit I didn't deny the rumors. Some of the guys in Accounting, she was on their tails all the time, some of those guys started wondering aloud, you know? They thought maybe she was really a man in drag living with her partner. No woman would act like her, so she had to be a guy. She *was* a real ball buster."

"It does sound like you had it pretty tough, Rita."

The waitress interrupted to ask if there were anything else they wanted. When they shook their heads, she tore off the receipt and placed it by Rita's side.

Rita leaned across the table to pick the conversation back up. "I know this will sound like I'm not a feminist or something, but women just don't make good bosses for other women. It's like I was in competition with her or something. You know, if I had a new dress or hairstyle, she'd look me up and down, and never say a word."

Alli nodded agreement. It was getting harder for her to give this self-centered woman her whole attention.

Rita stood up. "Listen, I have to go. Here's some money for my lunch. Would you pay the bill?"

Rita started to walk off then turned back. "You know the type, Alli. They act nicey-nice on the surface, but then they demean you and trash you and make you feel like dirt. No, I'm not *glad* she's dead, but I'm not sorry."

She teetered out of the restaurant on high heels, her perfect bottom wiggling back and forth as she bumped her way past tables.

Alli shook her head and began to dig around on the table for the receipt. There it was under Rita's napkin. And Rita's weird gun was beside it. Alli looked around to see who might have noticed, and then she slipped it into her own purse to return to Rita later.

Chapter 11

Things had been pretty quiet the last couple of days. Alli ate out and came home late to avoid the family. She only slept there. She let herself into her casita quietly so as not to announce her presence. The house across the yard was dark.

Nevertheless, Alli drew the curtains to block the light, and turned on just the bathroom fixture, with the door pulled to, to keep illumination to a minimum.

"It would probably be safer to have more light than that," a voice said as the lamp by the sofa clicked on.

Alli was blinded for a moment, blinking her eyes as she adjusted to the light. "Gina. Gina, what are you doing here? I thought..."

"I brought you some wine, it's kind of warm now, but we can put ice in it. It's your favorite. Nobilo's Sauvignon Blanc," Gina said.

Alli started to cry. "I'm so sorry, so so sorry. I know I'm a screw-up. And I know I make life harder for you sometimes, but your friendship, your love is more important to me than anything."

Gina wiped tears from her eyes as well. She rose from the sofa and put her arms around Alli. "No, I'm the one to apologize. I said horrible things to you, untrue things. I am so scared that I am taking all my fear out on you. I have to hold it together for Ma and the kids.

You, well, you and I have a history of fights going back to that playground battle in second grade. I crossed the line, though, and I'm sorry. Can you forgive me? Can we put this behind us?"

Alli squirmed out of Gina's arms. "First, in the interest of full disclosure, let me tell you what's happened this week. Then, if you still want us to be friends and business partners, I am so good with that. I need you, and I need your family. I was scared to death I was going to lose you. So, pour us another glass of this most excellent wine, let me get the nuts and cheese, and I'll tell you everything."

"I'd like that, Alli. I know you are not one to sit around, like me. I admire that risk-taking part of you, but I do worry about you."

"Oh, Gina, I missed having you around to run by all this stuff I've been thinking. I need your good common sense to balance out my intuition and rash action-taking. Evan gave me a little talk along those same lines!"

They arranged the food, sipped their wine, and Alli launched into the tale of her past week. Gina sat quietly, her face revealing to Alli that she was fighting down her impulses so she could let Alli finish.

Gina only interrupted once, as Alli described the lunch with Rita. "But, I thought you told Evan you wouldn't do anything else."

"Yeah, but I already had the lunch planned, and I did call him and Detective afterwards and told them what she told me. They have to check Paul Franklin. He could get into the house and the office. He had motive and opportunity. That's what I wrote in my crime book."

"Well, they say the husband is the most likely to have done it," Gina responded.

Alli grinned at her. "Who, 'they'?"

"You know, the crime shows. All of them say the husband is the most likely to have killed the wife, but then again."

"Right. How often does the husband *end up* being the killer?" Alli paused. "I really do like the guy, and just because they argued, well, that's not necessarily a pathway to murder. Still, they checked out Pete. They jolly well better check out Paul Franklin. There's something going on there, I'm sure of it."

"Alli! No. Do not get involved again."

"I won't Gina, but if information falls into my lap, what am I supposed to do? Put my fingers in my ears and sing tra-la-la-la?"

* * * * *

Friday afternoon, the family whole again, Alli set out to see what else she could do. She had promised Gina no more taking chances. Just paperwork stuff she could get legal access to. No confrontations or interactions with anyone. It seemed an easy enough promise at the time. And after all the wine.

Alli donned her disguise again. A friend of hers whose brother was a big-time poker player provided her with a sheet that told her how to play the odds. If she had this hand, she should discard two cards to get new ones. If she had another, she should bet more. It wasn't real poker playing, but it could make her look like she knew what she was doing. Alli spent the morning trying to memorize the sheet before finally giving up and digging in her Goldwater Drawer (the one on the far right in her kitchen) for a Sharpie pen. All she had was purple and orange. The purple showed up better on her forearm and hand. Alli copied the sheet onto her body, then practiced holding the cards while searching for the pattern of the card hand on her body hand.

She borrowed Maria's car to "run errands" and headed down the 101 to the Indian Casino. This time she had some singles and fives so she could look like a serious bettor.

Alli made her way back to the poker tables scattered around the high rollers room door. She positioned herself beside a table so she could see the comings and goings from the room. She pretended interest in the table betting, but she kept her eyes on the room. If Maria and Pearl's observations were correct, Paul Franklin was probably in there right now.

"In or out, Lady?"

"Huh? What do you mean?" Alli asked.

"Are you going to sit down and play? You can't stand behind players and see their hands. Play or go."

The dealer motioned to an empty seat. Alli sat down and began pulling her money out of her purse.

"We use chips. Is this your first time, Lady? Maybe you'd be better off at the poker slots."

"Chips? Oh, chips. Where do I get them?"

He sent Alli off to the exchange windows where she turned her cash stash into a tiny pile of chips.

She sat down at the table and the dealer eyed her small stack. But, he dealt her a hand to play. She checked her forearm and saw that she was supposed to change in three cards. She asked for them.

Alli followed the marks on her hands to see that she was supposed to fold. She did so. The next hand, she got luckier and actually got to bet. But she was quickly out because she didn't have enough to see the raise.

She won the third hand and now had a few more chips to work with. She was startled when a hand on her shoulder caused her to look up at the tall uniformed Native American man standing there.

"Would you please come with me, Miss?"

"Is there a problem, Stan? I know Miss Wesson. I'll vouch for her." Alli heard Paul Franklin's voice over her other shoulder.

Alli stood, confused by what was happening, and upset to be identified by the man she was stalking.

"Could we move over here away from the tables?" The security guard took Alli's marked up arm and led her to the side.

"I don't think I want to go with you. Can't a girl place a bet?" Alli blustered. "Hi, Mr. Franklin. Imagine seeing you here."

"Miss Wesson, did you say? Miss Wesson was engaged in some suspicious behavior at the table, so I was sent to check it out. I watched for a while, and then I approached her. Miss, what is written all over your arm? Are these codes for cheating? Are you sending signals to a partner at the table?"

"Cheating? No, I mean, does having this stuff that tells you how to bet, is that cheating? I've never played before and a friend of a friend told me to 'play the odds'. He gave me a sheet that told me what to bet if I had certain cards. See." Alli held out her arm and hand for them to investigate.

Paul Franklin bent over the markings with the guard. She watched the two of them exchange guy-looks that said, "What a ditz! Poker isn't a formula."

"I think she's okay, Stan, but I'll walk her out to her car and explain things to her."

Stan waved them away as Alli and Paul left the casino.

Alli was embarrassed to be ushered out, but she realized the futility of protesting. Besides, her prey was leaving, so she might as well, too.

"First of all, why are you in that get-up?"

Alli hesitated. Truth? Lie? Truth? Lie? Ah! Half-truth. "I didn't want to be recognized. I mean, what if one of our customers found out I had a gambling habit? We might lose a customer."

"Next time you don't want to be recognized, I'd suggest a wig. Your hair is pretty distinctive, and it does draw the eye. Once in the vicinity, it's pretty easy to tell who you are by your face. A gambling habit, eh? I wouldn't have taken you for the type."

"What type is that, Mr. Franklin?"

"Now don't take this wrong, Alli, but you seem to have lots of interests, and gamblers often have pretty barren lives. They crave the excitement, the expectation for quick riches. You don't seem the type, is all."

Alli decided to go for it. "And you? Do you come here a lot? You seemed to know the security guy pretty well."

"I know how this must look, too, coming so soon after Clarice's death, but I had to settle some things with someone, so I dropped by for a few minutes. But yeah, I come here sometimes. It's relaxing pitting my brain and instincts against these really good players."

"I'm so sorry, Mr. Franklin. I know we sent a card expressing condolences, but I haven't seen you. This must be really hard on you and the children."

"Thank you. It is difficult. My sister took the kids back to California. They needed to get away from all this. The police are still coming to the house to question me, search for god-knows-what, and I stay away from there as much as I can. Along those lines, I don't think I remembered to tell you we will be taking a hiatus from your wonderful meals. I still have several dinners in the freezer. So, can I get back in touch with you, once the kids are back and things are settled down?"

"Absolutely. Is there anything else we can do in the meantime?"

"No. But thank you for asking. Will you excuse me? The guy I was looking for wasn't in the casino, so I have to call him. Take care. And, thanks again for your great food."

Alli walked slowly so she could catch the phone call, digging in her purse as if searching for her keys.

"Prentice? Where were you? What? The police? What do they want? *The* dragon? How did *you* get the dragon? Oh, no. Don't tell them a thing. Call me tonight. We have to meet." Paul Franklin snapped his phone closed and turned back toward where Alli was standing, her hand clutching her keys.

She jingled her keys above her head, smiled, and trotted toward her car. At the first coffee shop, Alli pulled into a space and pulled out her crime notebook to record what she had heard. Next, she phoned Evan and asked him to convey the information to Detective Clinton.

* * * * *

By that evening, Alli and Gina's whole family had decided to hunker down with pizza and re-watch *Ratatouille*. Pearl, who had been a stalwart help throughout the whole ordeal, was invited, too. Craig though invited, had another commitment. Alli was glad it was just the family, with Pearl, of course, counted in that group.

Dessert, Alli promised, would be extra special, and something they had never had before. The adults were working very hard to keep things light and started telling knock-knock jokes after the movie until the kids joined in.

"Want to hear a World War III knock-knock joke?" Nicky asked.

They all nodded.

"Knock knock."

Alli bit. "Who's there?"

Silence. Then Alli, Gina, Maria, and Pearl exploded with laughter, while Carrie stood by puzzled.

"What? I don't get it," as her lip quivered, Alli bent down to her.

"Oh, Button. It's just a silly joke. Nothing important, but I could use your help with my special dessert. I'm thinking of naming it 'Carrie's Colossal Crumble Castle'. What do you think?"

They went into the kitchen and Alli started pulling stuff from the refrigerator and sent Carrie into the pantry to fetch graham crackers, cinnamon, nuts, and anything else she found that appealed to her kindergarten tastes.

The assemblage on the counter included whipped cream, blueberries, maraschino cherries, and chocolate syrup from the refrigerator and Carrie's assigned goods along with the container of Gina's homemade chocolate cake mix. Alli mixed the nuts, cinnamon, and chocolate cake mix and several crushed graham crackers. Carrie placed a graham cracker on a plate for each of them. Alli added a layer of whipped cream, blueberries and chocolate syrup. Carrie sprinkled on the nut mixture and added the next graham cracker layer.

They repeated layers until each dessert was three-graham-cracker-layers high. Alli slathered on more whipped cream and drizzled on chocolate syrup. Carrie topped each one with a cherry. They delivered the desserts to each.

Gina looked at the concoction and the clock. "Alli, with all that sugar, they'll never get to sleep."

"Sure they will. We're going to put on 'Love Story' next. They'll be out in ten minutes!"

Only the kids finished the dessert. The adults agreed it was not one to repeat.* As predicted, Carrie and Nicky fell asleep side by side in the beanbag chair as the women wept their way through the movie.

*Seriously, Reader. Do not make this dessert!

Chapter 12

Prentice Carlisle's apartment was on the top story of his shop in the Catlin Court antique district of Glendale. He struggled to consciousness, the alarm system buzzing into his drug-induced sleep. The sedative his doctor had prescribed was the only way he'd been able to get any rest since the murder. And now the jade dragon was back in his possession.

He wakened enough to realize that it was his shop alarm, not the house one that was so persistent. Sure he knew what it meant, he picked up his cell phone and punched in a number.

"Do you hear that? That's my alarm system. Want to bet someone took that jade dragon? Again? The police will be here in a few minutes. I'm going to tell them what I know. I don't want to be an accessory in this mess."

The voice on the other end answered. "The worst thing you can do is panic. I have plans to divert attention. Meet me later and I'll tell you what we need to do. Shut off that damned alarm and when the police show up, tell them you had a short circuit or something. You're a good liar."

Carlisle took a deep breath before answering. "Name calling won't get me to back you up this time. I'm out, I tell you. This has gone further than we planned."

"Oh, I don't think you're out until I tell you you're out. I have a little piece of evidence the police might like to see, some fingerprints on a tea caddy. Now shut up and do as I said. I'll meet you for lunch at the Sonic Burger place on 75th Ave. and T-Bird. 11:30."

Prentice stared at the silent phone in his hand. The red and blue flashing lights of the patrol car cast garish images on his closing in walls.

* * * * *

Alli, Gina, and Maria cleaned up the dessert from the night before and the Saturday morning breakfast debris. Though the room was quiet except for the clanking of plates and tableware, it was a comfortable silence after a week of friction. Life felt good again to Alli despite their continuing business and murder investigation worries.

Gina and Maria were right, Alli needed to butt out of this investigation and let the professionals handle it. She had to trust the system, something she had never been very good at. But peace in her life was worth it. She was back in her family, and nothing was going to get her out of it again.

* * * * *

Rita tossed in her bed, flinging her arm across the body beside her.

She awoke to Forester's "What the hell? Get up if you can't be quiet."

Rita mumbled "Sorry" and exited to the bathroom down the hall. She squatted on the toilet, releasing the hot liquid, as she rested her head in her hands.

Should she tell someone what she knew, thought she knew, she corrected herself? And if she told, what would that mean for her and her life?

Maybe she could work things out at her lunch date. She was sure he didn't want to meet her, but she could be persuasive in her own way. Yes, everything would be better later.

* * * * *

Forester stared at the door Rita had just exited through. *Damn broad. What time is it?* He picked up his cell phone to check the time right as it rang in his hand.

Cautiously. "Yes? I told you not to call me. I don't want a record of even knowing you." He listened to the caller, responded, and punched the off button. Maybe he could get in another half hour. Then, screw Rita, and off to his day. A busy one was shaping up. Forester smiled as he curled up on his side and shut his eyes.

* * * * *

Paul Franklin picked up the phone again to place a call. It was almost 7 in San Francisco. The kids would probably be up watching cartoons and eating cereal, their normal Saturday routine. Not too early to call, even if his sister was sleeping in.

Right before he hit the memory button for her number, he laid the phone back in its cradle. He couldn't talk to them yet. His guilt would reveal itself to them. He couldn't deal today with their questions about why and what next.

First, Paul had to finish what he had started with Prentice Carlisle. The antique dealer had told him he had the jade dragon, brought to his shop by someone. Paul had to get the dragon back and let the police know his suspicions about the theft and the part it might have played in Clarice's death.

Later. He would call his children later. For now, Paul put on his racquetball clothes and headed to the gym for a punishing workout.

* * * * *

Craig was already at the gym. He hated early morning phone calls. They were never good news, so he took it out on the gym equipment.

Sweat dripped off the ends of his beard onto the floor beneath the punching bag. Exercise was the best way for him to control his frustration and anger.

He couldn't understand why the police had not yet made an arrest stick in Clarice's murder. Surely there was enough evidence against that yard guy, Pete. Or what about that old guy, the one who used to be the hospital CEO? From what Rita had told him, Franklin Bailey Young had both opportunity and motive. Were the police even *looking* at him?

Meanwhile, the hospital's Board of Directors were being deliberately vague about who would be named to replace Clarice. He had even heard, through Rita, of course, that Young's name was in contention. He didn't think he could work for that egomaniac incompetent. He was just rid of one egomaniac. The thought of another directing him was enough to make him consider moving on. And that was just not in his plans.

Maybe the info he'd get at lunch would help him bring this to a close. That job should be his. He just had to figure out how to get it.

Craig threw a frenzy of jabs at the punching bag.

* * * * *

Evan ducked his head into Detective Clinton's office. "You're here early. And on a Saturday, too. What's up? You get a break in that hospital murder?"

Clinton was staring at his murder board wall. He pushed his chair back from his desk and leveraged himself up with the desk front. "Nah. This case is driving me nuts. It's like I'm not seeing something that's right there. You tell your girlfriend to butt out? Amateurs like her just mess up the picture more."

Evan felt his face heat up. "Well, whether she's my girlfriend or not, that's still TBD. But, yeah, I told Alli to keep out of it. I think she will this time, but, Jack, you have to see it from her point of view. She doesn't want to be a suspect. Who does? And she's always just been... impetuous, you know?"

"Yeah, I know. Damn good cookie baker, that girl. You oughta hold onto her. Now her partner...she's one cool customer. You heard the interview tapes. Calm, collected. Of the two of them, she's the one with the bigger ax to grind and she had opportunity working right down the hall from the vic as well as having access to her kitchen at home. My money right now is on Gina Smithson. I'm thinking of dropping over there for another little chat. Think it's too early?"

Detective Clinton grabbed his tablet and pushed past Evan. Evan stared after him. He was so tempted to call Gina to warn her, but he knew that was impossible. Why did he have to be friends with someone who did indeed, he had to agree with Clinton, seem like the frontrunner in a murder investigation?

His training, the mantra of motive and opportunity, resonated. Most murders weren't nearly as complex as the TV shows made them out to be. Mostly it was pretty easy to go out in concentric circles and identify the murderer in a close-in circle.

But he knew, he just knew it was impossible. Gina Smithson a murderess? When pigs fly. But Clinton had a nose for crooks. Could it be? Did Gina murder her boss? And if she did, what did that mean for Alli?

Evan walked over to Clinton's murder board and looked for a pattern, any pattern that would lead away from Gina and Alli.

Chapter 13

Gina answered the doorbell and stood aside to let Detective Clinton into the house.

"Ms. Smithson, I wonder if you could answer a few more questions for me. Do you have time right now?" Detective Clinton stared at Gina in a way that meant she had no choice, not really.

"Of course, Detective Clinton. I'd be happy to help if I can. Could I get you something? Coffee? Tea?" Gina blushed as she said "tea" then hurried on. "Anything?"

"Nothing thanks. Could we go in here?" He motioned with his arm into the living room off to the left of the entry way.

Gina led the way. She sat on the sagging sofa, brushing cookie crumbs into her hand as Detective Clinton sat in an armchair across from her.

She didn't look at him as she said, "Those kids. I've told them not to snack in here, but you know how kids are."

Clinton nodded. "Yeah, I have four myself. The wife has done a good job with them. I'm pretty busy, so it's up to her a lot. Sort of like your situation. You work, so your mother must be a big help. And your partner, Alli."

"What brings you by on a Saturday morning, Detective? Do you have a new lead?" Gina picked at a loose thread on the sofa cushion.

"Well, actually, it's like this. Every time I look at the facts, things keep coming around to the same place. I was wondering if you could help me move to another place."

Gina finally raised her eyes to look at him. "Oh, Detective. I know Alli seems a good suspect in this case, but she could never, would never hurt anyone on purpose. What can I tell you that would convince you of that?"

"How did you feel about your boss, Ms. Smithson? We've heard she rode you pretty hard?"

"Ms. Franklin could be hard on everyone, Detective. She is, rather, she *was* a perfectionist. She expected the best from everyone, and she mostly got it."

"And that didn't bother you? You were okay with that?"

"Detective, I'm sure people have told you that I'm a bit like that myself. Would I have liked some acknowledgment that I was doing a good job, sure? Who wouldn't, but that just wasn't Ms. Franklin's way."

Clinton stared at her. "Did you want her job? Did you think you could maybe run the hospital more humanely? Get results but have a happier staff? Did you see yourself doing that?"

Gina felt her face redden. "What are you implying? Am I a suspect?"

"Ms. Smithson, Gina, would you come with me to the station? I have some more questions and some things I'd like to show you. See if you can help me explain them."

"What...What do you mean? Are you arresting me?"

Gina's voice rose higher.

Alli peeked into the room. "What's going on? Oh, Detective Clinton. I didn't know you were here. Did you have a break?"

Gina stood and stared at him. "Are you forcing me to go with you? Is it my choice?"

Alli's face showed puzzlement. "Why are you going with him on a Saturday morning?"

Detective Clinton looked at the two women. "We can do this quietly or not. It is your choice. You surely don't want your children to see you in handcuffs. Just come along and we'll finish our conversation at the station house."

Gina looked over to Alli. "Call that lawyer we cook for on Thursday. Ask if he'll meet me at the police station. May I get my purse?"

At Clinton's nod, Gina exited the room and moments later returned.

"Don't say anything, Gina. Nada. Nothing. Zilch."

"Call the lawyer, Alli. I'll be fine."

Gina and Clinton went out the front door to his dark sedan in the driveway.

* * * * *

Maria sat still and watched Alli on the phone, her third call in fifteen minutes. "But why would they think this of my Gina? How could anyone think such a thing?"

Alli held up her hand to silence Maria's moans and remarks. "Oh, thank you so much. Yes, I'll be meeting you there, too. I told her not to say anything. This has to be a misunderstanding."

Alli laid the phone back into its place. "Third time works the charm."

"So why three lawyers? It takes three to help Gina?"

"No, Maria. She will have one lawyer. Our client, the one I called first is a patent attorney. Who knew? Anyway, he had a friend who does criminal law, but he couldn't help because he does contract law work for the hospital. He had a friend, however, call number three, who will take Gina's case. Did I just say that? Gina is a 'case'? Oh, Maria."

Alli stopped when she saw Maria's drawn face, tired eyes and cheeks covered with deep lines. When did Maria get old? "Listen, I gotta go. I'll call you as soon as I know anything. This is all just a huge mistake." Alli took Maria's arms and pulled her out of the kitchen table chair. Alli put her arms around Maria and hugged her. She buried her face in Maria's ample neck and kissed her, leaving a small tear along side.

Alli grabbed her purse from the counter and the car keys off the hook. "Call Pearl. Tell her to come over to be with you while you wait. Can you send the kids to one of the neighbors for a couple of hours?"

While Maria nodded, Alli yelled behind her, "It will be okay. I promise." She went through the door to the garage and screeched the car onto the street. Alli covered the two miles to the police station in three minutes.

When Alli arrived she found a reserved spot to pull into. She'd ask forgiveness later. The desk sergeant looked up from the log book he was working on. She stretched her neck over the top of the high desk trying to see what he had written about Gina.

He maneuvered the book away from her eyes.

"Hey, aren't you the cookie lady? Those were darn good. You bring some more?"

"No, uh, Sergeant Farley. I'm here to see Gina Smithson. She's with Detective Clinton."

Alli watched Farley's face cloud over. "Oh. The Franklin murder. They're in the interrogation room right now. You her lawyer?"

Alli was very tempted to answer yes, but behind her she felt the warmth of a body close by.

Evan's voice interrupted her. "No. Ms. Wesson is not an attorney." He spun Alli around. "What are you doing here? I thought you told me, told everyone that you were not going to be involved any more."

"Evan, you have to help me, help us. Clinton has Gina locked up in a room, and he's grilling her. You know that's wrong. Stop him!" Alli leaned into Evan as she grabbed both his forearms.

Evan broke loose, then taking Alli by her arm, he led her down the hall to his office. They entered and he closed the door behind them. "I've been watching the interrogation, Alli. Detective Clinton is being very respectful. She has a Coke and he's just showing her some things."

"But why? Why would he almost arrest Gina? He told her to come quietly or he'd use handcuffs! Evan what is going on?"

Evan stared down at his desktop then raised his eyes to Alli's. "As an officer of the law, I cannot tell you anything." He held up his hand as Alli started to interrupt. "But, as your friend, I can tell you that things don't look good. Oh, right now it's circumstantial, but you put enough circumstantial evidence in front of a jury, they might just convict." He turned to his window onto the parking lot.

"Like smoking, you mean," Alli mumbled.

"Huh?" Evan twisted around to look at her.

"You know. They never *proved* smoking caused cancer but they had enough correlational evidence piled up, that now everyone accepts that smoking is a cancer cause." She shrugged her shoulders as if accepting the inevitability of Gina's situation.

"No, not like smoking. A really good attorney demands they look for proof beyond a reasonable doubt. Gina will probably get off." Now it was his turn to shrug.

"In the meantime? What do I tell her kids? Her mother? Her friends? Our clients?" Alli broke into tears.

Evan had never seen her cry. Not through anything that had happened to them. Not through her many job losses. Alli was not a crier. He reached out to touch her shoulder but a loud voice from the outer office stilled his hand.

"I demand you release my client immediately. Since you cannot produce a warrant for her arrest, Gina Smithson is being held illegally. I'll have your badge for that Sergeant, uh, Farley. Direct your Detective Clinton to release my client this moment."

Alli's head popped up, and she smiled. He was here. The attorney she called, one of those TV lawyers who take impossible cases. One of those who fight for the little guy against all odds. And, he worked on contingency so they didn't need any money now. Good thing as their operating margin was pretty slim.

Alli jumped up from her seat in Evan's office and tore through his door. She bumped into the attorney, a squat, squarish-shaped fellow who had blustered his way past the desk sergeant.

"Mr. Osberg? I've seen your ads on TV. I'm Alli Wesson. I called you about my friend, Gina. Thank you for coming."

"Ms. Wesson. A pleasure. Now let's get your friend out of here." Osberg whisked out a card and handed it to Evan who stood right behind her. "Sir. If you would."

Evan stammered an "all right" and went further down the hall and turned left. Alli watched him go, then turned back to the attorney.

"She's innocent, Mr. Osberg."

He turned to look at Alli. "Of course she is. All my clients are innocent. Even the guilty ones. I'll get her off on some technicality and then she can get on with her life."

"No, that is, I mean, I, we, don't want her off on a 'technicality.' We want her name cleared. You have to prove she's innocent."

"Well, my dear, proving innocence is a lot harder than proving guilt. I'll do what we need to do. The important thing is she'll be back in the bosom of her family tonight Now, I can't promise the police won't file charges later; she may still go to jail tomorrow. But for tonight, she's free."

Alli wasn't sure that's what she wanted to hear, but then Gina came around the corner Evan had gone to. She rushed down the hall and the two women hugged. They held arms as Osberg ushered them through the front door of the station.

Outside were two radio stations and three TV trucks, a hovering helicopter, and a reporter Alli recognized from *The Arizona Republic*. Gina looked at Alli, and Alli turned to the attorney.

"What's going on?" she began.

"I thought we could use a little help in the clearance campaign. Let's get the public on our side. Don't say a word. Just look upset. Harridan killed by hardworking mother of two young children who cares for her invalid mother? I don't think that will play well, do you?" Harry Osberg turned away from Alli and Gina, held his hands up beside his body, and set his mouth in dismay as he addressed the media before them.

CHAPTER 14

It took all of Alli's wiles to keep the kids away from the TV. Gina's picture was prominently displayed in the news leads ("More at 6") on every channel. The phone rang constantly. No one was allowed to answer, which also puzzled Nicky and Carrie. After a couple of hours wrestling with both questions and bodies rushing to get to the phone, Alli called one of Gina's co-workers whom they socialized with and asked if she'd be willing to keep the kids overnight and away from the news.

The promise of seeing the latest movie and staying up late gorging on popcorn lured the kids away from the tension that was building in their home. Gina and Alli both promised a gourmet dinner for six as a thank you.

Fortunately, no media people were camped out yet on their front yard. Maybe reporters didn't like having to pull extra time on a weekend. After all, as Alli told Maria, Pearl, and Gina, it really was a nonstory until Gina was actually charged.

"So you do think I'm going to be charged with murder?" Gina's face paled.

Pearl reached across the kitchen table and took both of Gina's hands in hers. "No, no. Twit here is just saying that since you aren't charged, where's the story? The police questioned you again. Big whoop!" Pearl glared at Alli who understood the message.

Alli flinched. "Right, Gina. What's to inconvenience themselves over? Those reporters are probably off to Paul Franklin's house asking about that jade dragon. Uh, about that jade dragon. In the interest of full disclosure since I gave up the criminal life, or rather investigating criminals, uh, I have a small confession to make."

"Alli, tell me you did not take that jade dragon from Clarice's house," Gina demanded.

"Oh, no, no. Not from her house. I took the jade dragon from her office."

All eyes fastened on Alli.

Maria interrupted the silence. "You stole something? After all these years, you stole something, just like your family? Alli. How *could* you?"

"No. No, I didn't steal it, but Rita came across it in the Dragon Lady's office and while I was there, while I was still investigating, back then in the past, I, uh, I told Rita I'd return it to Paul Franklin."

Gina stared at Alli. "And did you? Return it to Paul Franklin?"

"Well, not exactly. Uh, actually, not at all. I took it to a dealer in Glendale's antiques district. I wanted to see what his reaction was. And his name was in a news report as being the place where the Franklin's bought it."

Pearl and Maria both said, "And?"

Alli squirmed in her seat. "He seemed nervous. He knew it was the jade dragon from the Franklin's house. I know he did. I watched him for a while and overheard a conversation with someone about it. He told me he'd appraise it and I should come back for it Monday. I already told Evan and Detective Clinton. I'm sure they'll follow up. But I want to go back and check myself."

Gina dropped her head into her hands and began to sob. "Alli, that was a piece of evidence that has been contaminated beyond all use to the police. Did you ever think that you might have messed up the fingerprints? Fingerprints that might help identify a killer?"

"I know, I know. Alli screws up again. But, he knows something, this Carlisle guy. And he's the nervous sort. I'm sure the police can shake him down."

Pearl shook her head. "Alli. You watch too much TV."

Maria, notably silent during this interchange rose to her feet, pushing off the table to help her stand. Pearl noticed the difficulty she was having stood and held her arm.

Maria turned to stare at Alli. "I am going to my room. If they take Gina away because of what you did, Alli, maybe it is time for you to find another place to stay." She and Pearl left the kitchen.

Gina turned to Alli. "She didn't mean that. I think the jade dragon thing is big, but my fingerprints aren't anywhere on it, so I can't believe it will be a factor. She's just upset. She'll settle down."

Alli stared down the hallway after Maria. Find another place to live? Maybe that *would* be for the best. All she touched these days seemed designed to hurt the ones she loved most.

* * * * *

At 6:00 exactly, the doorbell rang. Alli was closest so she checked the peephole before swinging open the door to Craig. She fell into his arms, forcing him to hug her with flowers in one hand and wine in another. After an awkward moment, Alli withdrew. She felt her face redden as she stammered an apology.

"Oh, that's okay. Not everyday I get a hug like that. Pretty tough day, was it?"

"Yeah, I guess I just needed some contact."

Craig studied her. "What about that boyfriend of yours? Why isn't he here hugging you?"

"Oh, Evan? Well, he's not really...I mean, I'm not sure we... anyway, he's a police officer, so he can't really, uh, you know, see me until this is all cleared up. But, you're here. That will help."

Maria and Pearl came out of Maria's room where they had spent the day. Pearl came over to greet him, but Maria stood back and watched.

"How are things going for you at the hospital now, with all that's happened, I mean," Pearl asked.

Craig tilted his head and scratched at his beard. "Well, it's tough. We don't have an acting CEO and don't know when we'll get one. Someone on the Board is signing stuff for us so we're limping along, but I can't think they'll allow it to go on this way much longer. Things are already falling through the cracks. I submitted a transition plan to them. I don't know what they thought of that," he gave a rueful laugh.

Pearl wondered aloud, "Might they bring back Forester?"

Craig looked quizzical so Alli jumped in. "Forester Bailey Young was CEO before Clarice. But I thought he got into some kind of trouble."

Gina entered the foyer. Craig left Alli's side and hugged Gina. "How's my girl doing? You okay?"

Maria sniffed. "Hmmph. How do you think she is doing with the police suspecting her and maybe they will lock her up tomorrow without even having good evidence?"

Gina waved the crowd into the family room. "Let's get out of this doorway. Wine? Thank you so much. Alli, would you open this and bring the other bottle of wine in here, too? I think I'll switch to Craig's pinot noir."

"I must say you seem pretty calm for a woman who was all over the news today. Of course, you were a short timer. That big wreck on I10 knocked you off center stage." Craig smiled and reached for Gina's hand and held it in his lap.

Alli and Maria's eyes met. Pearl raised her eyebrows. Gina and Craig were looking at one another.

"Hooboy!" Maria interrupted the moment. "Any cheese to go with this stuff? You know I'm not used to drinking without food."

Pearl snorted. "Since when? C'mon, let's you and me rustle up some snacks and let the young people talk."

Alli rose to accompany them.

"No, we can do it, Alli. You stay with Craig and Gina. We can manage fine, right, Maria?"

"Yes, do stay, Alli, if they are all right without your help." Craig turned on a full smile for the two older women.

Once Alli had seated herself again, Craig leaned toward her. "So what do they have, think they have," he amended, "that implicates Gina? What do your sources tell you, Alli?"

"Sources? If by sources you mean Evan, nothing. He can't tell me anything. It's against the police code of honor or something. Everything I know, or think I know, has come from my own investigation."

"So what *do* you know? Tell me. Maybe a fresh look from someone not so close to it will take you down another avenue?"

Alli looked between Gina and Craig. "Is it okay Gina? Do you want me not to talk about it anymore? It's your call."

Gina sighed. "Why not? It can't hurt at this point to see if Craig notices something we've missed. But first, who do *you* think murdered Clarice? Who could have done it? And why?"

Craig clucked his tongue. "Ah ah ah. Gina, you know that would be pure speculation, though of course everyone is speculating. And I shouldn't add to the cesspool of conjecture, but, if I had to put my money on someone, it would be Rita and her former boss. *Cui bono*, as the saying goes."

"Which means?" Alli challenged.

"Which means, the police will look to who stood to gain the most from her death. Was it the grieving husband counting on the life insurance money or was it revenge from someone Clarice done wrong?" Craig sat back with a smile on his face. "Elementary, My Dear Watson, er, Wesson."

"Okay, so why are you leaning more to Rita and Forester over the husband?" Gina inquired. She removed her hand from Craig's and leaned over to pick up her wine glass. She patted Tasha's head resting on the sofa beside her.

Craig twirled the liquid and then sipped his own wine. "I pick that pair because Rita had access to the tea at Clarice's office, for sure, and at home with some pre-planning. She did nothing but complain about how Clarice was always riding her. The rumor mill is that Young had a burn about her, too. Word I heard was that he blamed Clarice for everything from his loss of income to the divorce up to and including losing money over at the track."

Gina chimed in. "I know it was after you left the hospital, Alli, but surely you remember all the allegations that floated around that time. Young was supposed to be getting kickbacks from vendors, he was rarely at the office, stuff like that."

"Yeah, I guess, but with all of that, why would they think killing Clarice would get him the job back?"

Craig picked up Gina's hand again and traced figures on her palm. "Good point, Alli. But do killers really think things through? Maybe he thought the disruption would be so great they'd turn to someone with experience. He certainly has been into the office more this last month than in all the previous six months since I arrived."

Maria and Pearl walked into the room with a basket of assorted

Mission Impastable

crackers, three kinds of cheese, and slices of kielbasa that had been browned up.

Alli leaned over to spear a chunk of meat when the doorbell startled her into dropping it on the floor. Tasha immediately arrived to clean the floor.

Alli jumped up and peeked through the little glass hole in the door.

"Oh, no. No. Gina hide. Run out the back door. Go to my place."

"What are you saying, Alli. Why should Gina hide in her own house?"

The doorbell chimed again, more insistently.

Alli ran to the sofa and pulled Gina to her feet. She shoved her toward the Arcadia door. "It's the cops. They're here to arrest you!"

* * * * *

"Thank goodness the kids weren't here," Pearl exclaimed. Maria sobbed in her recliner while Pearl held her.

Craig and Alli made a quick plan after the police arrived and escorted Gina, handcuffed, out to the squad car. Craig called Gina's attorney while Alli packed a bag with toiletries and a change of clothes. In case they let her have them. They were going to the jail to see if they could have time with Gina before Harry Osberg arrived.

Alli could only hear Craig's side of the conversation, but it sounded like Osberg thought there was a night court that they could use to get her released on her own recognizance so she wouldn't actually spend the night in jail. Alli fervently hoped that was the case.

Alli and Craig were about to leave the house, when Maria called out to Alli.

"Come here, Alli. I told you that I did not want you to ruin my family. Please find somewhere else to stay, maybe at Evan's, maybe in the park, I don't care. Just don't come back here until this is all straight. Somehow this is your fault. And I can't bear to see you tonight. Or tomorrow, Maybe ever." Maria began to sob again.

Pearl gave Alli's hand a squeeze. "Maybe it's best. For tonight. Call me tomorrow. I'll stay here with Maria."

Craig drove frantically to the courthouse in downtown Glendale. Gina was not in the night court yet, if she even would be. Harry Osberg, dressed much more casually than he had been this afternoon, arrived a few minutes after them. They conferred in the back of the courtroom, Alli watching the door Osberg had pointed out as the one where prisoners entered.

"That's all I can tell you right now. I'm going to the charge officer to see the warrant and, then I am going to talk with Gina at the cell where they're holding her. Saturday nights tend to be busy, so it will probably be another hour or more before she sees the judge. Relax. They're just trying to scare her." Osberg patted Alli's hand and shook Craig's. Alli slumped in the bench. Craig put his arm across her shoulder and she leaned into him.

"Maria threw me out. I mean, I know that sounds petty given what Gina is facing, but it's not, Craig. It's not. Maria, Gina, they're my only family. If I don't have them, I don't have anything."

Craig squeezed her shoulders. "Not to worry. I have an extra bedroom. You can stay with me. This will all go away tomorrow, I'm sure. Maria gets...umm, how did Gina put it? 'Exercised', yes, that's the word. Maria is an emotional woman. She'll be fine once we get Gina back to her tonight. Now tell me more about this personal chef business. Where do you get your recipes?"

Even though she knew what he was doing, Alli was grateful for the distraction. She could always talk food. It calmed her and she chatted on about their clients and their food fetishes.

The Night Court Clerk entered the courtroom. "All rise. The Honorable Clementine Ferguson presiding." A petite woman in a black robe adorned with a lacy collar seated herself behind the tall desk.

"You may be seated," the clerk announced. Officers led the criminals, alleged criminals, Alli reminded herself, to the benches where they would await their turns. He read from a clipboard the name of the first person. Alli found herself trying to guess what the judge would rule based on her own perception of people's guilt or innocence.

The twelfth one to stand before Judge Ferguson was Gina. Alli noted that Osberg had been able to get some makeup to her. Gina, though pale, looked quite kempt. That should help, Alli thought. Gina looked too respectable to believe her a murderess.

Alli whispered to Craig that Osberg may look and talk like a dork, but he seemed to know what he was doing. Alli's confidence in a positive outcome rose.

Apparently the judge agreed enough with Alli's assessment of Gina's demeanor, or with Osberg's arguments, that she allowed Gina to leave. No jail tonight, but she had to keep herself available for questioning and couldn't leave the county until the Glendale police no longer considered her their prime suspect.

Alli and Craig hugged Gina and Osberg then hurried Gina out to Craig's car. Craig called Maria before he pulled out of the parking space.

When they got to the house, Maria flung open the door and ran out to greet them. She hurried Gina inside, saying not a word to Alli, though she did thank Craig for bringing Gina home.

Alli stared at the closed door as Craig backed onto the street for the twenty-minute drive to his condo, ironically very close to the courthouse they had just left. Neither spoke.

Chapter 15

Maria led Gina to the sofa in the family room while Pearl poured them liqueur glasses of Bailey's Irish Cream.

Gina was still stunned from the evening's events, but she looked around the room and noticed Alli's absence. "Are Craig and Alli still out in the car? Aren't they coming in?"

Pearl gave Maria a look. "Uh, no. They're going to Craig's place. Alli told me she's spending the night there."

Gina looked up from her glass. "Spending the night? With Craig? But, why, what? I thought he and I..."

Maria jumped in. "It was my idea. Not that they stay together because who knows what that man has in mind but it was my idea for Alli to go away from here for a while."

"Ma. That doesn't make sense. This is Alli's home. Why should she leave? And to stay with Craig? It just doesn't make sense," she repeated.

Gina saw Maria's face take on that implacable expression when she knew she was right and she wasn't going to back down.

"Ma. What did you say to Alli? Tell me."

"After the police came and took you away, I was so scared. I was mad. Mad at the hospital. Mad at Alli for getting involved in this mess. Mad at myself for not stopping her sooner. So, I just thought it would be best for all of us if she just went away for a while. Just until this gets settled. Then she can come back."

Gina felt her blood pressure rising. She stood up and faced her mother and Pearl. "This is my home, too, and you cannot make that kind of decision without talking to me first. How could you? You know how much this family means to Alli. She needs us. Even though she acts tough, she's not. You of all people know that the best."

Maria wrung her hands. "I'm sorry. You're right. I know I hurt her, and she's been hurt so much. Should I call her, tell her to come back?" Maria began to cry again. Pearl reached for her hand and squeezed it.

Gina quickly crossed to her mother and hugged her hard. She looked at her watch. Three-thirty a.m. "No, it's too late. They're probably in bed. I'll call in the morning and tell her to come home."

Maria nodded and gave a small smile and wiped her eyes. She blew her nose and told Gina, "You always were the one with a head on her shoulders. You could see things so clearly, even when you were little."

"Just one thing, Ma. Did you suggest Alli stay with Craig or was it his idea?"

Pearl spoke up. "Alli told me in the driveway just now that Craig offered when he heard that Maria tossed her out."

Gina's stomach flip flopped. She turned to leave the room. "I see."

*   *   *   *   *

Alli settled into a corner of Craig's sofa, legs tucked under her, a third glass of wine nearly finished. She stared vacantly out the window of Craig's condo at the lights of downtown Glendale.

She drew her gaze from the window and began examining his condo. Sparse, clean. No personal touches like knickknacks or photos. One corner, near the window, which would have been perfect for the sofa instead housed an elaborate terrarium system. A portable water tank fed a drip system to the dozens of plants set on tiered shelves.

Alli turned to Craig. "What are those? They don't look like any plants I know, except, maybe, is that an orchid?"

"My hobby. Remember? We talked about it the night we met. I

love the discipline it takes to grow exotic plants. There is little room for error. You can kill them with an inadvertent draft or overwatering." He smiled. "I'm not saying I have control issues, but..." He waggled his hand back and forth.

Alli nodded. She turned back to investigating the Glendale lights blinking off as its night owl citizens called it a night.

Craig interrupted her reverie. "We never did get dinner tonight. Could I make you an omelet? A PB&J sandwich? I make a mean *vichyssoise*."

Alli looked up at him. "Really? Just like that?" she let a small smile curve her lips.

"Well, Wolfgang Puck and I make a lot of soups together. He and some of his other cooking buddies drop off cans here all the time."

"Craig, this is really nice of you, and I feel so rotten because I haven't always been so nice to you. I mean, I grill you about your life, I question your background. I just want to say I'm sorry for my past behavior to you. You've been a great help through this mess."

"No need to apologize, Alli. I hardly noticed," Craig grinned at her.

"It's probably because you and Gina, well, you two seem close. I haven't seen Gina this interested in a guy since, well, since her husband Nick died. Maybe I'm afraid of losing her. Are you close? Oh, good grief, there I go again, grilling you." Alli held up her hands. "Sorry, sorry, sorry. And yes, a PB&J would hit the spot. Do you have milk, too?"

Craig smiled and went to the kitchen that opened off his living room. "I'll get that right now. Why don't you just relax. More wine?"

"Oh, that wouldn't be a very good idea. I might be a mean drunk. Lots of my family were. Oops!" Alli clapped her hand over her mouth.

"That's okay, Alli. Gina has shared some of your story with me. I know that her family took you in when your family left."

"Gina told you that?" Alli gargled the words. It was an unwritten law that nobody talked about her past. Nobody, no way, no how.

"Well, I kind of wiggled it out of her. I needed to know if I was right. Here. Eat this. And I have these great cookies a friend makes. They should taste familiar." Again Craig smiled at her.

Around the chunky peanut butter and apple butter clogging her throat, Alli managed to get out a sentence. "What did you mean, you wanted to find out if you were right? Right about what?"

Craig cleared his throat, stood up from the small table for two, and walked over to his plants. He adjusted the grow light hanging from the ceiling. It was an infinitesimal adjustment as near as Alli could tell.

She interrupted his fiddlings when it seemed he would not speak. "Is it because you wondered if you were going to get a nut case in the family, in case things got serious with you and Gina? Did you wonder if she and I were blood relatives?"

Craig turned back to Alli and a smile lit his eyes and whole face. "Is that what you think? That I'm interested in Gina? Romantically?"

Alli felt her face grow hot. "Oh, I am so sorry. How presumptuous of me. It's just, well, you two have worked late a lot and you have been out on several, what I thought were dates. You were holding her hand tonight. I mean, the clues seem to indicate something's going on."

"Ever the sleuth, eh, Alli?" Craig smiled more broadly. "No. No, it's not Gina that brought me into your life. It's you I'm interested in knowing more about."

"What? Me? Uh, that's a surprise, Craig. I have a boyfriend, well, sort of. Our relationship is complicated."

"You are too cute when you get flustered. Just like when you were a kid. You never could dissemble." Craig laughed aloud at her confusion. "I know you have a boyfriend. I'm sure he's a very nice fellow, police officer, right? Helping with this murder case?"

Alli nodded. Where was this going? What had Gina told him about her childhood?

Craig picked up their dirty dishes and rinsed them. He placed them in the dishwasher and wiped down the table and counters. Alli waited until he was ready to speak, determined to control her own impatience and let Craig tell this story his own way.

Craig dried his hands on a towel and poured two glasses of pinot noir. "Come sit with me, Alli." Craig slid open the door leading to a small balcony.

Nervously, she followed him outside and sat beside him in the wooden rocker that overlooked the city. She took the glass he handed her.

Craig reached for Alli's hand. He held loosely in his own. "I came to Glendale to find you, Alli. Don't I look at all familiar?"

Alli studied his face in the light reflecting from the living room floor lamps. She shook her head. "Why should you? Did you used to live near us?"

"Oh, yeah. Very near. Take off 20 years and this beard. I'm your brother, Cal. I came to find you, Alli, and take you home."

Chapter 16

Alli pulled her cold hand from Craig's. Or was it Cal? She peered at him, searching for something familiar in his face. "Take me home?" Alli asked. "*This* is home. If you are Cal, and I'm not sure you are, you would know that. I was born and grew up here. My life is here."

"But your family is not here. Home is with family, Alli, no matter where that might be."

Alli stood up and moved to the sliding glass door to the balcony. In the east the faintest tinge of pink limned the horizon.

Her back still to Craig-Cal, she asked. "Why are you here? Really? And don't give me any of that family bull. You and I both know what our house was like. Isn't that why you lied about your age to get into the Army? We never saw you again. You left us there with them. And now, now you come back into my life wanting to kiss and make up?"

Alli felt rather than heard Cal approach her from behind. He slid his arms across her front and crossed them, hugging her into his body. Alli struggled out of his grasp, bumping into his terrarium, and made her way to the kitchen.

"I need coffee. Where do you keep it?"

"Here. I'll do it." Craig entered the galley kitchen and pulled out grounds and a filter from a cabinet by the sink. He kept his back to her while re-opening the conversation.

"Alli, I know this must be hard. After all these years. I'm sure you have questions, and I can't answer them all. I wasn't here when the folks pulled up stakes and left. I know Mom is so sorry. She sent me to find you, to ask you to forgive her."

"Mom? What about Dad? Does he want forgiveness, too?"

"Dad's dead, Alli. He can't hurt you or anyone any more." He turned back to face her.

"What do I call you? And why use a false name anyway? What is this really about, Craig or Cal or whoever you are?"

Craig poured a shot of Bailey's into each cup then poured the coffee over it. He carried their two cups of coffee over to the sofa table.

"Call me Craig. At this point, I can't use my real name. I can't really explain why just yet, but I will. Trust me. Can you trust me? Telling you the truth was me trusting you. I need to know if I can count on the same."

"That doesn't make sense. I mean, you are who you are, right? So how can you be somebody else? There are papers, your service record, high school. Everyone has a paper trail."

Craig leaned back into the sofa cushion and sipped his coffee. "There are ways to create a new paper trail. A trail that is the 'who' you want to be not the 'who' your parents turned you into. I didn't want to be Cal Wesson any more. You must know what I mean. Haven't you ever wanted to erase our family from your life?"

Alli looked into Craig's eyes to gauge his sincerity. "I have erased them, you, everyone. I don't have a family except the one who took me in when I came home from high school that day and found an empty house and not even a good-bye note. You never wrote us, so I had no way to find you."

Craig stroked Alli's arm. "Oh, poor little Alli. I had no idea, not until much later. And by then, you seemed to be doing okay. Why drag you back into the mess they continued to make. I'll tell you everything Mom told me, but not now. Now you have to get some rest. There are sheets in the second bedroom for the bed there. I'll fix that up while you get out of your clothes. The closet has some old shirts of mine that you can use as a nighty. The bathroom has a toothbrush and toiletries. We'll get to everything else in due time.

Rest. Tomorrow is a busy day. You need to tell me everything you know about this case. We have to clear Gina's name. That is job one. Yes?"

Craig bent down to look into Alli's eyes. She stepped away from him and went off to the hallway bathroom. She closed the door behind her and sank onto the toilet seat. She bent her head to her knees, held her legs tight and sobbed into her jeans, muffling her cries as best she could.

* * * * *

Alli awoke to strips of sunlight warming her face. *Where am I? Oh, yeah. Craig's place. Cal?* The clock on the bedside table said 10:30. She sat up and shook her head, running her hands through her hair to unmat it. Apparently she had slept and that surprised her.

Alli sank back into the bed. She pulled herself into a fetal position and lay in bed, covers up under her chin even though it wasn't cold in the room. Could it be that Craig was her brother? How could that be true? And did he really return to Glendale to find her? What made her inner radar ping? And why couldn't he use his real name?

She needed to test him, she decided. Alli conceived of some questions to quiz Craig-Cal on this morning. If he were genuine, she'd soon know. Then she could find out why he concealed his identity. *I'm turning into a regular Miss Marple.* She shook her head and the covers off at the same time.

Alli got up and padded out into the hallway. The condo was still. Craig must still be asleep. After a quick bathroom stop, she went into the kitchen. A note there told her to push the button on the coffee pot. It was all set to go. She did and then made her way to the terrarium.

Alli reached out a finger to touch a leaf when Craig's "Stop, don't touch that" startled her.

"I'm sorry. It just looked so healthy. I wanted to touch it. Probably not good for the plants, eh?"

"Not everything thrives with touch, Alli. Plants don't like to be cuddled. That particular one is poisonous and touching it could inadvertently poison you. I can't lose my little sister now that I've just found her." Craig's laugh seemed forced to her.

"I started the coffee. Is there anything...?"

Craig waved his hand in denial of her offer. "No, I have some blueberry muffins in the freezer. I got the recipe from a friend of mine. Her mother used to make them all the time. I'll just defrost them for us. For now, I'd rather you catch me up with your investigation. Sit down over there, sip your juice, and tell me who you suspect and who you've ruled out."

[See Mrs. Roth's Blueberry Muffins]

Alli studied Craig. "Why?"

Craig sighed. "I told you last night, well, this morning, that I wanted to help you and Gina. Maybe a fresh pair of eyes can see something you missed."

"Yes, but why help us? This is probably illegal. At least I've been told what I'm doing is borderline illegal. Why get mixed up in this mess if you don't care for Gina?"

"Oh, Alli, I do care for Gina. Maybe not the way you thought. And maybe I will come to love her if we can get her out of this and we can spend more time together. Most of our interactions have been around work. That hospital is hardly the place to engender romance."

Alli looked into his face trying to gauge his sincerity.

He set the muffin basket between them on the table. "And there's you, of course, Alli. When you're in pain over your friend, it pains me. I want you to get this cleared up so we can get you back to the life you were meant to have."

"I told you. This is my life. And I'm happy with it."

"Really. So Maria's ability to toss you out of the house on a whim doesn't bother you? Don't you want a home with more stability than that?"

Alli bent her head. "That was a low blow, Craig. Maria loves me, I know she does. Besides, our parents made sure I understood instability long before Maria's family took me in."

Craig leaned back in his chair and dabbed at muffin crumbs he'd dropped on the tabletop. "But she loves Gina more. Blood tells, Alli. Blood always tells. Why do you think I looked up the folks when I got out of the service? When you see Mom again, you'll understand. She's changed."

Alli stared out the wall of windows in Craig's condo. "I'm not ready for that. But, okay, I'll buy that it might be soon for you to know how you feel about Gina. But you like her, right? You won't hurt her?"

"Never. She's important to me, but I don't know, I can't tell how important. Is that okay? But what about you, Little Sis? How worried should I be about that cop in your life?"

Alli shrugged as her face warmed. "Evan. He's fun. We date. We dated a few years ago and then broke up. Now this case has broken us up again. As long as I am 'a person of interest' he can't see me, personally that is. I seem to see him a lot professionally."

"What caused the break-up before?"

Alli shrugged again. "Evan wanted more. He thought we should take things to the next level. I'm just not ready for that. Better for me to play the field, unattached and loving it!"

Craig took her hand. He cocked his head. "Uh huh. Right."

Alli withdrew her hand from his. "You know so much more about me than I know about you. I mean, you kind of know what happened between the parents bugging out and you showing up here. So where have you been? What have you done? Apparently you made a success of your life. What about our little sisters? How come...?"

"Whoa! All in good time. I'll tell you at dinner tonight all about what's been going on with me and what happened to our family. For now, shouldn't we be talking about the case against Gina?"

"But I was wondering about Mom's family and how they all are. Is Grandma, uh, what was her name? still alive?"

"Granny Smith?"

Alli started.

Craig smiled. "Remember? She was such a tart old lady that we called her that. Grandma Appleton, really. Was that a test, Alli?"

Alli sat back in her chair. "Well, can you blame me? You've had more time to get used to this than I have. So you really are Cal? Really?"

"Really. But, please, until I explain more, will you keep that to yourself? I know it sounds crazy, but I must be Craig Phillips around here, at least for a while longer."

Alli studied Cal's face. "Why don't you look anything like I remember? You used to have green eyes, now they're brown. Your nose isn't the Appleton nose we all got."

"The same reason I can't tell you more about my life is the reason I had some plastic surgery and have colored contacts. It's all work related."

Alli thought for a moment. She ran over possible scenarios. "Oh, Cal, I mean, Craig, do you mean you're a spy? A government agent? Are you here investigating the hospital?"

Craig held his finger to his lips. "Shh. I didn't say that. I can't say that. Just let it rest for now, okay?" He smiled to encourage acquiescence.

Alli gave a conspiratorial smile in return. "Not a word." She zipped her lips closed and tossed the key away.

Craig reached out and grabbed for the imaginary key. Just as he used to do when they were kids.

Alli settled back into her seat. She had a brother again. A real family. Alli smiled and reached out for Cal's hand. Cal squeezed back and then got up to get them more coffee.

"Now, let me help. Can we use Evan's interest in you to try to get some more info about this case? The police can't be seriously considering Gina. Not really. I think the husband did it. For the insurance money. The hospital carried a two-million-dollar policy on Clarice, it was part of her compensation package when they recruited her."

"Seriously? Two million dollars? That kind of money might make a browbeaten husband consider murder. Wait. How could you know that, Craig?"

Craig squirmed in his chair. "Well, see, I have access to financial records, as part of my job, so I just took a peek into some files that weren't *technically* my business. And a good thing I did. Two million dollars could be a powerful motivator. But, I'm sure the police have checked all that out. That's why we need to know what they know so we can fill in the blanks for them."

"I see what you mean, Craig. Yes, I may have some information they don't have. But it's all in my notebook, back at my place. And I can't go there."

"Let me. I'll go pick you some clothes for you and bring them back here. Where's the notebook?"

* * * * *

Craig pulled away from Gina's driveway an hour later, clothes for Alli in his back seat. The notebook was hidden under a pile of underwear in her suitcase. Alli had told him the family was not happy she was recording all these notes. He thought it best not to advertise that he was going to help her with the investigation.

Maria watched him depart. Should she have let him into Alli's place? But what was she to do when he insisted she needed clothes? She was hurt that Alli didn't want to come back to get her things herself. Hurt that Craig told her Alli said she needed time away from them all. What was she going to tell Gina when she woke up?

Maria went back into the foyer and closed the front door. She leaned against it, her eyes closed. She felt and smelled Gina before she opened her eyes.

"Who was that, Ma? Did Alli call?"

Maria sighed heavily. "No, that was Craig. He said his phone is out of order, so he couldn't call before coming over. He came to get some things for Alli. She's going to stay with him for a few days, 'to think things through', he said."

Maria plodded into the family room and sank into her old recliner.

Gina followed her mother. "What? Alli, didn't come to get her own clothes? Oh, Ma! What did you say to her? I'm going over there. I have to see her and get this mess straightened out."

"Don't, Gina. He said Alli wouldn't answer the door. She doesn't want to see any of us, at least not for a while. Besides, he was going to pick her up and they were going out for the day, headed to Flagstaff for some Indian thing at the Museum of Northern Arizona. He said they'd be late getting back. He'll talk to you tomorrow at work, if you go in."

Gina headed to the sofa and curled up in a corner, resting her head against it's high back. She rubbed her watery eyes. She didn't look at her mother. "Oh, Ma. What have you done?"

Chapter 17

Monday morning found Detective Clinton knocking on Prentice Carlisle's apartment door. Carlisle had watched the detective haul himself out of the dark sedan parked in front of his shop. Another man exited from the driver's side. Carlisle dreaded the summons. He knew what was coming. He strode to the door and threw it open on the first knock.

"Ah, Detective. To what do I owe this early morning visit? May I offer you some coffee?"

"No, thanks, Mr. Carlisle. Would you have some time to answer a few questions for us?"

"Certainly. In what regard? Have you found Clarice Franklin's stolen jade dragon? Would you like me to inspect it for authenticity?" Carlisle wiped at a bit of moisture on his upper lip.

"Actually, we were hoping you could show it to *us*. We have information that the jade dragon was returned to you last week. Mr. Franklin knows of a particular coloration pattern, so he is willing to authenticate it for us."

Carlisle clenched his hands to his gut and pressed hard. "I can assure you, Detective. If someone had brought me a stolen piece, I would have called you immediately. I do get various and sundry jade statues in. I'm the only Orientals antique dealer in Glendale, you know, so of course if someone has jade to sell or wants to buy, I am the person to contact. Let me see. Last week you say?" Carlisle tapped a finger in the middle of his chin.

Detective Clinton looked around the small but elegantly furnished apartment. Ornate geegaws covered every surface. Silk paintings covered the walls. The furniture was low and modern as if not to compete with the décor.

"Oh, so sorry, please be seated Detectives. Perhaps some tea, if not coffee?"

Clinton waved a hand indicating "no." He seated himself on the sofa while Evan chose a chair opposite. Carlisle had no choice but the chair between the two men. That meant one of them could always be studying him but he wouldn't be able to see both of them at the same time.

"You were saying, Mr. Carlisle? About last week and the jade dragon someone brought you?"

"Oh. Was it a dragon? Yes, yes. I believe it was. They're rather common, you know. But, I don't have it any longer so I can't show it to you."

Evan flipped open his notebook and clicked his pen. Carlisle started at the sound and watched Evan as he wrote a few words.

Clinton waited until Carlisle's eyes returned to Clinton's own. "Look, Mr. Carlisle. We think you're in over your head here. We think someone took advantage of you and used you for his or her own purposes. We think you know something that could help us with a murder investigation."

Clinton stopped and scratched the top of his bald spot. "Look. We're not burglary or larceny or fraud. We're homicide. There are other guys who do that stuff. We just want to nail the guy who killed a nice lady. Can you help us?"

Carlisle snorted. "Nice lady? Clarice Franklin? She haggled like a fishwife with me over the price of that jade dragon so that I barely covered my costs and a little more. That she collected jade dragons was almost a stereotype. She was a dragon herself. Not to speak ill of the dead, of course." Carlisle turned pale. He seemed to realize too late how his words might sound.

Clinton interrupted Carlisle's discomfort. "Wait. She bought the dragon? We were told it was a birthday present from her husband."

"Oh, yes, indeed it was. But she selected it and bargained for the price. He just had to bring the money and pick it up so he could wrap it for her. She didn't like surprises, I gather."

Evan raised his eyebrows as he continued writing in his notebook.

Clinton asked, "So show it to us so we can take it to Mr. Franklin. We'll give you a receipt, but if it is the stolen dragon as we suspect, it will go to the evidence room for a while. After that, Mr. Franklin will receive it back. If it is not the dragon we are looking for, we'll return it to you later today."

"But I told you, I don't have it any longer. Yes, someone brought me a dragon that looked like the one, that could be the one that I sold Clarice Franklin, but it's gone. Stolen. Someone broke into my shop early Saturday morning and took it. You can check the police record. The alarm went off and a squad car showed up to check. I told them I was missing a jade statue."

Clinton looked skeptical. "Well, now, if that isn't just too convenient. Stolen you say? Anything else missing?"

"No. No. Isn't that odd? But I suppose she wanted to get just that one thing back. Or maybe the alarm frightened her off."

Clinton looked at Evan. "Her? You saw who broke into your shop?"

"It was that woman. The one who brought it here. I didn't recognize her at the time, but later I saw her picture in the paper. She was one of the cooks for the Franklin family. Alli Wesson stole the jade dragon from Clarice Franklin and then from me."

Chapter 18

Rita Kinney hated Monday mornings. She lit up her third cigarette of the day. She puffed frantically at it, drawing as much comfort from the nicotine as she could. It was a long time until her morning break. She stubbed it out in the overflowing ashtray, grabbed her purse, and opened her car door. *Time for another fun-filled week in this hell hole.*

Rita threw her purse into her desk drawer and slammed it shut. A sound from Clarice Franklin's office caught her attention. Not that she was superstitious, but she tiptoed to the door that was partially closed and peeked in. Forester was bent over Clarice's desk looking at her appointment book. What was his fascination with that thing?

"Ahem. Mr. Young? Did you have an appointment?"

Forester started at her voice. "Rita. You scared the living crap out of me! For God's sake, whatever happened to knocking on my door?"

"Your door? Isn't that a bit premature? Or have you heard something?" Rita slipped into the room and shut the door behind her. "You know, you really shouldn't be here. If people saw you, they'd..."

"They'd what? Think I came in to shtup you?" Forester grinned at Rita.

She felt her face redden and tighten.

"Ah, Honey. I was just kidding. C'mon. Where's my girl's smile? Gimme a kiss?"

Rita moved into Forester's arms. He grabbed her rear end and jammed her closer to him and then kissed her deeply.

"Oh, Forester. After this is all over, after you take over again, will we be able to be together?"

"Rita. I hate a whiner. I told you that a thousand times. When the time is right, I'll make an honest woman of you. But if my wife caught a whiff of this, she'd have me back in court to clean out the assets she just knows I have hidden. We have to keep a low profile. But just for a while. Soon, Baby. But since you're here and I'm here, you want to take advantage of that couch again? It's been a while since we warmed it up."

Rita looked behind her at the closed door. "No, I have to get back to my desk. People will wonder where I am. Now why don't you go out that door over there to the back hallway and leave. Don't come out this door, okay? Promise? And just what are you looking for anyway? The police pored over that appointment book, and I don't think they found a thing."

"But they didn't know what to look for, Rita. Clarice Franklin was raking off dough from this hospital. I have a friend in accounting who helps me out sometimes. He said there were some irregularities in the books, money missing. I told him to sit on it. Once I'm in, we'll do an audit and the whole mess will come out."

Rita scrunched up her face. "Forester, don't take this wrong, but, uhh, you didn't kill Clarice did you? I mean to get back as CEO?"

Forester looked astounded. "Why should I do that? By finding fiscal malfeasance, I'll justify getting my job back and the Dragon Lady will be remembered for more than purging this place of its good workers. Killing her would be unnecessary. My way would have involved public humiliation. By getting herself bumped off, she avoided that."

"Okay. I get it, but why didn't you call yesterday? You rushed off Saturday and said I'd hear from you. Then, nothing. Where did you go? What was so important?"

"Oh, it *was* important. I met with someone who is going to make sure I don't get covered with the muck flying around right now. Say, Honey, why don't you make yourself useful and get me some coffee."

"Rita? Rita are you here?"

Rita whispered. "That's Craig Phillips. He'd better not see you here. He's suspicious enough of me and you. Get out of here. Go on out the back door. Leave. I'll call you later."

Rita smoothed the front of her dress and opened Clarice's door just as Craig was about to knock on it.

"Oh, you are here. I thought I heard voices." Craig peeked past Rita into the office behind her.

"No, just me. Oh, I just turned off the radio. That must be what you heard."

"Right. The radio." Craig gave one more look into the office as Rita firmly closed it as she entered the reception area.

"What can I do for you, Mr. Phillips?"

"Rita, Rita. Mr. Phillips? After Thursday night?"

Rita blushed. Craig reached over and rubbed off a smear of lipstick from Rita's chin. "Been sitting under the apple tree with somebody else, have we?"

"I must have smeared it when I had some coffee. Would you like some?" Rita turned away and went toward the coffee maker on a credenza in her office. She shut the door behind her and made sure it clicked closed.

Craig followed her over to the coffee service and placed a hand on hers. "Rita. I need your help. I am trying to help the police with this investigation of Clarice's murder."

"Wow! You must be something for them to ask for your help."

Craig's lips turned up in a small smile. "Well, I have been involved in some investigations in the past. I suppose that experience could be valuable to the local police."

Rita looked around to see if anyone were listening and leaned into Craig. "That doesn't surprise me. You know the rumor mill around here is that you are here to investigate something big at the hospital. I've noticed, and so have some of the guys in accounting, that you have really paid a lot of attention to our books. Was Clarice raking off some money?"

Craig held up a hand. "You know I can't confirm anything like that. Let's just say that I was looking for irregularities. But, and this is just between us, I didn't find anything. The books are clean. Case closed."

Rita looked at Craig from under her lashes. "Does a man with your skills, your expertise ever think about settling down, you know, not going from city to city checking on the books? Maybe become a CEO of a hospital and not just investigate them?"

"You know. You're a mind reader, Rita. I am tired of wandering. I think I could bring a fresh approach to the hospital." Craig sighed. "But who am I kidding? I'm sure the Board is looking at some very highly qualified candidates. The former CEO being one of them, I'll bet."

"You know, there might be a way to increase your visibility, put you on their radar. Maybe I can help."

Craig looked over at Rita and put his hand over hers. "You'd do that for me?"

Rita withdrew her hand and straightened her shoulders. "Well, I'd like a little tit for tat if it works."

Craig grinned. "Me, too."

Rita blushed again. "You know what I mean. I want this job at the salary I used to have. And I want a new title, too—Executive Administrative Assistant."

Craig reached out to shake her hand. "Done and done. If you can deliver this job, the world is yours. I'd be honored to have such a highly qualified executive administrative assistant under me—so to speak."

Rita shook his hand back, determined not to give in to Craig's *double entendre*.

"Let me get this organized. The Board meets Saturday morning. I'll be there to record minutes of the meeting. That should give me enough time. By this time next week, you should be moving in here."

Craig's eyes became watery. "Really, truly Rita. If you can get me this job, I will owe you forever. Really forever. Think what that means for the two of us."

Craig gave a small wave good-bye and went back down the hallway to his cubicle.

Rita got her computer out of sleep mode and composed a document addressed to the Board of Directors touting the qualities Craig Phillips would bring to the hospital CEO job. She based her recommendation on her own experiences working with two former CEOs. Then she accessed her e-mail contacts and found the list of all hospital employees asking for them to read the attached letter and then come by her office to sign it. She clicked "send" and sat back to wait.

* * * * *

Prentice Carlisle followed the officers out onto on his porch to set out the antique porcelain table and metal chairs he kept as décor. Clinton turned at the bottom of the steps.

"Mr. Carlisle, if you think of anything else. Anything at all, please call."

"Of course, Detectives. I'll do what I can to help."

Carlisle went back into the shop and shut the door. He leaned against it, breathing heavily. When he felt more in control, he peeked out through the drapery and assured himself the police were gone. He put out the closed sign and pulled the draperies.

Under the counter was a small box. He opened it up and removed the jade dragon wrapped in a kid's t-shirt. Maybe there *was* a curse on the damn thing. Something set off that false alarm this morning. It scared him to death having this thing in his shop. No wonder he was so jumpy. That alarm was always going off. He looked for the card for the security system. They had damn well better fix it this time.

He had to get rid of the dragon and the guy who was behind all his troubles with it. Carlisle dialed a number and waited for a pick up.

* * * * *

In the car Clinton told Evan, "Let's go talk to Alli Wesson and see where she was early Saturday morning."

Evan put the car into gear and pulled away from the curb a bit more abruptly than he meant to. Clinton looked over at him and sighed.

Gina was home, taking a needed vacation day after her weekend with the court system. She told them that Alli was gone to Craig's place, but she didn't know his address. His condo was somewhere in downtown Glendale. It had to be on record at the hospital. Clinton looked over at Evan whose face had tightened up.

Evan asked, "Gina, do you know where Alli was early Saturday morning. About 6? Was she at Craig Phillips' place then?"

Gina reached out a hand and placed it on Evan's arm. "No. She was here. I heard her in the pool doing her morning laps, then she came in here about 6:30 for coffee and we had a mess to clean up from dessert the night before. Why? And Evan, it's not what you think about Craig. Ma got mad at Alli and threw her out temporarily. Craig told her she could crash there."

Clinton asked, "So there is no way she could be gone for say, 45 minutes early Saturday morning without you knowing?"

"No, Detective Clinton. My whole family were right here either asleep or cleaning up the kitchen. Too bad we don't have security cameras for evidence."

Clinton shrugged. "Thanks, Ms. Smithson. When you see her, would you let her know we'd like to ask her a few questions? Let's go back to the station, Detective Katz."

* * * * *

Back at the station house that morning, Detective Clinton and Evan were reviewing the notes from their meeting with Carlisle.

Clinton scratched his head. "This just keeps getting nuttier and nuttier. What's that girlfriend of yours doing running around town with the jade dragon we've been looking for? And where the hell is it now?"

"*If* it's the same jade dragon. We don't know that. But her alibi seems tight. Either Carlisle is mistaken or he's lying. When does Paul Franklin get here?"

Clinton checked his appointment book. "He said he'd be in during his lunch hour, so not long now." He slammed the book shut. "So the damn dragon's gone again. Where now? And why? And who? I tell you, I haven't had this many suspects since I was a rookie cop and everybody looked like the killer to me."

Evan laughed. "Yeah. I know what you mean. But, seriously, you can't think Gina Smithson killed her boss."

"I've seen stranger things, Katz, but, no. I don't think she did it, but why do things keep coming back to her? I think that Carlisle guy knows more than he's telling us, but he had neither motive nor opportunity. The killer had to be someone with access to Clarice Franklin's office and home since we found the poison both places."

"Well, that is a pretty long list. The husband is where my money is. That insurance policy?" Evan whistled. "Guys have done in wives for less."

"Yeah, I know. I know. Conventional wisdom. The murderer is likely someone close to the victim. Still, it doesn't feel right. Poison is a woman's thing more than a man's. What about that secretary, the foxy one?"

Evan smiled. "Rita Kinney. I don't think so. Rita doesn't have what it takes to pull off something like this. She's not a brain trust."

"Okay. I got that vibe, too. And hating your boss isn't a crime or most of Arizona would be out in the Tent City jail. But could she have had help?"

Evan thought about the question. "When I was dating Rita, I found out she was using me as a sort of beard, a cover for another relationship. Maybe if we found out who that was and if she's still involved, it could be a break for us."

Clinton's phone jangled. "Clinton...Yeah, send him in."

He replaced the phone in its cradle. "Paul Franklin's here. You got that file on him?"

Paul appeared in the doorway.

Clinton gestured to a seat. "Want some coffee?"

"No. No thanks. Have you had a breakthrough? Do you know who murdered my wife?"

Clinton cleared his throat. "Not yet sir, but we do have a few more questions. We had a tip that the jade dragon turned up in an antique store in downtown Glendale. Would you know anything about that?"

Paul rose from his chair. "What does that stupid statue have to do with any of this? I thought the burglary people were handling that? If you have nothing, I'm out of here."

Evan intervened. "Please sit, Mr. Franklin. Please."

Paul sat back down, but he sat forward in the chair as if ready to leave. "What?"

Clinton said, "We have reason to believe the dragon theft and the murder are tied. Forensic evidence and witness information leads us to think the dragon was stolen when the murderer by-passed your alarm system to enter your home and place poison in your wife's tea caddy. Didn't you comment to the personal chefs that your dog seemed out of it, logy, almost as if drugged? And didn't your slow cooker fail because the outlet overloaded and had to be reset?"

"Yes. Yes. Both true, but why would someone take the dragon?

That doesn't fit with murder. Or does it?"

Evan said, "That is a piece of the puzzle that's missing. I guess we'll have to find out from your wife's murderer. Maybe he or she liked the looks of it. Or maybe it was to throw us off if the break-in were discovered. Who knows? We'll find out, but for now the connection is what's important. Who knew about the dragon and its value?"

Paul dropped his head into his hands. "That dragon? I guess everybody knew Clarice collected dragons. She made no secret of it. And she was really proud of that one, a birthday present I got her right after we moved here. But...well, to be truthful, that dragon was not valuable at all. That's why I never turned it in to the insurance company."

Evan and Clinton looked at one another.

Clinton shook his head. "Wait a minute. Run that by me again. Why call the police about it when you discovered it was missing if it wasn't valuable?"

Paul clasped his hands together and looked Clinton in the eye. "Because my wife didn't know it was a fake. I lied to her. She negotiated a price with the dealer, Carson or Carlisle or something, but he and I arranged a swap. I paid him more than the fake was worth, and I pocketed the difference. I, uh, I was into some heavy debt at the casino. I wanted to pay it off. My wife doesn't, that is, didn't like me playing poker with the high rollers."

Clinton leaned forward. "So you're telling me that dragon disappeared and you don't care because it was not real. But somebody must have thought it was real or why take it? Did you know that the dragon turned up in your wife's office? Who could have put it there?"

"Detective, I honestly do not know. But, I suppose it could have been one of several of her co-workers. It does seem to come down to those who could get into her office, doesn't it?"

Paul stood up. "Listen, my kids are with my sister in San Francisco, and I am going to go see them for a few days. Is that okay? You have my cell number if there's a break. I just have to get away from here and be with my family."

Clinton nodded. "Sure. That's fine. We'll let you know what's happening."

After Paul went out into the hall, Evan heaved himself from the chair. "Well, that was interesting. Say, I'll drop by Rita's office. I'll try to make it look like a friendly visit, just to catch up. Maybe I can get something out of her. We might get lucky about who she's been playing footsie with."

"Or maybe *you* will!" Clinton laughed and clapped Evan on his back.

Chapter 19

The next morning, Detective Clinton rapped on Rita's open door and entered without an invitation. "Ms. Kinney? I was wondering if you could answer a few questions for us? Down at the station house."

Rita's face heated up. "I suppose this has to do with what your snoop you sent around yesterday was sniffing around about." Rita pointed a bony finger at Evan standing behind Clinton.

"Detective Katz visited you on his own time yesterday afternoon, Ms. Kinney. No, we're here because we have questions about that jade dragon that turned up here after the murder."

Rita's face felt even hotter.

"You should be asking Ms. Smarty-Pants Detective Alli Wesson. She was the one who found it. I think she put it there and just pretended to find it."

Clinton approached her desk and reached out a hand toward Rita's arm. "Well, let's just go talk about that. See where she might have messed up her story. Clear you once and for all."

"What do you mean, 'clear me'? Clear me of what? Finding a missing dragon? Shouldn't you be thanking me instead. That thing is probably worth in the six figures."

Evan took a step forward. "I thought you said Ms. Wesson found the dragon. Which is it?"

"You cops always twist a person's words around. Forest...uhh, somebody told me you'd try to do that and to just keep my mouth shut. I want a lawyer, that guy who got Gina Smithson off. You can't talk to me without him, right?"

"Would you please come with us? Quietly? Or we can make a stink. Which do you choose?"

"Don't talk to me like a kid, Clinton. Choice? Ha! That's not a choice. Okay. Let's go. But I want that lawyer before I talk to you guys."

In the back seat of Clinton's department-issued old blue sedan, Rita had her phone out and was punching buttons for an Internet connection. She needed that lawyer's phone number. Clinton told her she had to make her own call; that wasn't a service the police department offered.

Evan turned around when he heard a crash in the back seat. Rita hunched in a corner. "Anything wrong?" he asked her.

"Stupid old goat! His office can't take me on because of a 'conflict of interest' with defending Gina Smithson. Tell me the name of another one of those TV guys who advertise law services."

Evan shrugged and turned back to stare out the front windshield. Rita thought she saw a small smile tug at the corner of Clinton's mouth. Well, she'd show them. She punched the memory key for Forester's phone number. He'd just have to step up to the plate here!

* * * * *

Rita looked down at her watch, not bothering to conceal it. An hour already! Where the hell was Forester? She swung her crossed leg back and forth, arms folded. Clinton's office smelled of smoke, so the cops must allow smoking in here. "Do you mind?" Rita reached into her purse and pulled out a pack of slim cigarettes and a sterling silver lighter.

"As a matter of fact, I do," Detective Clinton said. "Mind, that is. Allergies. Doc told me to cut down on second hand smoke exposure. Pretty nice lighter for a secretary."

"Executive Administrative Assistant. But this was a gift, from an admirer."

"Right. You can smoke later. If you'll just answer a few more questions, we'll be done here."

Rita sat up straight and placed her arms flat out in front of her on the steel table. "And then I can go?"

She saw Clinton and Evan give one another a glance, and Evan shrugged.

"Maybe," Clinton said. "First, let's just over again who, other than you, had access to Clarice Franklin's office."

"I already told you. She was creepy about letting people into her office. I had to guard the door, practically. She made me move my desk so it blocked her door. People had to go around me if they wanted in. So nobody had access." Rita paused, "That is, no one without a key. I suppose somebody like the janitor or one of the execs with a master key could get in when the office was closed."

Evan leaned into Rita. "An executive? You mean like Gina Smithson? Was she an executive with a key?"

"Gina? Nah, she was low level, just a bit above me, actually. No, I mean like veeps and division heads, people like that had master keys. But that would only get them into my office. Hers was keyed separately. So, nobody could get in there. Well, except me, of course. But I always kept that key hidden."

Clinton sat down again. "It had to be tough working for Clarice Franklin." He leaned in closer to Rita. "I mean, we heard she had a nickname, 'The Dragon Lady'. That sounds like one hard woman boss."

"That's what I told Alli. Women bosses are the worst."

Clinton nodded as she spoke. "I hear you. We had a woman chief for a while. She didn't last long. When she tried to be tough, she just came across as a woman pretending to have a dick. We used to say she was a dick without one. You know a detective is sometimes called…Oops." He stopped and clapped a hand over his mouth. "Oh, I am *so* sorry, Ms. Kinney. My mouth gets away from me sometimes."

Rita waved her hand in dismissal. "That's okay. I've heard worse. But you got that right. They aren't men, and they got that penis envy thing going and that makes life miserable for the people they boss around."

Clinton nodded. "So I can see how it would go down. She rides you all the time. You can't do nothin' right in her eyes. She checks how many minutes you're at lunch. Am I right, here?"

Rita nodded, glad to have someone appreciate how difficult life had been with Clarice as a boss.

"So, you didn't want to kill her. Maybe you just wanted her to be sick for a few days, out of your hair. She loved that tea of hers, so it would be easy to put something into her cup."

Rita stopped swinging her leg and planted both feet on the floor. "Wait a cotton-pickin' minute! You think I killed her? You think I put poison in her tea at the office? But she died at home. Wasn't there poison in that tea, too? How could I get it into her house."

Clinton sat back in his seat and placed his two hands behind his head. "See, that bothered me, too, but then I heard that you made frequent trips to her house, one the day she died, in fact, to bring her some papers to sign. We heard you were alone in the kitchen while the two cooks were taking out some trash and wiping up a mess in the hallway. Motive and opportunity. What would we find if we checked your prints against those on that tea caddy?"

Rita sat back into her seat, stunned at the accusation. A commotion outside the room got her attention. She looked over at the door as Forester burst into the room.

He strode to the table and pulled on Rita's arm. "I've been watching this charade through the blinds over there. Rita, come with me. You haven't been charged with anything, these buffoons have no evidence, and they are just trying to get you to implicate me. Let's go."

Evan moved toward Forester as Clinton rose to his feet. "And why would we think you had anything to do with this, Mr. Young?"

Forester turned wild eyes onto Clinton. "Because that woman stole my job. She maligned me to the Board, and she took what was mine. She deserved to die. But I didn't kill her. Everybody hated her. Everybody wanted her dead. But I didn't do it, and you can't prove I did."

Evan responded. "Yes, we've heard she wasn't popular. And as former CEO, you had a copy of that office key, didn't you? The extra key you had made that one time and that you didn't turn in when you left your position. Could I see your key chain, please?"

Forester's hand went to his right pants pocket and patted the small lump there. "I don't have to give you anything. I want my attorney. Now."

Rita pulled her arm from Forester's grip. "You had a key still? Is that why you wanted her appointment book, so you could find out when she'd be out of her office?"

"Shut up, Rita. This is just a misunderstanding. My attorney will clear everything up as soon as she gets here."

Evan and Clinton watched the exchange between their two suspects.

"You called your attorney for me? Oh, thank you, Forester!"

"Don't be ridiculous, Rita. You couldn't afford her. I called while I was watching you make a fool of yourself in here. I could see where these dolts were leading you, so I took precautions."

Rita's eyes teared up. "Oh, Forester! You killed Clarice Franklin? Did you kill her because of how she treated me?"

* * * * *

Evan watched Forester and his very attractive attorney enter a room down the hallway. Rita trailed behind them. He sure wished he and Clinton could listen in on that little meeting. But attorney-client privilege blah blah blah. Was Forester a viable suspect?

Clinton clapped Evan's shoulder. "Let's go see if we can sort this mess out. Grab some coffee for the two of us, will you, and come into my office."

When Evan entered with two cups, one black and one with extra cream and sugar, Clinton had a file spread over his desktop.

Clinton turned and held out his hand for the coffee with everything. "I'm looking at the forensics report. I think we have to let him go. His fingerprints are all over Clarice's office, but none on the tea caddy in the office or at the house. I suppose he could have used gloves, but then why not have gloves on all the time so there'd be *no* fingerprints at all? He didn't think the office would ever be dusted, my guess is. Otherwise, it doesn't add up."

Evan looked over his shoulder at the grid he'd made for the various findings and suspects. "And Rita's were all over the tea caddy at the office but not the house. Gina and Alli's prints were on the tea caddy at the house, but not the office. Same with the husband. Only the victim's fingerprints were on both. No fingerprints from Carlisle anywhere. What are we missing?"

Clinton shook his head. "Let's back up. What did the tox scan say the name of the poison is?"

Evan flipped through the autopsy report. "Here it is. A-b-r-i-n. I'm not sure how to pronounce it. 'Ay-brin'? 'A-brin'? The M.E. attached some info on it. It's real toxic. Like ricin only more so. Dangerous to handle, so somebody would have to know what they're doing. The symptoms are what she had, bowel irritation, inflamed mucous membranes. Deadly poison. Kinda rare. It's not easy to buy, even over the Internet. Comes from the seeds of a plant, jequirity pea, sometimes called rosary pea. So, I guess the perp could have grown it, that way there'd be no paper trail."

Clinton nodded his head. "So who are we looking for here? Who had it in for the woman, had access to her office and home, and knew enough to wear gloves while touching the tea caddies to not leave prints?"

"Or who wore gloves to prevent accidental contact with the poison. Maybe no prints gave him or her a two-fer—protection and no prints evidence."

"Evan, if you had to rule out people, who would it be right now and why?"

Evan sat down in the chair across from Clinton's and leaned back and closed his eyes. He liked this game that he and Clinton played at some point in an investigation. Usually it happened when they were stuck and needed to think outside the box.

"The suspects so far are Gina and Alli, whom I rule out because I don't think there is motive."

Clinton interrupted. "But there was opportunity. Gina, at least, had access to both locations where there was poisoned tea. And Alli could have been in Clarice's office with Gina."

"Granted, but there is no strong motive. If everybody who hated their boss was a murder suspect, the courts would be even more clogged. Nah. Maybe opportunity, but not really motive. Besides, I do have personal info. I've known these people for years. I just can't see it."

"Okay, Evan, I'll give you that. They pass the smell test. I'd be real surprised, too, if they did it. And, I think they would both have to be in on it. It doesn't feel right. Go on."

"I'm doing the easy ones first. Prentice Carlisle is a slime, and I think the art forgery unit could have a go at him, maybe put up RICO charges, but I don't think he's a murderer."

Clinton nodded his head. "Agreed. And there's no motive or opportunity. It was in his best interest to lay low and let us think the jade dragon was real."

"Well, except," Evan began again. "I don't know how the theft of that dragon fits in. Was it just coincidence that two crimes happened to the same family two months apart? I don't believe in coincidences. There's something there, but what? You think we should get Paul Franklin in here again and dig deeper?"

Clinton nodded. "Maybe put Franklin and Carlisle in a room together? See what we get? Okay. Who else is out?"

"Well, I think Rita and Young are out. There's no forensic evidence tying Young to either location, and Rita just doesn't have it in her to murder somebody. Talk them to death, yes, but not kill. And any attorney would be able to explain her fingerprints on the tea caddy in the office. Heck, we can do that. She served tea to the woman all the time."

"So that leaves...?"

Evan sighed. "In my opinion, that leaves bupkis. We got no suspects. This case is colder than Flagstaff in February."

Clinton shook his head. "We're missing something, somebody. Let's go over the list again of who she worked closely with. It's got to be one of them. Hand me that list. I'm going to be real thorough this time."

Clinton took the top sheets off the list of alphabetized employees while Evan started with the last pages. They would meet in the middle. They did it this way all the time.

Evan and Clinton silently turned the pages, scanning the names and their positions at the hospital. Most of the employees would have had little to no interaction with Clarice Franklin, at least professionally.

Suddenly, Evan stopped at one name. "Hey, Clinton? What about this name? Didn't you do the initial interview because I might have a conflict? Could you get your notes? It might be worth following up on."

Evan sat at Clinton's computer while Clinton paged through his interview notes. Evan typed in the name and social security number of one administrator and waited for the search results.

Chapter 20

Alli looked up from the Sudoku puzzle she was working as Craig entered the eating area, buttoning his shirt sleeves. "You're leaving late for work, aren't you?"

He looked over her shoulder, took the pen, and wrote a "3" in one of her boxes. He handed the pen back to her. "I have comp time coming to me. I decided to take a little of it. What are you going to do today?" Craig asked.

"I thought I'd dazzle you with my cooking skills. It's the least I can do after you let me stay here indefinitely. Besides, I need someone new to test my recipe on."

Craig turned back from the door. "Whoa! A new recipe? Shouldn't you know if something is good before you serve it to others? It would be more prudent to plan it out, know for sure, wouldn't it?"

Alli laughed at the look on his face. "That's the beauty of it, see. Since it's new, nobody knows what it tastes like, so they won't know if it didn't work or they just don't care for the taste. I always try out my new recipes on people. Lots of times I'm very successful!"

Craig shook his head and gave her a grin. "Hard to believe you're *my* little sister. I am much more planful than that. What are you making?"

"Seafood Scampi with Angel Hair Pasta. And a lovely Caesar salad with homemade croutons. Ummm. Do you have shrimp or lump crab meat or scallops or lobster?"

[See Seafood Shrimp with Angel Hair Pasta]

"Here." Craig threw some bills on the table in the entry way. "Here's some money for groceries. There's a little market around the corner that's better stocked than you might think. I like to support the locals when I can. Oh, and an extra key is in this drawer." He waved and walked out, the door clicking shut behind him.

Alli threw on her clothes. She wanted to get the shopping done early so she could have the rest of the day for her visit to the antique store and chilling. She was tired from not sleeping well last night. Fortunately, the scampi sauce she planned was so easy she could start dinner when Craig got home.

As promised, the market had the ingredients she wanted. Though the seafood selection was limited, she did manage to find two she could use in the sauce. She tucked everything away in the cupboards and refrigerator. Left to her own devices, she would have left out some of the ingredients on the counter, but Craig was a neat-nik, so as long as she stayed here, she would do her best to stay tidy. Who knew he'd end up that way after the squalor their mother had called their home.

Alli was sweaty from her walk to and from the store, so she decided to read for a while before heading out for Carlisle's store. She could shower later and then walk over to the antique store that was a couple of blocks away. She wanted to see what Carlisle had to say about the jade dragon she'd left there.

Craig's small bookshelf was loaded with tomes on plants. Nary a novel in sight. There were also a couple of cookbooks, so she chose one of those. She murmured the title aloud, "*What to Eat and What Never to Eat*". Interesting. Even though she was an intrepid eater, she had never eaten plants beyond the conventional ones. She'd never tried nasturtiums in her chilled peach soup as she had once seen offered on a menu. Maybe she should expand her horizons.

She took the book and a cup of coffee out onto Craig's small patio. As she sipped and read, Alli found the sections on edible flowers the most interesting. The peppery flavors described did sound enticing. She decided to give it a whirl. She knew the kids and Maria would avoid them, but maybe she could get Evan to try some. At worst, it would make an interesting blog entry. Maybe she could get the Burpee seed people as a sponsor for her site if she developed several ways to use flowers.

Alli went back into the kitchen and began opening drawers to find a tablet of paper to write down some of her findings. In the back of a drawer, under some jar openers and old rubber bands, she found what she was looking for. The top page had some writing on it, so she carefully lifted that sheet so she could remove one further into the paper pad. As she started to replace the pad in the drawer, she realized that a recipe was written on the top sheet. Alli's mouth formed an "o" of surprise. Should she take the sheet? She thought probably not. What had she learned from all of this past week's mistakes?

Alli reluctantly shoved the tablet back to its previous location, heaping on the stuff to cover it. She leaned back against the counter to consider what to do next.

Where is Craig's phone? Alli hunted all over the condo and found two empty cradles where phones should be holstered. *Now why would Craig take or hide his phones?* Alli felt stirrings of alarm. She went back to the kitchen drawer and considered taking the tablet there, but maybe it was better to leave it in place as evidence. Instead, she copied it out, stuffed the recipe into her purse, and left his condo. She had to get out of there before he returned. Something was not right.

Alli turned right and walked a few blocks to the Catlin Court area of Glendale. She had to check in with that antique shop guy and find out what he knew about the jade dragon.

*   *   *   *   *

Gina left the house for work without speaking to her mother. At her desk, she kept trying Craig's home and office phones, but there was no answer either place. Craig's secretary told her that Mr. Phillips had come into the office this morning, but then he left for an off-site meeting. He told her he'd be back after lunch. Could she take a message?

Gina nodded her head. "Yes, please tell Mr. Phillips there's been some mix-up and I need to talk to him about it. As soon as he comes in. Thanks, Lisa." Gina headed back to her office.

Stacked up on a corner of her desk were the latest financial statements. Gina sighed and pulled the stack in front of her and began going over the reports. Maybe if she kept herself busy, she wouldn't feel the hole in her heart so much.

On the fifth statement, Gina sat back and cocked her head. *What? That doesn't make sense.* She took the last three months of reports from her file cabinet. *How could I have missed this?* Gina picked up the phone to call Accounting. Maybe somebody there could help her find an explanation for these numbers. Where was Craig? She needed to talk to him about this, too.

Gina put her head in her shaking hands waiting for a pick-up in Accounting. *Isn't anybody working today?* She replaced the phone and went back over the figures in the files. She and Craig would get to the bottom of it. His eyes would find what hers had missed. Somebody was skimming cash—maybe. Gina shook her head and went back to the budget columns.

* * * * *

Alli walked into *Carlisle's Far East Antiques* to the tinkle of the old-fashioned bell mounted on the door. No one was in the shop front, so Alli peeked behind the counter to see if the owner were hiding from her. Nope. But a cloth wrapping caught her eye. Wasn't that Nicky's old t-shirt she had wrapped the jade dragon in to bring to Carlisle?

A sound behind her made Alli jump to the side and seem to be examining some smeary blue teapots.

"Oh," Carlisle's voice expressed surprise. "Oh. It's you, Miss uh Miss West, was it? Or is that Wesson?"

Alli felt her face grow hot. "I can explain. Yes, you're right. I am Alli Wesson. I'm so sorry for giving you the wrong name, but it's just that…"

Carlisle interrupted her stammering. "It's just that you are a murder and theft suspect."

Alli nodded her head. "Yes. Well. True enough, but suspects don't a murderer make. And I don't steal things, either. I stopped back in because I wondered if you could tell me something more about the antique jade dragon I brought you."

"Oh, you must not have noticed in the paper. There was a robbery.

Someone took it. That dragon appears to move around a lot."

"Stolen, Mr. Carlisle? But...I mean..." Alli turned around and strode behind the counter. She picked up the wrapped bundle she had noticed earlier. "I believe this is the dragon I brought you. Another one must have gone missing. I'm taking this to the police station. I should have done that in the first place instead of bringing it to you. Thanks for keeping it safe for me." Alli turned to leave.

Carlisle began sputtering. "Here. You can't take my merchandise. That is my property."

Alli clutched the wrapped dragon close. "I don't think so. This is my nephew's t-shirt. I can describe the design on the front, the side that's turned in. Shall we call the police to come here? Maybe that would be best."

Alli picked up the phone while Carlisle stood with a stunned look. She punched in Evan's cell number and told him where she was and what she had. "Come fast, Evan. I think Mr. Carlisle wants to go someplace."

Alli replaced the phone and turned to Carlisle with a smile. "Do you have any teapots that aren't ancient? I could use a cup of tea while we're waiting."

Carlisle nodded and went back to the small kitchenette behind the counter. He and Alli went out onto the porch of the shop and sat at a small table to await the police. Carlisle's hands shook as he poured their tea. His lip was trembling, too.

Alli reached out and placed a hand over his. "Mr. Carlisle, may I ask how you got mixed up in all this mess? I mean, gee, stolen dragons with ruby eyes kind of get people's attention. What happened?"

Carlisle slumped into his seat and stirred his tea. "I never thought it would come to this. Theft and murder! You have to believe me, Ms. Wesson. I had no idea where this would lead. It was to be a simple subterfuge, a minor scam, but one with the full knowledge of the customers, well, one customer."

"Huh? What are you saying? The Franklins' knew about this?"

"Mr. Franklin needed an infusion of cash. Mrs. Franklin wanted a valuable antique dragon. He and I decided to substitute a fine quality, but counterfeit dragon. He would pocket the difference in cash, and I would still have the genuine antique to sell. Had Ms. Franklin gotten another appraisal, she would have discovered the ruse. But she seemed content with the documentation I provided. The insurance company took that documentation for their valuation as well. Neither Mr. Franklin nor I ever could have guessed that the dragon would end up stolen."

Alli nodded. "Did Paul Franklin consider filing an insurance claim?"

"Oh, heavens, no! Mr. Franklin, despite what I just shared, is quite an honorable man. But what I wonder is why *you* stole the dragon. Surely you knew you'd be a suspect, being in their home and all."

Alli shook her head. "That's what you think? You think I stole this dragon?"

Alli unwrapped it and placed the dragon on the table between them. "I told you, I don't steal things."

"Then how did this come into your possession? You brought it to me last week. I called Mr. Franklin and told him to come get it. He asked me hang onto it until things settled a bit more in his life. So how did you get acquire this piece?"

Alli nodded understanding. "I got it from Ms. Franklin's office, but I didn't steal it. Her administrative assistant found it hidden on a shelf behind some books. I've been trying and trying to figure out how it could have gotten there."

Carlisle looked startled at that information. "Her office? Then, maybe, no. That wouldn't make sense."

Detective Clinton's department car slid into a slot on the street. He and Evan approached the front porch where Carlisle and Alli sat.

Clinton looked at the unwrapped statue sitting on the table. "Holy, uh, moley, Mr. Carlisle. Is this the dragon you said Ms. Wesson stole from your shop? Why did you bring it back, Ms. Wesson?"

Clinton took handcuffs out of one voluminous pocket. "Put your hands behind your back, Ms. Wesson. You're under arrest for possession of stolen goods. You have the right to remain silent."

Alli tucked her arms together and looked over to Evan for help. "C'mon. We've already done this. Please listen to what Mr. Carlisle has to say. The dragon has been in his shop since last week. I came today to get it, to bring to you."

Clinton slipped the handcuffs into his jacket pocket, leaned against the porch railing, and took out his notebook. He licked the tip of his pencil and poised it to write on the pad. "Fine. What do you have to add to this story, Mr. Carlisle? And, FYI? We've already talked to Mr. Franklin about your scam. We know it's not technically illegal, so we're not here to arrest you, but keep to the truth or we'll charge you with calling the police for a false theft report. Now, what's your side of this dragon story?"

*   *   *   *   *

Clinton's car pulled away from the curb a half hour later. Alli relaxed back into the cracked leather seat of the back seat.

"Thanks for the lift, Guys. I was about call a cab to take me to the hospital. I have to check some things with Gina, then, maybe we could get together later this afternoon? I've been thinking about some ideas I'd like to run by you."

"Why not now, Alli?" Evan asked. "We're still ten minutes from the hospital."

"No, it's going to take longer than ten minutes, and, besides, I need to talk to Gina first. I don't want you to accuse me of going off on a tangent again."

Clinton gave a long look to Evan.

Alli leaned forward. "Hey! I know what that look means, Detective Clinton. But, this time, I think I am really on to something, but there's a personal aspect that...that interferes with my thinking. I have to have Gina help me process this stuff."

"Sure, Ms. Wesson. Whenever you're ready just give a call to us. We'll drop everything else we're doing and get right with you."

Alli harrumphed and scrunched lower in the back seat corner. She sat silent as they made their way into the hospital parking lot closest to the employee entrance. Alli hopped out as soon as the car stopped.

"Thanks for the ride. And, really, I think you'll want to talk to me later. Maybe. I mean, maybe I'll call if this pans out. Bye."

Alli watched the car depart and walked to the entrance. She decided to take the stairs to Gina's fourth floor office. She felt leaden. Was it from lack of exercise or from surplus anxiety. What if she were right?

Huffing, Alli opened the fourth floor door and entered the hallway near Gina's office. But when she rapped at the door and pushed it open, no one was there.

Alli wandered down the hall to Rita's office, but she was gone, too. Where was everybody? Alli tapped her foot then walked back to Gina's office. *Wait here until she returns from wherever, whenever? Or go back to the house and wait for Gina to come home? Maybe Maria can help figure this out.*

Alli straightened her spine. She entered Gina's office again and picked up the phone after checking a number. "Glendale Cab? Could you please pick me up at the front entrance at Glendale Community Hospital?"

Chapter 21

Craig stopped off at Gina's office when he got to the hospital. Her door was shut, so he knocked then turned the knob to enter. Empty. He turned around to leave, then paused. He checked the hallway to make sure no one had seen him enter. He closed the door behind him and locked it.

Gina's normally tidy desk looked a mess. Papers were piled on the top and spilled over onto her credenza. Spreadsheets. He moved closer to study them. He picked up her phone to check the most recent call in the phone log's memory. Accounting. She knew or thought she did. He could think of only one way to stop her until he figured a way out of this mess. He quietly unlocked her door and felt for his car keys.

* * * * *

Maria answered the insistent doorbell. "Well, Mr. Hospital Bigshot. What brings you here on a work day when you should be making sure people have what they need instead of driving around places which aren't at work. Did you and Gina have a fight? She won't talk about you anymore. What did you do to her because if you hurt my Gina I can't be responsible for my actions since she's my daughter and so good and she deserves better than to be treated like this."

Craig interrupted. "Good afternoon, Maria. Uh, I just dropped by to get the kids. Gina and I are good. She wanted me to bring them to her. Everything is fine, just a little tiff. In fact, that's why she wanted me to get the kids for her. We're taking them out to dinner."

"She didn't tell me that. Why wouldn't she call me with news like that since the kids are still in their school clothes and can't go out to dinner dressed like that?"

"Oh, don't bother. Truly, it's just an informal place, Mexican, you know, nothing fancy. As to why she didn't call? I don't know, but she was so busy when I left her that I had to insist on getting the kids so I could get her out of there sooner. You know how she is."

"Well. I guess that makes sense. Still, she is very good about calling. I'll just give her a buzz and make sure she's okay."

"No, Maria. No. I told you she is busy. She'd be upset if she knew you were worried. Just tell the kids to come."

Maria sniffed. "Hmm. I think I should just give her a call. It won't slow you down." She turned her back and picked up the phone on the kitchen counter and crossed to the sofa. She sat down and began to dial.

Craig came up behind her and hit her head with a sap. Maria fell back, knocked out.

"Sorry, Old Girl. You should have let us go." He pulled her legs up onto the sofa and arranged her head on a pillow. Craig covered her with an afghan and sprinted up the steps to the kids' rooms.

"C'mon. *Vite vite*. Do you remember what I told you that meant?"

Nicky answered. "It means to hurry. It's French."

"Good boy. Let's go."

"Is Gram coming?" Carrie was looking down at her grandmother on the sofa.

"No, no. She told me she would take a little nap with you out of the house."

"Gram never naps," Nicky responded. "She says naps are for kids or people who don't have enough to do."

"Well, she's napping now, as you can see. Let's go to your mother. My car's out front." Craig ushered them through the doorway.

Craig escorted both kids into the back seat of his black Volvo. They buckled up.

"You're supposed to check that we buckled up. We can't be in a car without seatbelts on," Carrie reminded him.

"Fine." Craig glanced at both children. "You're good. Let's go."

Nicky protested. "Why can't I sit up front? I'm older than Carrie. I should get to sit in the grown-up seat."

"But you're not a grown-up, now are you? Don't be a pest, Nicky. Sit back. We're not going far."

"I want my mama, are we going to meet Mama? Where is Gram? Why can't she come with us? Is she still asleep?" Carrie whined.

"It's gonna be dark soon. We have to be back for dinner. Will you take us home for dinner?" Nicky asked.

"Shut up. Just shut up." Craig turned around from his seat and glared at them. He took a deep breath. "Look, I'm sorry I yelled at you. But, I'm upset, too. I wouldn't have come to get you if your mother hadn't asked me to. We're going to meet her. She said she'd bring dinner."

"Oh goodie!" Carrie brightened. "Pizza? Chicken fingers? Tacos?"

"I don't know what your mother is bringing. She didn't tell me. She told me to take you to her. So, please, be quiet. No more questions." Craig turned the radio on to a popular music station and turned the volume up loud to circumvent further conversation.

Ten minutes later, Craig pulled into a circular driveway. He grabbed a backpack from the front seat. "Get out of the car." Nicky helped Carrie undo her seatbelt.

"Where are we? Whose house is this? Is this your house? It's nice, isn't it, Nicky?"

"Yeah, this is a cool house, Mr. Phillips. Do you have a pool? Look, Carrie, it's got an upstairs. But it looks bigger than ours."

Craig stood at the front door with the leaded glass windows fiddling with the key in the lock. "Now, you have to be quiet. We're going to surprise your mother. Can you do that?"

"I thought you said she was meeting us here. If she's already here, how can we surprise her?" Nicky asked.

"Because...because we are going to a special room in this house, and then I am going to go get her while you stay quiet. She thinks we're going one place, but we have to go to another one, so I'll go bring her here. Stop asking questions. Just do what I told you to do."

"Why are you being mean to us? You didn't used to be mean,"

Carrie asked, her eyes filling with tears again. "I want my mama."

Craig finally got the door open and ushered the children into a dimly lit hallway. He closed the door behind him and relocked it. He motioned for them to follow him down the hall, putting his finger to his lips to indicate they were to be quiet. He turned on the lights in a room that was clearly an office.

Inside were file cabinets and shelves with books. There was no window, and the room was silent, the air dead and stale. He locked the door behind him. Two chairs sat side by side in front of the desk.

"Sit down, Kids. You can wait here to surprise your mom." As they sat, Craig stood behind Nicky, put a handkerchief over his face, and grabbed his arms as Nicky struggled against the chloroform. Carrie began to scream. When Nicky slumped in his arms, then he drugged Carrie. He tied each child upright into their chairs, binding a handkerchief over their mouths so they could not make much noise when they regained consciousness. He hated the sound of brats screaming and crying. It was too much like his childhood.

Craig turned off the lights and left the room, locking the door behind him. Now to attend to Gina. Then he and Alli would leave the state.

* * * * *

Alli paid the cab driver and stood in front of the house. Should she knock? Maria would be home. What if she wouldn't let Alli in? Should she just slip around to her place and wait for Gina to come home? Alli, not liking the idea of confronting Maria alone, opted for the sneak-to-the-back choice.

She opened the creaky side gate, the one she always wished she had WD-40'd each time she came home late from a date. But, she had learned how to minimize it's sound, so as quietly as she could, Alli opened and latched the gate and made her way to her casita. She glanced at the family room through the Arcadia doors and saw Maria napping on the sofa. The kids were nowhere around. They must be playing some quiet game in Nicky's room.

Alli opened her door and went inside the sweltering hot apartment. The air conditioning hadn't been on in days. Well, with her gone, why would it be? She dropped her purse on the counter and opened the refrigerator to get some iced tea she had made the day she left unexpectedly.

Alli poured a glass and took a deep swallow and then she choked. "Maria doesn't nap! She has to be sick!"

Alli dashed out her door and slid open the unlocked Arcadia door. Maria was lying under an afghan. *In this heat?* Alli knelt beside the prone woman and picked up her wrist to check for a pulse. Alli didn't even realize she'd been holding her breath until she suddenly expelled it. Alive.

Alli gently tapped Maria's sunken cheeks. "Maria? Maria? Are you okay? Wake up."

Maria's eyelids fluttered then shut again. Almost immediately, they flew open and Maria tried to sit up.

"Where are the kids? Did he take them? Oh, my head." Maria put her fingertips on a knob showing through the thin hair on the back of her head.

Alli spread the hair to get a better look at the bump. "Did you fall? How did you hurt your head? Maria, are okay?" Alli helped Maria to get upright and then ran to the kitchen for a bag of frozen peas to put on the bump. "Here. Let me hold this for you."

Maria looked up at Alli and huge tears filled her eyes and slid down her cheeks. "Alli, I am so sorry. So sorry. All that's happened is my punishment for what I did to you, how I treated you. I love you. I love you like I love Gina. I don't know that I ever told you that, but you knew, didn't you. You knew how much I love you, right?"

Alli dropped the bag of peas and had to pick it up and reposition it. "You're not going to die. You don't have to go doing penance and saying stuff just to make sure you go to heaven. We'll talk about that later. What happened to you? And where are Nicky and Carrie?"

"Craig Phillips has them. He told me Gina sent him. When I tried to call her, you know, to check, I never did trust that man you remember, and I was right I guess after what he did. He hit me with something. I don't know what happened after that. Alli, why would he hit me just for checking like a grandmother should?"

Alli handed the bag of peas to Maria. "Craig hit you? Craig knocked you out? Why? What could he want? I'm calling Gina. There has to be some explanation for this."

Alli went over to the phone and punched in Gina's number. The phone rang and rang. No answer. Where was she?

Alli replaced the phone and came over to Maria. "There's something I have to tell you, something I found out while I was gone. Maria, Craig Phillips isn't his real name."

"I knew it! I knew it! He just seemed so smarmy around me, always trying to get on my good side."

Alli smiled at the thought of Maria having a good side somebody could get to. "You're not going to believe this, then again, maybe you will. Craig is really Cal Wesson, my older brother. Do you remember he went off to the Army when we were in middle school? He came back for me. He loves me. He wants us to be family again, a healthy one this time."

Maria sat back and regarded Alli, gauging how much she should say, Alli thought.

Maria apparently decided to jump in with her info. "Yeah, well, the way I heard it was it was the army or jail time. He was young enough they thought the discipline of the Army would straighten him out more than being put in with the hard guys."

Alli tried to process this view of things. "So it must have worked. Look at him. Holding a responsible job. Searching for me. Except..." Alli stopped speaking and dropped her head into her hands.

Maria put her arm around Alli. "Except why would he need to change his name and why would he bop me on the head and steal Nicky and Carrie? Right?" She hugged Alli to her.

Alli took a deep breath and drew back from Maria. "And except why would he have books about making poisons from houseplants and grow a bunch of them in his apartment greenhouse?"

Alli stood up and moved to the phone. "I'm calling Evan. I should have told him earlier today about Craig or Cal."

Maria looked puzzled. Alli said, "Never mind. Long story about seeing Evan today. But, I'm calling him now and tell him what I found out."

The phone rang sharply to interrupt Alli. "Maybe that's Gina. She must have seen I called her."

Alli grabbed the phone, "Gina? Where have you been? Craig took the kids."

"Yes, I did," Craig's voice cut her off. "Alli. Stay out of this. As soon as I clear a few things up with Gina, we can leave. I've decided this hospital job isn't for me after all. I know a great town in Florida we can go to, start over, send for Mom to join us. You'd like that, wouldn't you?"

"Uh, Craig, or rather, Cal, why did you hit Maria? Why did you take Nicky and Carrie? What's going on?"

"I'll explain it all later, Alli. But for now, I have to talk to Gina. Would you put her on the phone please?"

"Cal, she's not home yet. She must be on her way because she wasn't in her office a few minutes ago."

"I see." He paused, "Then, tell her when she gets home I want her to meet me. Alone. And if there is even a whiff of the police, and trust me, I have a nose for cops, if there is even a whiff, she'll be very sorry. Very sorry. Do you understand what I'm saying, Alli?"

Alli stammered, "Yes. Yes, I think so. Where shall I tell her to meet you?"

"At the Franklin's house. She can meet me here. We'll go to where the kids are. Alone, Alli. Tell her I'm serious." The phone line went dead.

"That was him, wasn't it? Where are the kids? What does he want? We don't have much money, but I can cash in some of my DC's tomorrow."

Alli had to smile in spite of the situation. "CD's, Maria. No, he doesn't seem to want money. He wants to meet with Gina. He didn't say why."

Alli looked down at the phone still buzzing in her hand. She put it back in place. "Maria. I have to go. Can I have your car and your cell phone. I'll call Gina on my way."

"Yes, of course, but where are you going? What should I tell Gina?"

Alli grabbed the keys from the hook and snatched the cell phone off the kitchen counter. "I'm going to get Nicky and Carrie back."

Chapter 22

Alli parked down the street from the Franklin's house. There was Cal's car in the driveway. She peeked inside the vehicle. No kids, but one of Carrie's barrettes lay on the floor in back. He did have the kids, or had them.

Even though she knew this place pretty well from all of her visits, Alli didn't see how she was going to get in. Maybe she could trigger the alarm system to get the police there. She worked her way around to the back yard gate, crouching beneath windows to avoid detection.

Alli jiggled the gate latch leading to the yard. Locked of course. She found a toehold in the stucco on the pillar the gate attached to, and she hauled herself up and over the locked gate. She landed and rolled into a ball to keep from getting more damage than a bruise. Right next to the gate was the electric box. Maybe she could find the one for the alarm and trigger it.

Alli opened the metal door and found that all the wires were cut. No electricity. No alarm. *Well, that makes it easier for me to get in, too.* Alli went toward Baby's doggy door. Lots of time people forgot to put the door guard in the slot. She'd used doggy doors a lot as a kid. But she wasn't kid-sized anymore. And Baby was smaller than usual.

Alli put an arm through the doggy door and rested her hand on a tile floor. She twisted her body so she could take advantage of the door's diagonal space. After much wiggling and scraping, and ripping a tear in her sleeve, Alli found herself in what she assumed to be the laundry room. She stood quietly listening for a moment before tiptoeing to the partially closed door. She leaned an ear against it. Not a sound.

Alli slipped out the door and made her way down the hallway. The heavy air was stale, still. The house felt abandoned.

Along the hallway on the way to the foyer, all doors were open. Except one. She paused at the shut door. Alli turned doorknob slowly. She didn't want the handle to click. Locked. Why would one door be locked? Was that where he had Carrie and Nicky?

Alli kept moving slowly past another partially opened door. The door beyond that was the half-bath then the foyer she had entered many times.

Where would Cal be? In the locked room? In the kitchen? The family room? He could be anywhere, upstairs even. She stopped to listen again for any sound that could be human.

An arm grabbed Alli around her waist, pinning her arms to her sides, while the other hand closed over her mouth.

Cal's voice spoke softly in her ear. "What the hell are you doing here? I told you to stay away, stay out of this. Don't you trust me?" He sighed and placed a cloth over her face. She felt herself going limp as she struggled to get free.

When Alli regained consciousness a few minutes later, Cal was sitting beside her. He held her hand lightly in his.

"I chloroformed you, Alli, but I only gave you a whiff, just to get you to settle down. You have to listen to me. Oh, Honey. Why wouldn't you wait for me to come get you? This is no place for you, nothing to do with you."

"Of course it has to do with me, Cal. Those are Gina's kids. I had to see they were all right."

Cal cocked his head to one side and gave a small smile. "You're right. I should have known you'd show up. When is Gina coming? She's may be about to make a big mistake. I have to stop her."

Alli sat up, withdrawing her hand from his. "I tried to call her again before I got here. Something must be going on. She's been away from her desk all day." Alli shook her head to clear it more and then took a deep breath and exhaled it. "What's the mistake? Is it a mistake...about you?"

Cal got up and walked into the kitchen. "How did you get in, by the way? I used a key she gave me when she wasn't feeling well, there toward the end. She had me bring by some paperwork a few days she wasn't up to coming in."

Alli shrugged. "Doggy door. Like we used to do when we were kids. Remember how you'd make me crawl through and steal change on people's dressers or bologna from the refrigerator? I haven't done it in years."

"You're bigger now," Cal smiled. "Must have been tight."

Alli shrugged. "Yeah. Cal, will you tell me something honestly?"

"I would never lie to you, Alli. I'm done with lies and all the rest of it. I've kind of like hit bottom, you know? Like those AA guys? I want us to start over again. I thought I could do it here, but things sort of got out of control."

"Out of control like poisoning Clarice Franklin?"

Cal came back into the family room and sat in a chair across from her. "What did you say? You think I tried to kill The Dragon Lady?"

"I was reading some books at your place, and then I found a recipe in a drawer. Ways to kill people with plants."

Cal leaned back into his chair and waved his hand in dismissal. "Oh, that. Well, yes, I do know about those things, but I never wanted to kill anyone. You have to know that about me. I have done some... well, let's just say I regret some past events."

Cal got up from his chair. He seemed jumpy. "Clarice was more of a tea addict than I thought. She was just supposed to be sick enough to stay away from the office until I cleared up some things."

Alli swallowed. "Cleared up some things?"

"Yeah. There was a, well, a small discrepancy in the food department's account. But I had gotten some money from Paul Franklin to replace the funds. I was working on that when she died. She wasn't supposed to die, Alli. You have to believe me."

Alli made herself put on her sincere face. Not always being truthful sometimes came in handy. She knew she could be convincing even in the face of contradictory information.

"Craig. Cal, listen to me. Gina won't say a thing. Honestly. I can promise that. All she wants is her kids and her boring life back."

"I was going to have my life back, too, until Clarice began to suspect me. She started asking questions. Started digging into the books. That's when I made her sick. Take her mind off me. Then when she died, I thought maybe I could still have that life by becoming CEO in her place. Lots of people at the hospital like me. I'd have been a much better boss."

"Wait. You said Paul Franklin gave you money? Why?"

Cal smiled. "It was my connections that Carlisle used to get the phony dragon. When I told him I knew about it, and it might leak out to Clarice, he paid me to keep quiet. I hid the dragon in her office. He was going to get it one day when he dropped by. But then, she died. Things spun out of control."

"But why take Gina's kids, Cal. Let's just go. Let's call or send a note to her to tell her where she can get them."

Cal looked over at Alli. "I panicked. I never panic, Alli. I always plan for everything. Then, it all came unraveled. I couldn't let Gina tell the police about the account books. I mean, they're okay now, the money's back, but a good auditor would figure it out. I thought if I told her I'd let her kids go, she'd promise not to tell anyone. She's the kind of person who keeps promises. And after all, what harm's been done once the money's back?"

Alli nodded. "You're right. She does keep her promises. I learned that from her family. That's not how we grew up. I'm sure if we just go, she'll keep quiet. Please? Can we go?"

Cal shook his head. "Easy for you to say. It's not your life she holds the key to. I can't go back to jail, Alli. I can't stand being locked up with animals who aren't as smart as me. All I wanted when I came here was to find you and start over. Our own family. We'll get it right this time."

"If you only knew how much I want that, Cal. It's all I've ever wanted."

Cal looked over at Alli. "Really?"

"I think the reason I've screwed up so much over the years is that I haven't been with my family. I've been pretending to fit in, pretending these people were my family. But they're not. Now that you're here, I see that."

Cal nodded throughout her comments. "Yes. Yes, that's how I feel, too. We had an awful childhood, but we can fix that now. We're in charge now. We can make a good family."

"Right. But you have to let the kids go. Cops get real upset when kids are hurt. Where are the kids?"

Cal nodded toward the hallway where the locked door was. "I put them in that room. They're just chloroformed. They'll be okay."

Alli let out the breath she had been holding. "Cal, please. Let them go. I can't lose you again. And I will if the cops get involved."

Cal looked around, his eyes wild, searching the corners of the room and out the window. "Cops? Do you think she's already called them? Maria might have called them."

Alli reached for her purse. "Yes, but they don't know where we are. Let me call Gina again. I'll get her here alone. She can come pick up the kids, and you and I can blow this popcorn joint. No harm, no foul. Where shall we go? Where can we start over? Didn't you say something about Florida."

Cal walked toward the door "Okay. Call her. But tell her if any cops come, the kids won't be worth picking up."

Alli flinched at the implication, but she squeezed out a smile meant to reassure Cal. She opened her purse and searched around for Rita's weird gun. She wrapped her hand around it and withdrew it from her purse.

"Wait," Cal interrupted. "You don't have a cell..."

Alli pulled the trigger. Two probes shot into Cal's thigh. He crumpled to the floor. His body curled into a fetal position.

Alli looked at the gun and the insulated wires sticking in Craig's leg that led back to her gun. "What the...? That's not a gun!"

Cal moaned, paralyzed on the floor. Alli turned at the sound of pounding on the front door. She ran to the door and let Evan and Detective Clinton into the house. Two uniformed officers cuffed Cal and dragged him out to the squad car, reading him his rights as they went. Two other officers stood behind Clinton.

Alli led the way down the hallway. "The kids are in here." Alli called in to them. "Carrie? Nicky? It's Aunt Alli. We're coming in to get you."

Clinton leaned in to the door as well. "Kids? We're going to make some noise here. Don't be scared. We have to break the door."

The uniformed officers crashed into the door until it broke open. Alli pushed past the splinters and gathered the kids into her arms while Clinton and Evan undid their bindings. They were still groggy but okay. She helped them stand.

They all heard Gina's voice in the foyer.

Carrie started crying. "Mama?"

Nicky ran toward the door and was swept up into Gina's arms as she entered. Gina sank to the floor and Carrie piled into her arms, too. Gina's tear stained face lifted to Alli. "Thank you."

Alli was crying, too. Evan came over to Alli and pulled her into his arms. She sobbed into his chest. When Gina rushed into the house, Evan pointed down the hallway.

"How did you find us, Evan? I didn't know how to let you know where I was. I was so scared."

Evan held her tighter. "You had Maria's phone. It has a GPS locator. It was pretty easy to find you. Then, when we got closer, we realized he had to be in the Franklin's house. Perfect place to hole up with all the Franklin's in California."

Alli's teeth chattered. "Evan. Craig is my brother. My brother Cal. I...I shot him. I shot my brother. How could I shoot my brother? I could have killed him. Am I a killer, too?"

Evan whispered into Alli's ear. "You did good, Alli. Shh. Shh. It's over. He's alive. You shot him just right with that taser."

Alli shivered. "Taser? I thought it was a gun. Evan, I was willing to shoot my own brother with a gun! It doesn't matter that it wasn't a gun. I wanted to kill him. How could I want to kill someone?"

Evan hugged her again. "I don't believe for a minute you wanted to kill him. But you did want to stop him. And you did. You aimed for a non-lethal part of his body, and you took him down. Good thing we had those Saturday morning shooting lessons, wasn't it? I told you it might come in handy some day."

Chapter 23

Alli and Gina had just wrapped the last entrée for the freezer when Jack Farnsworth walked into the kitchen.

Alli started. Gina gave her look and offered a warm greeting. "Mr. Farnsworth! We didn't know you were still home. Mrs. Farnsworth left about an hour ago. We're nearly done here. We'll just wipe down the counters and be on our way."

Jack held up two hands in a supplicating manner. "Yes, I knew you were here. I've been waiting to talk to you. Can you wait a few more minutes after you're done?"

Alli blushed. "It's my fault, Mr. Farnsworth. Really. Gina never screws up like that. It was me, er, I."

Jack and Gina both looked puzzled.

Jack broke the silence. "Uhh. I'm not sure I…"

Alli rushed into the gap in speech. "I know we are supposed to put the recyclables in the big brown can, but last week, I got them mixed up, and it wasn't until I was almost home that I realized the mistake. You know how things niggle at your mind, and later you figure out why? I know the city sometimes sends a violation letter. I want you to know, I'll pay whatever the penalty is."

Gina, who had been staring at Alli with her mouth open, said,

Mission Impastable

"Alli! How could you mix that up?"

Jack Farnsworth threw his head back and roared. "See. That's exactly why I want you two. You have integrity. You have more, of course. Your cooking is amazing, and your work ethic, commendable." Jack continued chuckling.

Alli tilted her head. "Want us? Want us for what? You already have us. Do you have a big dinner party coming up like that one last month that we prepared?"

Jack smiled. "Oh, no. Nothing like that. That's Celia's turf, but there probably is something she's involved in. No, this is a job offer of a different sort. Have you ever considered teaching?"

Gina stood staring at Jack without uttering a word. She didn't know what word to utter.

Alli started giggling. "Teaching? Now that's funny, right Gina? If any of my teachers ever thought I would enter their profession, there would be mass resignations throughout the Deer Valley School District."

Jack wasn't laughing now. "I'm serious. I have a teaching offer to make the two of you."

Gina finally stammered out a response. "What? Excuse me, Mr. Farnsworth. What are we missing here? We're cooks, not teachers."

Jack pulled out a couple of chairs around the kitchen table. "Please. Sit." He pulled out another for himself.

"I bought a floor about a year ago in the old Sugar Beet Factory in downtown Glendale. You know, they turned it into a liquor place? Well, I got a floor to start the Culinary Arts School of Glendale, CAS-G. There's no cooking school in the West Valley, and we need one. Why send all that money over to Snottsdale, right? There are several chefs, and quite a few students, but I want to expand the course offerings. I'd like you to help me plan and then teach classes in how to cater and how to run a personal chef business. Are you available?"

* * * * *

On the ride home, the Farnsworth job was their last one of the day, Gina was trying to tame Alli's enthusiasm. She would have accepted Farnsworth's offer immediately had Gina not said they needed time to think about it. They would let him know the next day.

"Alli, I am already stretched to the max. I'm almost out of comp time and vacation days since 'Dinner is Served' took off. We cannot take on another customer unless you are willing to do it all yourself. You are going to have to take on some of our existing customers when I run out of days to take off from the hospital. We have to tell him no."

Alli shook her head. "Gina, Gina, Gina. Look at the big picture. Think about our goals. Quit your job at the hospital."

Gina, who was driving, pulled over to the curb six doors down from their own driveway. "Quit my job? Are you nuts? What will pay the bills? How will we pay back the home equity loan Ma took out to fund us?"

"Do the math, Gina. We have already turned down three new customers. We call them tonight to see if they still want us. We advertise to get more customers. We give a bonus to existing customers who refer us to someone who hires us. And, with the part-time salary Farnsworth will pay each of us for teaching a couple of classes each a week, we can do it! I know we can!"

Gina put the car into gear and drove to their house. As the garage door opened, she said to Alli, "When we walk in that door, get the calculator."

* * * * *

Two weeks later, Gina walked in the door from the garage at 10:31 a.m. The house was quiet with the kids at school, Maria at her Bunco group, and Alli cooking at a customer's home. She brought in the boxes from her office. She put them on the counter and considered that her past professional life fit in three medium boxes.

She noticed her mother's special pound cake on the counter, cooling. She considered cutting a piece, but she figured it was for dinner that night. Instead, Gina walked to the freezer and got out a new pint of Ben and Jerry's "Heath Bar Crunch." She ate it all.

[See REAL Pound Cake]

* * * * *

At six o'clock the next morning, Maria, trying to tie her robe around her considerable middle, entered the kitchen. Alli stood at the counter crushing garlic cloves.

"Isn't it a little early for garlic, Alli? Or maybe not. Remember that morning I was feeling down and out maybe you were in 9th grade and you said you'd fix breakfast for you and Gina before you went to school and I thought that would make you late? You made garlic toast, and I got calls from your teachers all day saying how you stank up the classrooms. Hoo boy, you didn't have many Italian cooks for teachers I could tell that from their attitudes and how they had such delicate noses."

Alli turned around and saw Maria standing by the door. She grinned at the story as she rinsed garlic juice and papery fragments off her fingers. She held them out to Maria. "Want a sniff?"

"No. I can make my own hands stinky, thank you. Move over. I can dice those tomatoes for you. What are we making?"

Alli scooted over. "Since everyone is coming to dinner tonight, I thought I'd make stuffed shells. The recipe feeds hordes and once we do this part and refrigerate it until almost dinnertime, we can relax while it is baking."

[See Three-Cheese Stuffed Shells and Alli's Quick Marinara Sauce]

Maria didn't look at Alli while she diced tomatoes. Alli had moved on to the onions for the sauce. Neither spoke for several minutes.

Maria broke the silence. "Sort of like old times doing this. Even though Gina loved to cook and she was good at it, you and I seemed to have the best times cooking together. It was sort of like we knew at the same time what to do. I don't know. Maybe that's just me and my memory."

Alli wiped her fingers. She turned to Maria and slid her arms around Maria's waist. She hugged hard and kissed Maria's neck.

"You remember right. We just cooked together so much when I moved in here, a dumb, screw-up kid with no one who wanted her. I think cooking with you saved my sanity."

Maria hugged back. "We wanted you. I always loved you. You should have been my daughter, so I just pretend that's the way it really is."

"Really? You really did want me here? You weren't just doing charity work?"

Maria teared up. "Alli, what happened? Why did I get so mad at you? I am so sorry. I can never make it up to you."

Alli laughed. "Sure you can. Keep chopping. There's more where that tomato came from." She hugged Maria again and went back to the onions.

* * * * *

Alli, Gina, Maria, Pearl, and Evan gathered in the family room for drinks before dinner. Alli sighed and leaned back into Evan. "Mmm. This feels so safe after last week."

The kids were splashing in the pool off the family room as some grown-ups sipped tart, icy wine and others enjoyed a warmer red. They couldn't stop re-hashing what had happened. Pearl stood by the Arcadia door since it was her turn to watch the kids in the pool.

Evan rubbed his growling stomach. "That smells good. What's for dinner? I don't think I've had anything but fast food since Clarice Franklin's murder."

Maria rose from her recliner and waddled over to Alli. She patted her hair, leaned over, and kissed Alli's forehead. "My Alli took my great recipe for shells and she messed around with it and now we have to eat something even better than I made and nobody will remember it was my recipe that she started with and like better. C'mon, Pearl. Help me make the garlic bread and salad. Dinner will be in 15 minutes, Mr. Hungry Cop."

Pearl got up. "Glad to lend a hand if that will make dinner quicker. Gina? Tag, you're it. Watch the kids." Pearl followed Maria into the kitchen.

The two older women busied themselves with the dinner sides. With only a counter separating the kitchen from the family room, they could still hear and participate in the conversation about Cal Wesson.

As she pulled the romaine from the refrigerator, Maria chimed in. "I never did like him, you know. Not from the beginning. Something about him, sly like, that must have reminded me of your family, Alli."

Pearl punched her in the side. "Oh, sorry, Alli!" Maria recovered.

Gina gave a small laugh. "Yes, I remember what a hard time you gave me about seeing him. Still, he is, or rather was charming."

"All of us Wesson's are charming," Alli preened. "No, really. How could any of us know? We don't live in a world where people are crooks. Well, except for you, Evan."

Gina said, "But you shot him, Alli. Knowing he was your brother, you still shot him."

Alli thought about it. "Well, it would have been more impressive if the gun were a real gun. I thought there'd be blood everywhere. I was glad the kids were in another room."

Evan added, "The taser zap did the job, Alli. Bullets are much messier. Thanks to you, Cal Wesson will be going away for a long time."

"No, thanks to Rita and her taser and to you for showing up when you did. I'm just glad I remembered I had it. Will she get it back soon?"

Evan shook his head. "Not until after the trial. She was one pretty upset lady when we told her we had it. She started whining about needing protection in the parking lot. Asked if I'd escort her." Evan shook his head. "She blames you, me, and, who knows, maybe even the hospital auxiliary league, for her life being in danger after work hours since she doesn't have her taser. I bought her a can of pepper spray to use meantime."

Gina said, "But, still, real gun or no, you pulled the trigger. You shot him. To save my kids. I can't thank you enough."

Alli patted the seat beside her. "Give me a hug. That is more than enough payment." Gina scooched closer and they hugged hard.

Evan smiled at Gina then added, "I'm not sure he would have hurt them, but you never know. He was pretty desperate to escape at that point. He just couldn't see his way out of it. Imagine not being able to prove you weren't trying to kill someone you poisoned. His attorney has his work cut out for him."

"Do you think it's true, Evan?" Alli asked. "Do you think his story about just wanting to incapacitate Clarice so he could doctor the books to conceal his embezzlement was true?"

Evan shrugged. "Who knows? When we tracked his various aliases, he has lots of arrest warrants out for theft and fraud, but never anything violent. So maybe he wasn't trying to kill her."

Alli got still. "I'd hate to think I have killer blood in me, too. Along with larceny and fraud. Those are bad enough."

Gina reached over for Alli's other hand, the one Evan didn't have hold of. She squeezed it. "You don't have a violent or criminal bone in your body. That's why I am still surprised you could shoot Cal, especially since you knew he was your brother. It must have been very hard."

Alli squeezed back. "Yep. But, Cal is only a blood relative. This is my family." Alli looked into the kitchen. "Would you make it official and adopt me, Maria?"

"I already started the paperwork. Mr. Osberg is dropping by with it tonight. For dessert."

Everyone got quiet. All eyes turned to Maria.

Gina asked, "Ma? Is that why you made your special pound cake yesterday?"

Alli shook her head to process what she just heard. She cleared her throat and asked, "Maria? You're kidding right?" Alli sat very still watching Maria. She squeezed the hands of Gina and Evan.

Maria smiled. "Well, yes. About the adoption." After a pause, she resumed. "But Mr. Osberg is coming for dessert."

Recipes in *Mission Impastable*

- P183—Alli's Tangled Linguini with White Clam Sauce
- P185—Maria's Chunky PeanOat Cookies
- P187—Lasagna Roll-Ups
- P189—Sorta-Skinny Alfredo Sauce
- P191—Alli's Super-Easy-but-Elegant, Never-Fails-to-Impress Cream Cheese Cracker Spread
- P193—Gina's Teriyaki Sauce
- P195—Fettucine ala Alli
- P197—Replacement Dinner-in-a-Flash Menu
  - Dipping Oil and Bread
  - Bruschetta Rounds
  - Bruschetta Pasta Florentine
  - Honeydew Slices with Cinnamon-Honey Drizzle
- P201—Linguine Aglio e Olio (Linguine with Garlic and Olive Oil)
- P203—Chocolate Chovolate Kick Cookies
- P205—Buttermilk Chicken and Rice
- P207—Mrs. Roth's Rich Blueberry Muffins
- P209—Seafood Scampi with Angel Hair Pasta
- P211—REAL Pound Cake with REAL Whipped Cream and Fruit
- P213—Three Cheese Stuffed Shells and Alli's Quick Marinara Sauce

Alli's Tangled Linguini with White Clam Sauce (Serves 6)

Sometimes when you rename a dish, as Alli did to make the movie tie-in, kids will eat what they would normally spurn.

Ingredients

12 ounce box whole-wheat linguini

2 tablespoons butter

4 tablespoons flour

¼ cup white wine

¼ cup olive oil

1 cup clam juice

2 garlic cloves, crushed

2 garlic cloves, sliced

2-6.5 ounce cans of chopped or minced clams

1 tablespoon dried basil (or 2 tablespoons fresh basil)

Shredded Asiago cheese for the table

Directions

1) Cook linguini to al dente in boiling salted water.

2) While pasta is cooking, melt butter in a skillet. Add flour when butter just begins to turn brown and whisk until smooth. Whisk in the wine. Heat the mixture to bubbly.

3) Add olive oil and clam juice. Whisk again over heat. Add in garlic and simmer for a few minutes until the mixture begins to thicken.

4) Add clams and basil. Stir well and serve over pasta. Add Asiago cheese to taste.

MISSION IMPASTABLE RECIPES

Maria's Chunky PeanOat Cookies (makes ~6-7 dozen small cookies)

Maria felt left out of the Wild Cinnamon business. Since she taught both Alli and Gina to cook, she wants to make a contribution. This recipe can be varied so many ways. For example, leave out the peanut butter, chocolate chunks and peanuts and substitute cranberries and pecans instead. Maria invites you to create other combinations.

Ingredients

1 cup plus 2 tablespoons butter, softened

¾ cup packed brown sugar

½ cup granulated sugar

¾ cup chunky peanut butter

2 large eggs

3 teaspoons vanilla extract

1 teaspoon baking soda

½ teaspoon salt

1 ¾ cups flour

2 ½ cups oats

¾ cup chocolate chunks (can substitute chocolate chips.)

1 cup peanuts, chopped

Directions

1) Heat oven to 375°.

2) Beat butter and sugars in a bowl with mixer on medium speed until fluffy.

3) Beat in eggs, vanilla, baking soda, and salt until well-blended.

4) With mixer on low speed, beat in flour.

5) Stir in oats, chocolate chunks, and nuts.

6) Drop heaping tablespoonfuls (or use small cookie dough scooper) 1" apart on ungreased baking sheet.

7) Bake 10-12 minutes until golden brown. Cool 1 minute on cookie sheet, then put on cookie rack to cool.

Lasagna Roll-Ups
(serves 4-6)

This is the second of the book's pasta recipes. The book titles in this series will signal what the focus is for recipes in each book.

Ingredients

9 lasagna noodles

10 ounces frozen chopped spinach, thawed and drained

1½ cups ricotta cheese

1½ cups shredded Asiago cheese, divided

1 teaspoon dried basil (or 2 teaspoons fresh basil)

2 cups Sorta-Skinny Alfredo Sauce (recipe follows)

Directions

1) Heat oven to 350°. Cook noodles to al dente in boiling salted water. Drain and cool to handling temperature.

2) Mix ricotta cheese, 1 cup of Asiago, and basil in food processor until slightly lumpy. 3) Pour into medium bowl and blend in spinach.

4) Put one cup of Sorta-Skinny Alfredo sauce in bottom of 9"x13" pan sprayed with Pam.

5) Put spinach-cheese mixture down the middle of a noodle and roll-up from the short end to make a pinwheel.

4) Place pinwheels in the pan. Cover with remaining sauce. Sprinkle on remaining Asiago.

5) Bake for ~35-45 minutes or until bubbly.

Sorta-Skinny Alfredo Sauce

Ingredients

1 cup low-sodium chicken broth
1 cup low-fat evaporated milk
2 large garlic cloves, minced
1 tablespoon butter
3 tablespoons all-purpose flour
¼ cup shredded Asiago cheese
½ teaspoon nutmeg
Salt and pepper to taste

Directions:

1) Heat broth, milk and garlic until steamy hot (about 3-4 minutes).

2) Melt the butter in a small skillet. Whisk in flour then immediately add hot milk mixture and continue whisking.

3) Whisk until sauce thickens (1-2 minutes). Add cheese, nutmeg, salt, and pepper.

4) Simmer for 5 minutes. Use on pasta or in Lasagna Roll-Ups.

MISSION IMPASTABLE RECIPES

Alli's Super-Easy-but-Elegant, Never-Fails-to-Impress Cream Cheese Cracker Spread

Alli dearly loves making appetizers and has a bunch of them. Check out this February, 2014 for a month of appetizers at "Parsley, Sage, and Rosemary Time" (www.sharonarthurmoore.blogspot.com).

Ingredients

8 ounces cream cheese

4 tablespoons best-quality chutney

1 box Carr's Water Crackers or other expensive cracker

Directions

1) Unwrap the block of cream cheese and place on an elegant plate with a silver butter spreader to the side.

2) Place the chutney in tablespoons equidistant from one another down the middle of the cream cheese. With the spoon, arrange the chutney so it artistically drips down the sides of the cheese.

3) Serve with a small basket of crackers.

Gina's Teriyaki Sauce (about 2 ½ cups)

Gina lets chicken thighs marinate in this sauce for several hours before grilling. Then she serves the chicken with extra sauce at the table. Sauces and marinades are one way to escalate taste.

Ingredients

½ cup soy sauce

½ cup pineapple juice

½ cup water

¾ teaspoon fresh grated ginger

2 large cloves garlic, minced

3 tablespoons honey

3 tablespoons cornstarch

½ cup cold water

6 chicken thighs

½ cup diced pineapple

3 tablespoons grated coconut

Directions

1) In a small saucepan, heat soy sauce, pineapple juice, water, ginger, garlic, and honey.

2) Mix cornstarch with water in a cup and stir to dissolve.

3) Add several tablespoons of hot sauce to cornstarch in the cup and stir.

4) Add cornstarch to sauce in pan slowly, stirring constantly. Heat until thickened.

5) Cool to room temperature. Place one cup in zipper bag with chicken. Reserve remaining to reheat.

6) Grill chicken until juices run clear, about 20-30 minutes.

7) Before serving, mix pineapple into re-heated, reserved sauce and serve with chicken sprinkled with coconut at the table.

Fettucine ala Alli
(serves 6)

Can be a side or an entrée. Sometimes Alli makes this quick supper with leftover pasta. But for company, as when Craig came to dinner, she cooks fresh pasta.

Ingredients

12 ounces fettucine

3 tablespoons best-quality olive oil

3 green onions, finely chopped

2 garlic cloves, sliced

¼ cup flour

1 garlic clove, minced

½ cup pasta water

½ cup shredded Asiago cheese

1 tablespoon fresh ground pepper

Directions

1) Cook fettucine until just al dente in boiling salted water. Drain and reserve ½ cup pasta water.

2) While pasta cooks, heat olive oil in medium size skillet. Add onions and sliced garlic. Cook until garlic just begins to change color.

3) Whisk in flour, minced garlic, and pasta water. Simmer until thickened. Remove from heat.

4) Add drained pasta to skillet. Toss together with cheese and pepper. Serve with Gina's Teriyaki Chicken or by itself for 3-4 people.

Replacement Dinner-in-a-Flash Menu (Serves four)

Dipping Oil and Bread

Bruschetta Rounds

Bruschetta Pasta Florentine

Honeydew Slices with Cinnamon-Honey Drizzle

Fruit Tarts (bought at store)

Alli and Gina had to scramble to feed the Dragon Lady's family when their crockpot dinner failed. This comes together fast and is tasty and nutritious.

Ingredients: *Tomato Mixture for Bruschetta and Pasta:*

9 Roma tomatoes, chopped fine

3 large cloves of garlic, minced

4 tablespoons shredded Asiago cheese

3 tablsespoons chopped fresh basil

2 tablespoons best-quality olive oil

Directions

1) Mix together in a bowl. Cover and let sit so the flavors get acquainted while other items are prepared.

Ingredients: *Honeydew Melon Slices with Cinnamon-Honey Drizzle:*

½ melon, cut into quarters and thinly sliced

1 tablespoon honey

¼ teaspoon cinnamon

Directions

1) Cut melon in half. Save one half for later use.

2) Peel melon half and cut into fourths. Thinly slice each quarter and arrange on plates in a crescent.

3) Mix honey with cinnamon. Drizzle over melon slices. Refrigerate until ready to serve.

Ingredients: *Bruschetta and Dipping Bread:*

16-1" slices of French bread

½ cup best-quality olive oil, divided

3 garlic cloves, sliced

¼ cup Asiago cheese, shredded

Directions

1) Slice garlic into olive oil and set aside.

2) Slice French bread loaf into 1" pieces. Brush slices lightly with ¼ cup olive oil, and sprinkle on Asiago cheese. Put under broiler for a couple of minutes until very lightly browned. Set aside.

3) Right before serving, spread one teaspoon of the tomato mixture onto 8 bread slices and sprinkle on more Asiago cheese.

4) Serve another 8 pieces of bread with remainder of oil for dipping. Keep remainder of bruschetta mix to toss with pasta.

Ingredients: *Bruschcetta Pasta Florentine*:
12 ounces pasta
8 ounces mushrooms, sliced
1 red pepper, chopped
12 ounces fresh spinach
1cup Asiago cheese, shredded plus extra for the table
remaining dipping oil
remaining Bruschetta mixture

Directions

1) Cook pasta to al dente in boiling salted water. Drain then return to cooking pot.

2) Toss drained, hot pasta with mushrooms, green pepper, spinach, and Asiago cheese.

3) Add leftover brushcetta mixture and remaining dipping oil. Toss. Serve immediately with a bowl of Asiago cheese, any remaining bread, and melon slices.

Linguine Aglio e Olio
Linguine with Garlic and Olive Oil
(serves 6)

You do know Alli loves garlic, right? Well, this is not a date-night dish, but it's mighty tasty! And it qualifies as a Quick Cook recipe.

Ingredients

12 ounces of linguine

3 cloves of garlic, sliced

1 clove of garlic, crushed

½ cup best-quality olive oil

10 basil leaves, chopped

½ cup Asiago cheese, plus extra for the table

Directions

1) While linguine cooks, pour olive oil into skillet and heat to sizzling.

2) Add sliced garlic and stir until just beginning to turn color. The sliced garlic will get bitter if browned too much.

3) Immediately add minced garlic and remove from heat.

4) Toss with drained linguine. Toss again with Asiago cheese. Add in chopped basil. Serve with extra cheese on the side.

MISSION IMPASTABLE RECIPES

Chocolate Chocolate Kick Cookies
(makes 4 dozen)

Both the cocoa and the coffee have caffeine giving these chocolate cookies quite a kick!

Ingredients

2 cups flour

¼ cup cocoa powder (not cocoa mix)

1 teaspoon baking soda

½ teaspoon salt

1 ½ cups butter, softened

¾ cup granulated sugar

¾ cup packed brown sugar

2 eggs

2 teaspoons vanilla

1 cup chopped walnuts

11½ ounces 60% Cacao Chocolate Chips

¼ cup fresh-ground coffee beans

Directions

1) Preheat oven to 375°F. Stir flour and cocoa powder with baking soda and salt; set aside.

2) In a large bowl, cream butter with white and brown sugars. When fluffy, add eggs, and vanilla. Gradually blend dry mixture into butter mixture. Stir in nuts, chocolate chips, and coffee grounds.

3) Drop 1 tablespoon of dough per cookie onto ungreased cookie sheet. Bake 10-12 minutes. Cool slightly then remove to rack. Delicious for making ice cream sandwiches, too!

Buttermilk Chicken and Rice (serves 4 with leftovers)

Chicken is so versatile. One thing Gina likes about this dish is she can prepare it one day and cook it or re-heat it the next. Nice for busy working moms!

Ingredients

6 chicken thighs

2 cups buttermilk

1 tablespoon granulated sugar

1 teaspoon each salt and pepper

2 tablespoons fresh tarragon (or 1 T dried)

Brown rice

Directions

1) Wash chicken and dry with paper towels. Set aside while combining buttermilk, sugar, salt, and pepper in a gallon-size zippered bag.

2) Squish and swish to mix milk ingredients together. Add chicken and let marinate in refrigerator for at least 2 hours, turning often to keep chicken evenly covered with buttermilk mixture.

3) Prepare 4 servings of brown rice as directed. Put cooked rice into a casserole dish sprayed with Pam. Set aside.

4) Remove chicken from refrigerator, rinse off buttermilk mixture, and dry chicken. Add chicken, skin-side up on top of rice. Sprinkle pieces evenly with tarragon.

5) Cover and bake at 350° for 30 minutes. Uncover and bake for 15 minutes (or longer until chicken is done and skin is browned).

Juices should run clear when pierced.

6) Best served immediately, but can be refrigerated or frozen for reheating.

Mrs. Roth's Rich Blueberry Muffins (12 muffins)

Not overly-sweet, this recipe isn't Gina or Alli's; rather it comes from the mother of my high school best friend. I'm planning a blog post on the story behind it, so check out "Parsley, Sage, and Rosemary Time". One day it will appear!

Ingredients

¼ cup butter, softened

½ cup granulated, plus additional for sprinkling on top before baking

1 egg

1¾ cups flour

2½ teaspoons baking powder

¼ teaspoon salt

½ cup milk

½ cup blueberries (frozen okay)

Directions

1) Cream sugar into softened butter. Add the egg. Mix well.

2) Sift the flour, baking powder and salt and sugar together into the bowl.

3) Add milk. Beat until smooth.

4) Pour into greased muffin tins. Press 4 or 5 blueberries into each muffin. Sprinkle tops with sugar.

5) Bake at 350 for about 25 minutes.

Seafood Scampi with Angel Hair Pasta (serves 4)

All's simple version of Shrimp Scampi is meant to impress Cal or anyone else who eats it. It is rich and textured.

Ingredients

8 ounces angel hair pasta

¼ cup butter

¼ cup best-quality olive oil

4 cloves garlic, crushed

2 large cloves garlic, sliced

1 cup dry white wine

¼ teaspoon pepper

Any 1-pound combo of raw shrimp/scallops/lump crab meat

1 tablespoon cornstarch

¾ cup shredded Asiago cheese, divided

1 tablespoon chopped fresh parsley

Directions

1) Cook angel hair pasta to al dente in boiling salted water. Drain and keep hot.

2) Melt butter with oil in large saucepan over medium heat.

3) Stir in garlic, wine and pepper.

4) Add seafood and cook 3-5 minutes. Remove seafood to heated dish.

5) Mix ½ cup hot pan liquid with cornstarch and pour back into the pan. Stir until thickened. Cook for 3-5 minutes.

6) Raise heat to bring to boil. Add ½ cup cheese. Remove from

heat and add seafood.

7) Stir and *immediately* mix seafood and sauce with pasta in a serving bowl.

8) Sprinkle with remaining cheese and parsley and serve.

MISSION IMPASTABLE RECIPES

REAL Pound Cake with REAL Whipped Cream and Fruit (serves 12)

This dessert impressed Mr. Osberg, the attorney visiting Maria. Wonder if it will get him to return in the next book!

Ingredients

1 pound box of confectioner's sugar

1 pound of butter (four sticks), softened

1 pound of large eggs (7)

1 teaspoon vanilla

1 large pinch of nutmeg

1 pound of flour (fill empty sugar box or use kitchen scale)

1 cup Baker's heavy whipping cream (or regular whipping cream and 3 tablespoons powdered sugar)

3 cups cut-up fruit (strawberries, blueberries, bananas)

Directions

1) Heat oven to 325°. Mark the level of the powdered sugar on the outside of the box. Spray a bundt cake pan with Pam.

2) Cream butter with electric mixer and add the box of sugar in three segments, beating after each addition. When the box is empty, spoon flour into the box up to the mark made earlier.

3) Mix in eggs, one at a time, to the butter and sugar mixture. Mix well after each egg. Add vanilla and nutmeg.

4) Gradually add the box of flour in three additions. Mix until smooth.

5) Pour into the bundt pan and bake about one hour. Check done-

ness with a toothpick.

6) Remove cake from oven and allow to cool in the pan for 15 minutes. Turn onto serving plate to finish cooling.

7) Right before serving, whip Baker's cream until it is fluffy and holding stiff peaks. If using regular cream, add sugar gradually once soft peaks form and continue to whip to stiff peaks.

8) Serve a dollop on the cake and garnish with cut-up fresh fruit.

Three-Cheese Stuffed Shells and Alli's Quick Marinara Sauce (serves 6)

Alli learned how to make the sauce from Maria, but the combination of cheeses in the shells is her own invention.

Ingredients: *Marinara Sauce*

2 tablespoons best-quality olive oil

1 medium onion, diced

5 cloves garlic, crushed

2 cans diced tomatoes (or use 12 Roma tomatoes, mashed)

1 can tomato paste

1 teaspoon granulated sugar

2 tablespoons dried basil

½ cup red wine

½ cup pasta water

Directions

1) Saute onions in olive oil over medium heat in a pan. When just turning translucent, add garlic. Cook about 1 minute.

2) Add tomatoes, tomato paste, sugar, and basil. Stir together.

3) Add wine and pasta water. Simmer for about 2 hours. Even better made the day before.

Ingredients: *Stuffed Shells*

16 ounces large pasta shells

1 quart ricotta cheese (some people use cottage cheese, but it is

different)

    1 cup shredded mozzarella

    1 cup shredded Asiago cheese plus more to sprinkle on top

    1 egg

    2 tablespoons dried basil

Directions

1) Cook pasta shells to al dente in boiling salted water as directed. Drain. Reserve a half-cup of pasta water for the sauce.

2) Mix together the ricotta, mozzarella, and Asiago cheeses. Add egg. Blend well. Mix in basil.

3) In a large baking dish sprayed with Pam, ladle enough marinara sauce to just cover the bottom.

4) Fill shells to heaping with cheeses mixture. Place cheese-side up in the baking dish.

5) Spoon the remaining marinara over the top. Sprinkle on more Asiago cheese.

6) Bake at 350° for about 30 minutes or until cheese is bubbly.

About the Author

After 39 years as an educator, Sharon Arthur Moore "transitioned" to the life of full-time fiction writer. She's an intrepid cook, game-player, and miniatures lover.

She writes culinary mysteries, women's fiction, historical fiction, short stories, plays, paranormals (under the pen name River Glynn), and erotic romance (under the pen name Angelica French).

Sharon has lived in every region of the country except the Pacific Northwest and loved every single one of them. Her current favorite region is the desert Southwest. She is married to the most extraordinary man and claims four children, one daughter-in-law, a grandson, and yellow lab Maudie.

Contacts

Thank you so much for reading *Mission Impastable*. I hope you enjoyed it and will read more of Alli and Gina's adventures as personal chefs who just happen to get involved in murder. Please leave a review--good, bad, or indifferent--at Amazon or in an e-mail to let me know what you thought of Alli and Gina's debut book. I love to talk with my readers, so please feel free to send questions and comments to: authorsam@gmail.com

You can check out my blogs at:

"Write Away", www.samwriteaway.blogspot.com

"Parsley, Sage, and Rosemary Time", at www.sharonarthurmoore.blogspot.com

Or follow me for recipes and cooking tips on Twitter: @good2tweat

I am on Facebook at Sharon Arthur Moore Fan Page.

Please, let's connect, and share our love of cooking and culinary mysteries.